THE LAST COACHMAN

John Michael Doyle

The author was born at Beaufort Co. Kerry, the son of an Irish father and English mother and lived there until moving to England at the age of 17.

He worked in the engineering industry, mainly in aerospace, and served three years in the British Army.

In 1988, the author graduated from the Open University with a Bachelor of Arts degree and achieved BA (Honours) three years later. He then joined the staff of The Institution of Engineering Designers with responsibility for Continuing Professional Development.

In 1998, John was appointed as Associate Lecturer at The Open University in the field of Professional and Career Development in Engineering.

In 2005, the author retired but continued to work for the OU in a consultancy capacity.

John has always had an interest in history and hobbies, which now include writing, walking and photography.

The author is married to Shireen and has one daughter, two granddaughters and a dog.

THE LAST COACHMAN

John Michael Doyle

THE LAST COACHMAN

Olympia Publishers
London

www.olympiapublishers.com
OLYMPIA PAPERBACK EDITION

A CIP catalogue record for this title is
available from the British Library.

ISBN: 978-1-84897-088-5

This is a work of fiction.
Names, characters, places and incidents originate from the writer's
imagination. Any resemblance to actual persons, living or dead, is
purely coincidental.

Cover illustration by Walter Paget: *'Birth of the Irish Republic'*

First Published in 2010

Olympia Publishers
60 Cannon Street
London
EC4N 6NP

Printed in Great Britain

Dedication

For Joanne and Jacqueline,
in memory of your Great Great Grandfather

The Coachman, Michael Doyle, at Beaufort, circa 1910

Prologue

Had it not been for the little white wooden marker thoughtfully placed there by the Cumbria Bereavement Service it would not have been recognisable as a grave. But we had finally found it, and we were conscious that had we failed to locate the spot it would have remained undiscovered for another ninety years, known only as Plot 99, Section K, Ward 5 of Carlisle Cemetery. In all probability we were the first, other than cemetery staff, to visit him there since he was laid to rest at 2.30 pm Wednesday 26th April 1916. My wife had thoughtfully remembered to buy some flowers and she shed a tear as she gently placed them on the green grass.

The graveyard itself was neat and tidy and even in this forgotten corner, designated as the dissenters, or non-Church of England, section when the grave had first been dug, the grass had been cut and the path swept. The plot, according to the cemetery records, was 'un-purchased and remained the property of the Council'. So it was a pauper's grave, and as such he could have been buried with 'someone unrelated' and a proper memorial could not be allowed. The search for the grave had inevitably led to the uncovering of the story behind how he came to be here, buried with neither the wake nor the requiem that would have marked his passing had he died at home.

It was a strange set of circumstances that had led a man like him to find his last resting place in this pauper's grave within sight of the hills and lakes of Cumbria, yet so far removed from the hills and lakes of his native County Kerry. It was war that had brought him to this, the war so foolishly termed 'the War to end all Wars'. That he remained here was a result of another and equally misconceived war: the conflict that raged in Ireland during that fateful Easter Week in 1916 and which prevented his return home to a peaceful spot in an Irish country churchyard to be lovingly tended by those he left behind.

Across the cemetery I could see the neat lines of white headstones in the war graves section and thought that he was just as much a casualty of war as the men who had been buried there with full military honours. He had never been a serving soldier; rather he had served the soldiers by helping to supply them with the means necessary for them to carry out their duty. It was not patriotism, or revenge, or the search for glory or any of the other reasons why men go to war that had brought him to the great munitions factory being built in a Scottish peat bog, a bog not unlike the bogs he knew at home. What motivated him was the simple expedient of caring for his family.

The Great War with its thousands of guns voraciously gobbling up and spitting out the high explosive material he helped to make, and the many thousands of gunners who manned those guns would have occupied only a peripheral corner of his mind. Central to his thoughts would have been just one gun and a single gunner, his son, serving in a far off place which before the war he had never even heard of. He would though, have remembered in his prayers the casualties those guns caused. His thoughts regarding the second conflict, that Irish 'war within a war' for which he had little sympathy, would have revolved around preventing a second son from becoming involved.

He would, I was certain, have survived the First World War had it not been for the parallel world that accompanies the fighting in all wars, the world of plots and counter-plots, the world peopled by nameless, faceless shadows. That was what had finally brought him to this.

In the end the thousands of guns and the millions of deaths for him came down to a single pistol shot and a lone body tumbling from a lofty viaduct to be washed out into the treacherous waters of the Solway Firth.

Chapter 1

In nomine Patris, et Filii, et Spiritu Sancti: the priest greeted his flock in the hush of the little country church then turned to the altar and began the Mass. On this dull November morning the candles flickered brightly and the sanctuary lamp hanging from the roof before the altar cast a reddish glow. Although not understanding the Latin words the assembled faithful bowed their heads in reverence. The pews were almost exclusively populated by women and children in their Sunday best, their ranks interspersed by just a few of the more conscientious men. The single transept to the left of the altar, housed the local dignitaries, doctor, schoolmaster and postmaster with their families. As was the custom in the south-west of Ireland at that time, the second decade of the twentieth century, the men stood or knelt on one knee, caps in hand, at the back.

Kyrie eleison: hardly noticing the plea for mercy, one man was not his usual attentive self; obviously distracted he almost disregarded the habits engendered by two thousand Sundays and omitted to stand for the *Gloria* until nudged by the young man by his side. Michael Quinlan was indeed uncharacteristically distracted, his missal – unlike the majority of the worshippers he owned and referred to a Sunday Missal with an English translation during the Mass – remained unopened in his calloused hands. The size of his hands reflected his general physique. Being best described as stocky; short in stature but with powerful chest and shoulders above an expanding waistline. The calluses on his hands were the legacy of years spent working with ropes and stable equipment, hands which for all their strength could guide a team of horses with no more than a gentle pull on the reins; the expanding waistline was the result of hours spent sitting high up on the driving seat of a carriage. He was by trade, he would have preferred 'profession', a coachman, employed to convey the owners of the nearby Beaufort House in stately fashion wherever they had occasion to go. His profession also determined his mode of dress. Today he wore a well-cut three-piece tweed suit, supplied by his employers it would have been well beyond the capacity of his personal means; but the coachman was expected to reflect the status and dignity of 'the family' on every occasion. On duty he would wear a uniform as well turned out as the coach and horses in his charge.

Dominus vobiscum: as the priest read the Epistle, Michael Quinlan considered the decision he had to make as a result of the letter delivered just a few days previously – probably the most important decision of his fifty-four years on earth. He had got over the anger felt at the first reading, and the anxiety which followed, now he had reached the point where he had to put anger and anxiety aside and decide how best to deal with a problem he had never before been asked to confront. Never before in his life had he been unemployed, and although this dismissal did not constitute unemployment per se – he had been promised that he would be re-instated after the war and the letter included a good character reference – but he was perceptive enough to know that his life would never be the same again. The war would change everything.

Per evangelica dicta deleantur nostra delicta: the congregation in the pews rose and stood for the Gospel – the men at the back being already on their feet. The most immediate effect of the war which, with foolish optimism had been expected to be over by Christmas the year before, was that his English aristocratic employers were obliged to close their Irish country house until the end of the conflict; an event not now expected until some far off blessed day in the uncertain future. In the meantime only a few outdoor, and no indoor staff, would be required to keep the house and grounds in reasonable state of readiness while the senior, and as such highest paid, members of the household which included the coachman, would be laid off until the day when the world returned to sanity. It was not simply the duration of the war which worried Michael, it seemed obvious to him that whatever the outcome of the conflict there would be no return to 'normal'. Even in the relatively remote south-west of Ireland there was no escape from the images coming out of France and other blood-soaked theatres. He had read enough in newspaper reports and seen enough in the flickering silent images on the cinema screen to deduce that the dominance of the horse in transport was rapidly coming to an end. Although there were still appeals being made for horses to boost the war effort, the use of the new fangled internal combustion engine was rapidly increasing and there was no reason to believe that the trend would not continue after the eventual restoration of peace. The demise of the horse would bring about the demise of the coachman.

Laus tibi, Christe: the Gospel ended and the priest moved to the pulpit to deliver his sermon. As the people in the pews sat to hear the sermon several of the men at the back surreptitiously moved further back and out of the door for a disrespectful pipe or cigarette. As the young man standing next to Michael moved to follow he was restrained by a firm hand. Michael's seventeen year old son James had now, reluctantly it must be said, been granted the concession of standing with the men at Mass, but he was still expected to abide by the code of conduct preached by his father. The other Quinlan children, two boys and two girls, sitting with their mother in their usual pew four rows from the front, being conscious of the presence of their father at the back, were attentive and well behaved. If challenged, Michael would have admitted that he was a man moulded very much by the way of life he had been handed as a boy, a life of service to those whom circumstances had defined as his betters. As he had risen from the position of humble stable boy to the rank of coachman he had accepted without question, and indeed come to respect, the strict hierarchy which governed life in a Gentleman's Household. Now that he was the senior member of the outdoor staff he expected an equivalent level of deference to that he had once been required to show. He was therefore, always referred to as 'Mr Quinlan' among the staff and addressed as 'sir' by all except the butler, who was his equal. As a father he thought of himself as firm but fair and he did not consider it unkind or out of place to insist that his children also called him 'sir'. It was the way of things, just as it was the way of things for him to be known simply as 'Quinlan' to his employers.

Credo in unum Deum: his mind still wandered as the people stood to make their Profession of Faith. The anger at being required to make such a monumental change to his life of ordered routine had been replaced by a worry about how he would be able to function in this new, and unfamiliar world he would be forced to inhabit. But adjust he would have to, he had a family to feed, and as charity would never be an acceptable option, he would have to find a way of providing for them himself. Now, however, he thought that he had found a solution, and unpalatable as it had appeared on first entering his thoughts, he believed that it would provide an answer to his problem. All that was required was faith and a readiness to adapt, albeit for the first time in his life. What had at first been rumours was now confirmed by newspaper articles and advertisements: an enormous new building project was under way 'across the water' and large numbers of tradesmen and labourers were being recruited from across the whole of the British Empire to complete it. Nothing specific was known regarding the purpose of the construction, it was being kept secret and that fact alone pointed to it being connected with the war effort. Going by what he had heard from those who had relatives working there the pay was good although the work was strenuous. Michael knew that if he were to take this route to supporting his family he would either have to accept the indignity of becoming a common labourer or break the habit of a lifetime and lie. He had faith however, that he could pass himself off as a carpenter, for which he could thank the hours spent helping tradesmen employed at 'The House' in the days before his elevation to coachman. As well as care of his family there was a second pressing reason for seriously considering applying for work away from home.

Sanctus, Sanctus, Sanctus: the sound of the bell announcing the holiest section of the Mass interrupted his thoughts and brought him back to his Sunday obligation.

Memento, Domine, famulorum famularumque tuarum: the priest made silent mention of those for whom the Mass was being offered, and Michael knelt and prayed for his eldest son. Jack was now a serving soldier who had, together with thousands of other youthful Irishmen, enlisted in response to Kitchener's expression

16

of the country's need. He still felt that nagging sense of guilt for not doing more to prevent Jack from going off to the war, and this, he was aware, stemmed from the fact that it was expected that at least one of the coachman's four sons would answer the call to arms. He had no knowledge of where Jack, who was serving in the Royal Field Artillery, was at this precise moment but his son's last letter home had indicated that his unit was being made ready to embark for the Middle East. He thanked God that Jack had, for the time being at least, been spared the carnage on the Western Front; and as the latest war news inferred that British forces were at last being withdrawn from the equally bloody slaughterhouse called Gallipoli, it would seem that Jack was somewhere at sea. But where he was bound would not be revealed until another letter reached home. Michael prayed, as he knew Jack's mother would be praying, that God would protect their eldest son. While Jack's letters brought a curious mixture of relief and anxiety to his parents they served to stimulate a desire in his brothers to share in the great adventure. Michael was well aware that it was only the news of his father's loss of livelihood that had prevented the youthfully excitable James from following in Jack's footsteps. As soon as the question of feeding the family had been resolved even his father would not be able to hold him back. Perhaps if he went away to work and took James with him then this might satisfy his second son's determination to prove his manhood. The third son William, at fifteen and working for a local farmer, was equally bent on adventure but Michael was sure that he would obey his father's wishes and stay to look after his mother and sisters.

Hoc est enim corpus meum: as the priest raised the Host, Michael was resolved that he too must be prepared to make a sacrifice for the good of his family. He did not, however, as yet fully understand the nature of the cross he would eventually be asked to bear.

Memento etiam, Domine: remember also Lord, the dead we wish to pray for. George, the eldest son and heir to the owners of Beaufort House, had perished in the unholy slaughter known as the second Battle of Ypres. Although not a man given to cynicism, Michael could not help but wonder if the tone of his dismissal had something to do with the fact that his own son still lived. He was confident that His Lordship, a true gentleman, would not have entertained such thoughts, but who knew how a mother's grief may have affected the Lady of the House. Such thoughts were, he quickly realised, neither in keeping nor helpful and were quickly banished.

Pax Domine sit simper vobiscum: the Peace of God seemed a long way away. Even in this remote corner of Ireland the effects of the war were being felt, and most thinking men could sense that another and more immediate conflict was likely to erupt much closer to home. Michael could see that within the paradox that was early twentieth century Ireland trouble of a different type was brewing. It was plain to see how The Irish Home Rule Bill put before the House of Commons a few years earlier had divided opinion in the country, with the main opposition coming from pro-British factions in the North. Soon, Michael thought, extreme nationalist organisations such as the Irish Republican Brotherhood and the Irish Volunteers were likely to take advantage of Britain's entanglement in the war overseas and cause trouble at home. There was little popular support for an armed uprising in the country generally, but he feared that many young men would be persuaded to rally to a cause they did not fully understand, just as they were being persuaded to join the regular army to fight against the Germans. He had already counselled James that any involvement with a rebel faction would constitute an act of disloyalty to his brother Jack at the battlefront. It seemed to be a wise precaution to remove the young man from the path of temptation.

Agnus Dei: he looked up the church to where his two youngest, Elizabeth and Mary, knelt between their mother, Annie, and son William. Beyond them on the steps of the altar itself his fourth son served the priest as an altar boy. Named after his father, Michael at eleven did not exhibit the lust for life that was such a feature of his older brothers' nature. Instead he had begun to demonstrate a sense of duty akin to that of his father, as was evidenced by his attention to his schoolwork, and by his volunteering to be an altar boy. And this without any pressure from parents, priest or teacher. It was thought that he would be the one to follow the well established Irish family tradition of giving up one son to the priesthood, an ambition dear to his mother's heart. If this ambition were to be fulfilled, and Michael hoped it would be, then he would have to provide for his son through years of training in the seminary.

Domine non sum dignus: as the priest proclaimed his unworthiness to receive the host, Michael made up his mind. He would have to steel himself to do what he was certain to be his duty to God and family and, unworthy or not, accept the prospect of exchanging a well ordered past for an uncertain future.

Ite missa est: the Mass had ended, the congregation genuflected and trooped out into a misty November morning. In common with several other men, Michael Quinlan unhitched his pony and harnessed it to the trap, while his wife chatted with the other women. The children played quietly under the watchful eyes of their parents, any deviation from behaviour appropriate to the Sabbath Day being immediately nipped in the bud. Michael loaded his wife and younger children into the trap and, signalling to James and William to leave their friends and follow on their bicycles, the Quinlan family set off home. They would share the Sunday meal together as Michael had always insisted that they should.

He was determined that by the following Sunday he would have finally made up his mind and would inform them of his decision. There would be no debate – it was not his way.

Chapter 2

"Dia daoibh." The Man from Dublin deliberately used the Gaelic form of greeting as he entered the room. He noted with some degree of disappointment that only three among the ten or a dozen men seated around the rough wooden table or leaning against the walls muttered the traditional Irish reply: *"Dia is murie duit."*

The meeting would have to be conducted in English and this would require him to be more than usually mindful of possible eavesdroppers, even if they were merely satisfying the demands of curiosity. They were assembled in the back room of a building which, as was usual in rural Ireland, contained both the village shop and public house; this particular one also serving as a working farmhouse. The room was in fact the farm kitchen, typically the largest room in the house. It had been provided for the occasion by the farmer/grocer/publican, Pat Devlin, a committed Irish Nationalist sympathiser, who had also quietly publicised the meeting throughout the parish by dropping a quiet word here and a guarded suggestion there. Rather than actually attend the meeting, he already knew the gist of what would be said, he had stationed himself behind the bar from which vantage point he could act as lookout. The Man from Dublin had been aware of the curious looks on the faces of the women in the grocery section at the front of the house, and the knowing glances that passed between the men drinking pints of porter in the bar further in, as he made his way through. Outright betrayal was not a major worry as he was confident that no Irishman would intentionally inform on him whether or not they agreed with his extreme political views, but he would have preferred not to become part of their idle gossip.

"Is this all that's coming?" It was not so much a question as an observation on the paucity of numbers.

The men looked up at him as he stood in schoolmasterly fashion with his thumbs hooked in the armholes of his waistcoat, for indeed a schoolmaster he had been before giving his life over to The Cause. With his back to a fire well built up with turf against the frosty November evening, he deduced from the shrugged shoulders and blank expressions that everybody in the locality remotely interested in attending the lesson he was about to conduct that evening was already present.

"God save Ireland," was his only comment.

Those present were, as he had come to expect in rural areas, mostly young men together with just a few of older heads. The ages of the younger element, he judged, ranged from perhaps seventeen to no more than twenty-two or three years of age. Apart from one, who was known to him, they were the usual collection of adventurous youths and faithful 'old hands' which typically formed the sum total of interest, and therefore support, in country areas. Most were farmers, or sons of farmers, who scraped a living from small family farms or were employed by the few larger farms in the neighbourhood. They were dressed roughly in plain farm clothes and, having come directly from the evening milking they had not had time to change into what passed for their 'best', and so they still carried the sickly sweet odour of the cowshed. A few smoked and ignored the envious looks on the faces of those who could not at present afford to indulge in the habit. In previous years many of them would have supplemented their income by offering their services as guides and providing traps and jaunting cars to drive the rich tourists who came to view the Lakes of Killarney and the Gap of Dunloe. But the war had brought with it a fear of travel, and a fear especially of crossing the U-boat infested Atlantic. By late 1915 the stream of tourists had been reduced to a tiny trickle, and times, therefore were hard. The only exceptions to the farmers were the village postman still in his uniform, and the man standing back in the flickering shadows cast by the fire and the single oil lamp on the table, which provided the only light in the room.

Although it was not generally known, Liam Daly was a man fully committed to 'The Cause'. He was known to The Man from Dublin as a member of the Irish Republican Brotherhood and a trusted ally who had secretly trained with the Irish Volunteers – a paramilitary organisation initiated by Eoin MacNeill in response to the formation of the Ulster Volunteer Force in the North. Daly, a tall lean man in his early thirties earned his living as a jarvey – a jaunting car driver – and was dressed in the uniform of his trade, waterproof cape, riding breeches and leather gaiters. He ferried people to and from the railway stations in Killarney and Killorglan, and even with the demise of the tourist trade seemed to make a living from it. His real purpose, however, was to travel around and about the area and keep abreast of local events and opinions. The speaker had been fully briefed on the local situation by Daly before the meeting.

The mission entrusted to The Man from Dublin was to gauge support and, if possible, create an appetite in Ireland's rural communities for a military campaign by Nationalists aimed at ending British rule. He was an excellent speaker with a consummate knowledge of both his subject and his audience, but experience gained from many meetings across the country told him that the only real support for armed rebellion was in Dublin and to a lesser extent in a few of the other large urban areas. Yet even in Dublin most Irish people believed that at the present time, the second year of the war, Irishmen should be fighting the Germans rather than the British. His superiors had come to accept his findings but were set in their opinion that once the shooting started most loyal Irishmen would rally to the flag and fight for the right to become a republic. They believed that the spilling of Irish blood, even if not immediately effective, would inspire future generations to carry on the struggle. So he had little choice but to do the best he could. He had some time ago given up the tactic of basing his arguments on the notorious Dublin lockout of 1913 when a federation of 400 Dublin businessmen refused to employ members of the Irish Transport and General Workers Union, and on the brutal attack by police on a public meeting of striking tram-workers in which three people were killed. It was one thing to tell people in the country areas that Dubliners suffered the worst housing conditions of any city in Europe, but expecting them to accept this as a reason for military action when life outside the capital was in its own way equally hard was, he had learned, a lost cause. Recently, however, he had been dealt a new and more powerful card to play.

He began his well prepared oration:

"Now I know very well that you good men down here in the County Kerry have no time to be worrying about what is happening up in Dublin. God knows you have troubles enough of your own, but I'm here to tell you that what happened in Dublin in 1913 is happening all over our beloved Ireland this very day."

As he went on to outline yet again the situation in Dublin he was aware of the lack of interest among those present, the majority of whom had never found cause to venture outside the mountainous confines of their native Kerry; but as he finished he looked directly at the young man by the window."I'm telling you again things like this are even now happening all over the country, and if you don't believe me you only have to look two miles down the road at Beaufort House."

At this James Quinlan, whose attention had been half on the speaker and half on the window where he was keeping a wary eye out for his father or any busybody who might report him to his father, visibly pricked up his ears as the speaker had been led to expect he would.

"The war is hitting our British masters hard. They are pulling up sticks all over Ireland like they did here in Beaufort taking their money with them and leaving thousands of good Irish people destitute!" Aware of the increase in attention he stepped forward and thumped his fist on the table and raised his voice.

"Now is the time to do something about it, the time for all Irishmen to rise up and throw off the yoke of oppression." His voice lowered and they had to strain to hear him. "And make no mistake, thousands of our countrymen have already joined the fight: I take it you've all heard of *Ruairi Mac Easmainn*?"

Only a couple of heads nodded. "All right Sir Roger Casement if we have to use his English title." This, as he had expected, raised little by way of further recognition but it provided him with the opening he needed to introduce the story of Roger Casement the British consular official turned poet, Irish patriot and revolutionary.

Roger Casement, who had been born into a Protestant family

in County Dublin in 1864, had in his youth been a supporter of Irish Nationalism. Having worked in Africa for some years however, he joined the British Foreign service and served in the Congo and later in Peru. His report on human rights abuses in the Congo was largely responsible for the Belgian king, Leopold, relinquishing his personal interests in that country and for the Belgian parliament taking over the administration of the Congo Free State from the king. In Peru and later Brazil, where he was promoted to Consul-General, he again brought to light atrocities committed in this instance by the major rubber interests against the native Indians. This work, coupled with his experiences in the Boer War, eventually led Casement to resign from the British Consular service and to adopt anti-Imperialist views. He moved inexorably back to his Irish Nationalist roots and helped in the formation of the Irish Volunteers, an organisation he eventually served as Chief of Staff. In November 1914, two months after the outbreak of war, he went first to America and then Germany to solicit German support for the cause of Irish Independence.

"Now there is a real Irish Patriot," said The Man from Dublin as he ended his potted history of Casement. "And do you know what he's doing now? No. Well I'll tell you. He's over there in Germany forming an Irish Brigade! That's right, an Irish Brigade, just like the one the great Patrick Sarsfield died fighting with in France all those years ago. Only this time they won't be fighting in France" – again he banged the table shaking the lamp and further agitating the shadows – "but here in Ireland herself; fighting for Irish freedom!" He let this sink in. "Where are these Irish fighting men coming from you might be thinking. They are Irishmen taken as prisoners of war by the Germans who have seen what fools they were to be conned into joining the British and are now determined to put that right by fighting against the real enemy, the Imperialist British. It's up to us, all of us, to support them."

The Man from Dublin looked closely to see if anyone there realised that what he had told them was far from the truth: Casement's grand design for an Irish Brigade had actually come to nothing. All Irishmen fighting in the British army were volunteers and so only a tiny few of those held as prisoners-of-war by the

Germans had taken up the option of joining Casement. He had not been able to recruit enough to form a company let alone a brigade and so the plan had been abandoned. The Man waited a moment wondering just how far he should pursue this line of argument. If he said too much he was taking the risk of compromising a covert operation of the utmost importance to his cause. On the other hand the news was not likely to remain secret much longer and might just be enough to make up the ambivalent minds of at least some of his audience.

So the homily continued: "You will want to know how we will arm ourselves for the fight. Well I'll tell you, and woe betide any one of you who breathes a word outside of this room. You tell nobody, neither father, nor mother, nor brother, nor priest, because if you do, make no mistake you will have the blood of hundreds of brave Irishmen on your conscience and for this you will burn in Hell! and that," he added, "after you have been branded an informer and found an early grave."

He paused. With any luck this would instil in them a sense of being privileged insiders, while at the same time making it plain that punishment for any indiscretion would certainly be more immediate than that which their parish priest never ceased to remind them was the fate of sinners.

He lowered his voice conspiratorially and they had to strain to hear his words: "The Germans are this minute supplying Casement with more guns and ammunition than we will ever need to drive the British out of Ireland."

This he reasoned was the right note to finish on. "Well there you have it. Now it's up to you. It's time for every man Jack of you to make up his mind, and don't take too long about it or you'll miss your chance."

The Man from Dublin left the room, but failed to tell them that all Casement had managed to extract from the Germans, who always remained sceptical of him, was the promise of some captured Russian rifles and a few machine guns with a minimum supply of ammunition; far less than was hoped for.

Chapter 3

The time was approaching ten in the evening, far too early under normal circumstances for the bar to be empty, but tonight was different. On hearing from Pat Devlin that the meeting in the kitchen was nearing a conclusion the regular drinkers filed out. Better, they thought, not to get involved. So when the men came through from the back into the bar they found it deserted save for Devlin who, following instructions, had placed several glasses of black stout on the counter. He invited them to 'have one on the house'.

Anxious to appear a man amongst men, and with a bravado instilled by the tone of the meeting, James Quinlan helped himself to one; as he sipped the unfamiliar liquid he found himself standing next to Liam Daly.

"So you're old enough to drink now eh Jim." Outside of the family, and out of hearing of his father, the formal 'James' was usually replaced by the more familiar 'Jim'.

"Oh sure I am."

"Well now, and what did you think of what your man had to say. Will you be joining the lads when the day comes?"

"And why wouldn't I?" came the impulsive reply. "I'll have to see how things turn out at home with me Da losing his job things are tight, me and Bill are the only ones bringing any money in. But when the day comes I'll be there."

"Good man yourself," said Daly, "but what will your father have to say about it?"

James hesitated, "I don't know, maybe he won't say anything at all, and anyway he has to find out first."

"Jesus Jim," said Daly, "you're not still afraid of the old man are you? You should be your own man, do like your brother Jack and bugger off away from here to lead your own life, and that doesn't, mean you have to join up and fight for the Brits like your brother either. There'll be plenty of fighting to be had here at home soon enough."

Daly moved on to spread the message among the rest of the company.

One of the first to leave, James was met outside by his younger brother Bill – William in the presence his father – who had obviously been waiting for him in the bright moonlight. He couldn't help but notice that Bill carried two fat rabbits freshly retrieved from his snares.

"You'll get caught by the gamekeeper one night soon," said James.

"Sure there's no gamekeeper anymore," said William, "he got the sack like Da." James considered this in the light of what he had heard earlier.

They walked homeward in the light cast by a Hunter's Moon. Down the rough road that passed for a village street their hobnailed footsteps rang out in the clear frosty air. "What did the fella from Dublin have to say?" asked an obviously excited William.

James passed on to his brother the gist of what he had heard in the pub kitchen, and exacted from William a solemn promise not to breathe a word about Roger Casement and the guns or it might go hard for both of them. "It's well known what happens to informers Bill."

"I'm no informer," said an indignant William. "Are you going to join the rebels and fight for the Republic."

"I am," came the determined reply.

"But I thought you were all set to follow Jack and fight the Germans."

"I was, but I've changed my mind, I'm not going to help the very people that put Da out of work."

William, who had long ago learned to take all of James' far-fetched dreams with a pinch of salt, suddenly realised that he had never seen his brother seem so serious about anything. James was showing a determination he had not previously noticed. He became concerned enough to look for a counter argument:

"But what if a rebellion starts against the British and you have to fight against Jack?"

"The Brits won't send Irish troops to fight over here, and if they did Jack and his friends would never raise arms against fellow Irishmen." James sounded confident but it was a disturbing thought.

The tone and form of James' words disturbed William, but he said no more as they continued the journey home. As they reached the cottage gate James, reverting to his former self, said ,"When we get in don't forget we were together all night up at The Gap snaring rabbits."

.   .   .

Later on that night The Man from Dublin sat in the bar with the pub owner passing on the latest news regarding the political situation and in particular the proposed rebellion, or at least that portion of the news he deemed it prudent to impart.

A dog barked in the yard and The Man moved into the darkened grocery shop while his host went to the window.

"It's all right it's only Liam Daly," he said and went to open the door. Daly was, he suspected, a trusted member of the Nationalist movement, but he said nothing of this.

Daly entered the room. "Could you leave us for a minute Pat," said The Man.

Devlin left without any sign of resentment at being excluded – he was experienced enough to know how things were done.

"Well Liam what do you think? How did it go?"

"Not bad," replied Daly, "I think we're sure to get a few to join us. The bit about Beaufort House hit home."

"Good," said The Man. "Now listen Liam we have a little job for you that will mean you giving up the jarvey work here. You'll have heard about the factory being built by the Brits over in Scotland, anyone with eyes in his head can see that it's a munitions factory and they're crying out for labour to get it working for them. There will surely be men from around here applying for the work there if they haven't already."

"And I'm to be the man to stop them." Daly was not averse to the idea.

"Not at all Liam, just the opposite, we want you to drop in over there yourself. Have a sniff around and find out what's what. And anyway they say the money's good."

Daly was certain there was more to it than that. "And what happens then?"

"Now don't get ahead of yourself Liam me bucko. I'll only say this: the Brits have been clever enough to build this place where it can't be reached by German bombers, and they can't send ships down the Irish Sea to bombard it, they would be blown out of the water before they got anywhere near the place. I'll leave you to work the rest out for yourself. Let me know as soon as you land over there and I'll tell you more."

Before the sun rose the next morning Daly harnessed a horse to his jaunting car and drove The Man into Killarney to catch the Dublin train.

Chapter 4

Lance Bombardier John Joseph (Jack) Quinlan had enlisted in the Royal Field Artillery in the Spring of 1915. Now, almost a year later, he found himself sitting on an empty ammunition box writing a letter home. Having had no more than a basic education he was not comfortable with the task of letter writing, but he was conscious of the worry the lack of news must be causing his family.

He thought over what little he had so far learned about this alien land he had just arrived in and pondered how much of the military situation the censor would allow him to relate to his family. He was conscious of the fact that they had not heard from him for some time and he was anxious to let them know that he was fit and well.

His last letter home had been written two months previously, just before he joined the troopship bound for Gallipoli. But with that misguided campaign grinding to a close, and the British Army being withdrawn, his battery had been forced to spend many weeks cooped up on board ship in the Mediterranean Sea waiting for orders. They were eventually directed to form part of a force being assembled in Mesopotamia, and after all those weeks on the ship, he was glad to find his feet back on dry land, wherever in the world it might be. He felt that the censor would not object to him telling the family where he was, and he smiled as he imagined them frantically searching for Mesopotamia in a dog-eared school atlas. They would be amazed to learn that he was at that moment within sight of the river Tigris in the land where the ancient Biblical city of Babylon had once stood. He had been told that it had not altered since the time of Christ.

They would be happy at the news that he had been promoted to the rank of Lance Bombardier, but he knew that he could not tell them the full circumstances under which he had achieved his first stripe. The fact of the matter was that so many soldiers, including several NCOs had succumbed to a range of illnesses as a result of exposure to the terrible conditions: boiling hot with unbearable humidity by day and below zero temperatures by night. He finished his letter by reiterating that he was safe and enjoying life and hoped and prayed that all was well at home.

What Jack could not pass on to his family was the detailed account of the military situation that officers and NCOs had been given by their Battery Commander.

Mesopotamia formed part of the Turkish Ottoman Empire. At the outbreak of the war in September 1914 Britain sent units of the Indian Army with some Western troops to secure the oil installations in the region on which the Royal Navy depended. They were initially successful and captured Basra and its oilfields without encountering resistance from the Turks. This gave them impetus to move further up the Shatt-al-Arab and the town of Qurna fell to British forces in December 1914.

In April 1915 a Turkish attack on Basra was repulsed and as the enemy retreated British troops followed and captured Amara in May. Following this more troops were sent to Mesopotamia and it was decided that an attempt should be made to capture Baghdad. This city marked the end of the line for the Constantinople-Baghdad railway. Built by the Germans the railway formed the principal Turkish supply line and her main link with Germany.

Nasiriyeh was taken in August and Kut-al-Amara in September. But at this point the advance faltered due to lack of supplies. Turkish reinforcements had also arrived and the British force was defeated at Ctesiphon in November. They were forced to retreat back to Kut-al-Amara where they were besieged by the Turks.

When he had finished his letter Jack hurried off to Battery HQ to ensure that it reached home as quickly as possible. Rather than cause undue anxiety he had deliberately said little in the letter about what he thought might lay ahead, but he was certain that it would not be long before he saw action for the first time. Things were proceeding swiftly and the battery was being made ready to move. They had been told that the Indian troops surrounded in Kut would not be able to hold out much longer.

As he returned from posting his letter Jack looked at the six 18 pounder field guns which made up C Battery. When the battery had disembarked the gun crews had unpacked and prepared the weapons for action. What was obvious to even the lowest ranking artilleryman was how little ammunition had been unloaded, and Jack feared that this did not augur well for the future.

He would have been even more worried had he known how right he was. It soon became clear that British commanders had failed to recognise the difficulty of supplying an army in an area without proper roads and prone to flooding. The only practical means of transport proved to be camels and flat-bottomed boats. These were always in short supply as was everything else the army needed. There were never enough guns, ammunition, food or medicines. Supply columns were also constantly harassed by the local Marsh Arabs who made no distinction between the British and the Turks and were ready to raid both. Conditions for the troops were appalling: extremes of temperature, mosquitoes, flies, sand and dust. What was arid desert one day became a severely flooded swamp the next. All of which lead to high levels of sickness and therefore a shortage of men

With his promotion he would now have command of the 6 man crew of one of the 18 pounders and with God's help he determined to acquit himself well.

Chapter 5

The Mass was slightly shorter this Sunday as the *Gloria* was not included on this the First Sunday of Advent, the beginning of the Church's year.

As the Quinlan family made their way homeward the children, including the two older boys, were not aware of what their father had decided. They would be told immediately after the midday meal what the future held for them.

Home was a cottage close by one end of the bridge which spanned the river Laune. It stood just inside the ornate wrought iron main gates of Beaufort House, and belonged to the estate. Occupancy of the cottage brought with it a requirement to act as gatekeepers, which duty the Quinlan family carried out whenever the owners were in residence.

The interior of the cottage consisted of five rooms on two floors, three on the ground floor and two upstairs. The kitchen, with its stone-flagged floor was by some margin the largest room in the house and at this time also served as the main living area. It was well, if plainly, furnished with a solid wooden table around which stood a set of eight sturdy dining chairs unmatched but of good quality. There was a wooden settle along one wall with a built-in chest under the seat, and a dresser for crockery and cooking utensils stood against the wall by the door which led directly in from the front garden. Where this room differed from the typical Irish country kitchen of the day was that it boasted a turf burning range rather than the usual open hearth. A large coarse mat lay on the floor in front of the range and on either side were placed two upright armchairs, these were the exclusive property of the master and mistress and trespassing by other members of the family was not encouraged. To the rear a door led into a single story scullery containing a large stone sink fed by a hand-operated water pump. Off the kitchen was another sizable room originally designed to act as the parlour but which, to accommodate the needs of a growing family, had been converted into a bedroom for James and William who shared a double bed. There was also a narrow single bed, unslept in but kept in a state of readiness by their mother in anticipation of her eldest son's return home. From the kitchen a staircase led up to a landing large enough to accommodate a single bed for young Michael. A door led off the landing into the main bedroom furnished with a double bed, a wardrobe and a washstand. Beyond this was a smaller bedroom again containing a double bed for the two girls, Elizabeth and Mary.

At the front of the cottage was a small flower garden behind a painted metal railing. It was the duty of the occupants to keep the garden cultivated to a standard befitting a gatehouse and the railings were regularly painted by estate staff to match the main gates. Woodland grew up almost to the wall on one side with a small fenced-in clearing where the family kept some chickens, and a few turkeys for the Christmas trade. Behind the cottage a vegetable garden led down to within a few yards of the river bank. The bridge carrying the road over the river sloped down on the other side of the cottage where a low dry arch, the last on this side of the bridge, had been boarded up to form a shelter for a winter turf supply; beside this stood the wooden 'outhouse'.

Although not grand, this accommodation was far better appointed than the majority of working peoples' dwellings, including many of the farmhouses, in the neighbourhood. Only ever meant to be occupied by a senior estate worker, in this case the coachman, it had been designed to reflect the general status of the main house. When the main house had been temporally closed for the duration of the war it had been decided that the coachman and his family could continue to live there rent free.

Michael Quinlan was conscious of the fact that it was not just his family but also his home he had decided he must leave behind.

The previous night, while the older boys were out, and with the younger children in bed, Michael had discussed the situation with Annie who, though not accustomed to questioning his judgement even when consulted, had raised some objections. She expressed concern about his age and state of health and reminded him of the chest pains he sometimes experienced following any strenuous activity; pains he thought he had kept from her. She worried that he was no longer the vigorous young man he had once been and so would have difficulty in standing up to the demands of unaccustomed hard labour, while at the same time having to change the habits of a lifetime in order to adapt to life in an alien world. But, once he had explained his reasons, concentrating on the possibility of James being lured into supporting the expected 'troubles' and his desire to do something in support of Jack, she had acceded to his wishes as he had known she would; although she was quite certain that there was a more compelling reason for his decision. Knowing that her man would be much too proud to sit back and leave his sons to act as breadwinners, she could see how the thought of being able to earn good wages, most of which would be sent home to her and the children, would be too strong for him to resist. He tried hard to disguise the fact that his pride had already taken a severe knock from being laid off, but she could sense his hurt. She was proud of the man she had met and married in County Kildare, had travelled with to Silvermines in County Tipperary where their three eldest had been born and, over ten years ago, had followed here to County Kerry.

"You must do what you think to be right as you have always done '*gra mo croidhe,*'" she told him, "but go easy on James, sure he's only half way between being a boy and being a man, he is easily led and he's trying hard to live up to you and Jack. Anyway," she added, more to hearten herself than anything else, "'tis only until after this cruel war is over, and then God willing we can go back to where we were before."

"I wouldn't count on that Annie," said Michael. "I'm thinking that the days of the horse and carriage are numbered, and the war will be the last nail in the coffin. The motor car is taking over and to my way of thinking it will be the only winner to come out of these troubled times. We can only do what we can today and pray that tomorrow brings something better."

She said nothing more but promised herself that she would be behind him as always and she would say nothing to the rest of the family but leave it to him to break the news himself.

"But why can't I come too Da?" This was the reaction he had expected from William (whose mother sharply reminded him "to call your father Sir") when he revealed that he intended to seek employment for both himself and James as building workers at somewhere called Gretna in southern Scotland where a new factory was being built, and they would be leaving in a few weeks time after spending Christmas at home.

"No William, you have to stay here to take care of your mother, young Michael and your sisters. I know you are up to the job, and if I were to let you come who would look after the garden and the pony, who would drive your mother into Killarney and to Mass on Sunday? You will have to take over as head of the house while we are gone." His new responsibility as head of the family went some way to pacifying William but it was obvious that he would have preferred to play a more exciting part with his father and brother.

"And you Michael," he continued, "will have to help William and your mother as well."

James had taken several minutes to digest the news. He was of course aware that some local men had gone 'over the water' to find work in the building boom brought about by the war. It was not known exactly where in Britain they went, but there were strong rumours that the building they were working on was a munitions factory. James had not, however, even in his wildest dreams, thought that his father would deign to join them as a labourer. It came to him that if he was to go with his father then he would have to modify the plans he had been quietly forming and was close to putting into action. The idea of going off to the British mainland with his father did in fact hold a great appeal, but since the meeting in the back kitchen of the pub the imaginative James had begun to see himself as a leading figure in the fight for Irish freedom.

"But won't that only be helping the British, the very same British tyrants who gave you the sack Da? That factory makes ammunition and any day now they'll be using it against Irishmen as well as the Germans. And I don't want to be helping them to do it." James had blurted it out before he could stop himself.

In any other circumstances Michael would have turned on James, but he was sure now that what he feared had already happened. James, whom he had prevented from following Jack into the army, had been influenced by the Nationalist rebels and had taken their message to heart. Rather than shout at his son he realised that, however much it went against the grain, it would be more beneficial to try and resolve the problem quietly.

"It wasn't the British who put me out of work," he told James. "It was the war, His Lordship had no choice. If anyone is to blame it's the Germans, the sooner they are beaten the sooner we can all go back to where we were before, and if I can help to do this I will." He followed this up with the one statement he knew James could not argue with in front of the family:

"Your own brother Jack is fighting in this war. If we don't help him by helping the British we're putting him in worse danger than he is already." He regretted having to say this in front of Annie who he knew would worry all the more, but he could see no other way of ending the argument.

"Now you think about that James. Your duty is to this family and it's not only Jack, you have to look out for your mother and brothers and sisters too before you start thinking you know all about politics and getting mixed up in something you don't understand."

He paused for a moment. "And if it's joining the rebels you're after don't forget that the greatest of all Kerrymen, Daniel O'Connell himself, was opposed to blood being spilt in the cause of freedom."

The rest of the family were aghast at the unexpected way Michael had dealt with James' mutinous behaviour, never before had they seen their father react with such lenience at a direct attack on his absolute authority. But it served to bring home to them the severity of the situation. Even James was taken aback. After a long pause during which Michael looked across at his wife to see what anxiety he might have caused and was gratified to find her giving him a nod of approval.

"We'll leave it at that." Michael stood up, reached over to the mantelpiece for his pipe and Sunday afternoon slowly returned to normal.

The three youngest sat up to the table to do their school homework under the watchful eye of their mother. James, aware that everybody except his father who seemed totally occupied with his pipe and newspaper had their eyes on him, eventually rose and went out. After what he thought was a decent interval William followed. He caught up with James who was making his way across the bridge.

"Sure didn't you get away with it there Jim," he said. "He must be getting old and thought he was talking to Jack. But hard lines, you'll have to go with him anyway."

"I'm getting fed up with everybody talking about Jack all the time. I'd go off to the war too if I didn't think I'd be helping the bloody Brits." James regretted it the moment he said it, but would not retract in front of his younger brother.

William, who had wanted desperately to talk about the momentous news their father had broken, was taken aback by James's sudden and uncharacteristic attack on the older brother he had always seemed to venerate. He had a mind to reprimand James, but sensitive of the mood of the moment, he changed the subject:

"I'm off up The Gap to see if there are any deer around, this hard weather might have driven a few down from the mountain, will you be coming with me?"

"No" said James. "I think I'll stop here for a while."

Chapter 6

James sat on the cold stone parapet alone with his thoughts. He bitterly regretted his spur of the moment remark about Jack, he certainly hadn't meant it, and hoped that he would be able to make amends to William, who he knew he must have hurt.

Thinking on it he began to realise that he would soon have to make up his mind about what direction he wanted his life to take. On the one hand he desperately wanted to be his own man and go his own way, while at the same time he did not want to fall out with his father, which would cause a rift within the family. It was not that he hated his father or even feared him, far from it, it would have hurt his pride to say so but deep down he loved the man and he readily acknowledged that he respected him. This was why he had felt such anger at the seemingly off-handed way the masters of Beaufort House had treated their coachman. Added to this was the fact that his father's sacking had laid on him a responsibility that had not previously been his. The necessity of bringing in a regular wage had prevented him from marching off to war like his brother. Resentment had been festering over the weeks, and so what he had heard in the pub kitchen a few nights ago had a profound effect.

He knew little about Nationalist politics, Home Rule or the desire for an Irish Republic, certainly not enough to quarrel, even if he had been of a mind to, with the lessons he had heard preached in the back kitchen. But it seemed to him that only by embracing the rebel cause could he go his own way and live life as he wanted to live it. He had briefly considered the obvious contradiction between fighting for Britain and fighting against them, but in his mind he had been able to pass this off and put it down to the change of circumstances. At least, he thought, he had learned about the duplicity of Ireland's British masters before signing up to fight for them. But now he was expected to go and help the British build a factory to produce munitions to be used against the Germans, who he had been told were Ireland's allies. To confuse things even further he could not dismiss the persistent voice that kept reminding him of the attraction of going away to work and earning what he felt would amount to 'a man's wage'.

Winter darkness was beginning to fall when his thoughts were interrupted by the sound of an approaching horse. He looked and saw Liam Daly turning onto the bridge, perched high on the seat of his jaunting car.

"Well now there's a sad sight if ever I saw one," said Daly, halting the car and looking down at James. "You have the look of the man who lost a penny and found a farthing. What are you doing out here in the cold when you have a warm turf fire at home?"

"Sure I'm only thinking about things Liam," said James.

"Thinking is it? Well I'm thinking that if you don't come up here off that cold stone wall you'll catch a cold in your arse and your thinking days will be over. Come on I'll give you a lift home."

James hesitated then rose and climbed up on the side seat of the jaunting car.

"Now there's a quare thing," said Daly when James was seated. "Jim Quinlan thinking, you always struck me as more a man of action, what brought this on?"

"My father wants me to go across the water with him to work at building some big factory."

"Christ Almighty!" exclaimed Daly. "Michael Quinlan? Now I've heard it all. He's the last man alive I thought would turn his hand to labouring, sure I had him down for doing nothing but polishing his fancy carriage up at the house there for the rest of the war."

James resented hearing his father spoken of in this manner, but he was beginning to learn the dangers of saying too much too quickly and so kept his thoughts to himself.

"Would I be right in thinking that you're not too keen on the idea yourself?" was Daly's next remark.

"I'm not sure yet what I'll do," said James. "I don't want to go against Da, but I don't want to fight for the Brits either."

"I hear there's good money to be had over there. Sure wasn't I thinking of taking a shot at it myself. There's nothing to be made from the jarvey business any more. Since the British sank the 'Lusitania' and blamed it on the Germans the Yanks aren't coming over any more."

It was James' turn to be shocked. "You mean you're going to help the Brits win the war instead of staying here to fight for Ireland?"

Daly touched the side of his nose with his finger. "Ah now Jimmy boy there's more than one way to fight for Ireland. There are a lot of loyal Irishmen over in America raising money for The Cause, and isn't Roger Casement himself in Germany this very minute doing his bit. A lot of good work can be done in many strange places."

Before James had time to fully consider this they had reached the cottage and Daly stopped the car. "Listen Jim, when I get over there I'll look you up and we'll have another chat."

Over the next few weeks James tried to find Daly in the hope of learning more about what had been said about being able to serve Ireland from afar, but the jarvey seemed to have disappeared from the face of the earth. As the days passed without any sign of Daly, his thoughts turned more and more to the prospect of accompanying his father to Scotland and, without further outside influence he became reconciled to the idea. His father was relieved that his son seemed, for the moment at least, to have put aside any further thoughts of joining the rebels.

Jack's letter arrived home just in time for Christmas 1915 where it immediately relieved the air of uncertainty engendered by the lack of news and the pending departure of Michael and James. The reply to the letter took the form of a united family exercise. William, whose handwriting was judged to be best did the actual writing while the others chipped in with ideas of their own. Michael and Annie thought carefully about how to break the news to Jack and eventually agreed to tell him the full story, omitting only their worries regarding James' nationalist leanings. Young Michael added a little prayer for Jack's safety, Elizabeth proudly penned her name to show how good she was at school, and Mary's contribution amounted to a line of unsteady ' A B Cs'. Finally satisfied with their work, William was dispatched off to the village post office to mail it.

As they left Mass on a rainy Christmas morning, Michael gathered up his family and looking at James he remarked. "That's the last Mass we'll have here for a while Jim." It took a minute to sink in, but then James realised that it was the first time he had ever heard his father use the shortened form of his name. Annie smiled to herself as she watched a sense of companionship develop between her husband and son.

But five hundred miles away to the north-west in a peat bog along the Solway Firth, not unlike the one where they dug their own turf, events were taking shape that would test their new-found relationship to the limit.

Chapter 7

Michael did not like Dublin. On the few previous occasions when he had visited Ireland's capital he had felt uncomfortably out of his depth and found the dirt, the noise and the crowded streets unpleasant. At home he was a man at ease with his environment; here, in spite of his good tweed suit and bowler hat, he felt like just another clumsy countryman lost in the big city. The train had been on time, arriving at Kingsbridge Station at midday following the three hour journey from Killarney. It was a mere five hours since they had left home, but during those hours their world had been transformed.

By seven that morning, William had harnessed the pony to the trap and they were ready for the sorrowful ritual of saying goodbye; a ritual which had been carried out tearfully by Annie, young Michael and the two little girls, while James suppressed his emotions and tried to emulate his father's dignified air. William, who would drive them into Killarney, felt embarrassed by his wishing to be going all the way with them, and busied himself with loading his father's well worn leather suitcase and James' newly acquired carpet bag into the trap. The threatened rain held off as the pony trotted the five Irish miles into the station and at one point the watery early morning sun broke through and was reflected off the surface of the Lower Lake. To the south, MacGillicuddy's Reeks were topped by a recent heavy fall of snow and the high ground to the north around Aghadoe carried a light dusting, which would soon be washed away by the pending rain. When they arrived in Killarney, the town itself was still asleep as if not wishing to be party to their departure, the only activity being centred round the station where porters helped the handful of winter travellers load their luggage onto the Dublin train. Having purchased tickets that would take them all the way to Gretna in Scotland, Michael and James said their goodbyes to William and found an empty compartment in a third class carriage at the back of the train.

The rain started as soon as the train left Killarney and accompanied them all the way to Dublin. "William will have a wet drive home," said Michael as he sat on the uncomfortable wooden seat. The movement of the train over the tracks and the confining space of the compartment made him miss the high driver's seat of a well sprung carriage and the more gentle movement generated by a team of well schooled horses. But all that was behind him now and it was best not to look back.

The train travelled eastwards to Mallow in County Cork, turned northwards and eastwards through Carlow and into Tipperary, then on through Laois and Kildare to Dublin. Passengers got on and passengers got off at the various stops but only the persistent rain seemed to be travelling with them all the way to Dublin. On several occasions people, in their usual talkative Irish way, tried to strike up a conversation, but Michael, not an accomplished conversationalist at the best of times, was too preoccupied with his own thoughts. James on the other hand was too busy glued to the carriage window looking out at places he had heard of but never seen. As they neared Dublin they ate the sandwiches lovingly prepared for them that morning.

Michael was stiff and sore by the time they got off the train at Kingsbridge Station but was relieved that he felt no physical pain in his chest, just the emotional ache brought on by leaving home. So, with a couple of hours to kill before catching the boat train north to Belfast he suggested that they take a walk around the city; a suggestion eagerly accepted by James whose only previous experience of urban life had been limited to the town of Killarney. He had wondered at the sheer size of the city as they travelled through the outskirts into the centre, but his first sight of that cavernous railway station had left him dumbfounded. Michael at least knew what to expect but to James it was another world. If the size of the station surprised him, it was the number and diversity of the people that really took his breath away. There were businessmen, tradesmen and labourers, soldiers, sailors and railway staff in uniform. Grand ladies, gentlemen and beggars, priests, nuns and a brown-robed friar with sandaled feet; crying babies and older children being kept under strict control by parents; young and old, military and civilian, sacred and secular alike and all too intent on their own affairs to notice the two new arrivals. Travellers boarded trains and travellers got off trains, first second and third classes all mingling together on the platforms. Luggage was being moved around on porters' trolleys or carried by hand. The hiss of the steam from the locomotives, the whistles of the guards, the calls of the vendors and the general chatter made James' head spin.

To catch the boat train for Larne they would have to make their way to Amiens Street Station and as they had plenty of time, and the rain had stopped, Michael decided they would walk and he could show James something of Dublin. They left Kingsbridge Station and Michael, not at all certain of finding his way around the capital, followed an uncertain circular route, but this did allow him to point out some of Dublin's famous landmarks: Trinity College, which James knew from his school lessons housed the Book of Kells. They walked along the Quays past the The Four Courts and saw The Guinness Brewery, which ran from St. James Gate to Thomas Street. Several times Michael had to ask for directions especially when they got lost in some of the poorer districts of the city – a city which at that time had the highest rate of infant mortality in Europe. On a few occasions he was helped by Dublin's 'shawlies' – women wearing a black fringed shawl with a child wrapped in it. As they walked past the Imperial Hotel, Michael recognised it as the place where the trade union organiser James Larkin, known as 'Big Jim', had addressed a crowd from a balcony during the infamous Dublin 'lockout' in 1913. Michael, whose entire working life had been based on the principle of loyalty to his employers, and with a son serving in the British army, considered men like Larkin to be nothing more than troublemakers.

Eventually they found their way over the river Liffey into Sackville St. (*later to become famous as O'Connell St*) Michael wore his smart coachman's coat and James a well worn raincoat, which had until recently belonged to his brother Jack. It started to rain again and, having walked the length of the street, they took shelter in the massive portico of the General Post Office and James tried to come to terms with the hectic everyday life of a major city.

"When were you up in Dublin before Da?" James asked.

"I think it was about twelve years ago Jim, you were just going to school. Her Ladyship had me here for a week to drive her around, We stayed in a big house out near Pheonix Park. Would you believe she shipped the small carriage, a horse, myself and her maid up here on the train."

"Was it the same as it is now?"

"No, it's changed since then," said Michael.

The last time he had been to the city, horses had seemed to bear sole responsibility for transporting both people and commerce through the streets. Now there were very few to be seen. Motor cars and lorries had taken their place, and even the omnibuses relied on the new form of horse power as they vied for street space with the trams. What horses there were seemed to have been reduced to drawing milk carts and bakers vans. He was strangely saddened to see a motor car drive over a small pile of horse manure as if even that would have to bow to its total dominance. He was more certain than ever that his predictions regarding the future of horse-drawn transport had been correct; the horse would be reduced to labouring in the fields. From what he had seen of the war it was plain that even on the battlefield the horse was only of use for hauling guns and supplies. The days when the cavalry decided the outcome of a battle were gone, yet like the soldiers the horses were dying in their thousands.

The other change he noticed was the posters, and he was aware that James had seen them too. He had seen several examples of Kitchener's appeal for volunteers being defaced and inducements to join the Irish Republican Brotherhood or the Irish Volunteers scrawled across them. There were also posters specifically bearing the same message. He said nothing about them as he thought it best not to get into a discussion about the rights and wrongs of Irish Nationalism with James.

He shook himself out of his doleful mood and motioned James to follow. "Have you seen enough? I haven't tasted railway tea for years, come on and we'll see what the station tea room can do for us."

This time Michael got detailed directions from a friendly policeman and soon found his way to the Amiens Street Station. He went to the counter to get the drinks and as he turned back with the cups in his hands he saw James in conversation with a flashily dressed and powdered young woman. It took him a moment to recall that Dublin boasted one of the largest red light districts in Europe and with the coming of the war this had clearly spread to Amiens Street Station where it catered for the needs of the army of servicemen passing through. James was being propositioned and it was obvious that he didn't know it. His only experience of girls had been at school, and although these girls mostly remained friends, both he and they were still considered far too young for anything other than their own private romantic notions. Anything more would have invited the wrath of both family and The Church which constantly preached against the taking of 'forbidden liberties'. He had sometimes been teased by the maids at Beaufort House but had not fully understood why their remarks caused them so much mirth. So now he was completely out of his depth, and not understanding what she wanted or what was expected of him he touched his cap and turned away leaving her standing there muttering something about not being able to spot a 'red necked culshie' as country folk were known to Dubliners. Finally seated and drinking their tea it would be hard to imagine who suffered most embarrassment, father or son, as Michael tried to explain to James things the lad had only heard in sniggering conversations with his equally woefully misinformed friends. But it did not escape Michael's notice that the son he was still inclined to think of as a boy had been taken for a man by the prostitute.

They left the tea room and collected their belongings then went to catch the train north for Belfast and the port of Larne. As they searched for their platform they inadvertently wandered through an open archway and were prevented from going further by a burly member of the Royal Irish Constabulary. They did, however, see enough to realise what was happening in this secluded part of the station. The girls here wore cloaks beneath which could be glimpsed long white aprons and their white headdresses were marked with red crosses. The train standing at the platform also bore red crosses in a white circle on the sides of the carriages; all along the platform rested a long line of stretchers on which lay blanket wrapped figures some with resigned looks on their white faces and others whose faces were obscured by bandages. At least one figure was totally covered by the blanket; nearby a soldier with one leg was being helped along on crutches and another in a wheelchair had no legs at all; white coated doctors moved among them with the nurses. This was an aspect of war James had not previously considered. What he had just witnessed was disturbingly very much the real thing, totally removed from the pictures he had seen or the censored newspaper reports he had read. He was badly shaken, but as they walked away he managed to put into words what both were thinking:

"What'll we do if something like that happens to Jack, Da?"

"We can only pray that it doesn't," Michael quietly replied.

Chapter 8

In the buffet room at Citadel Station in Carlisle the ill-assorted trio sat at a corner table. Ill matched they may have been in terms of appearance, but they were united in their unwavering adherence to a single purpose. The Man from Dublin had removed his raincoat and Liam Daly had shaken off the rain and removed the waterproof jarvey's cape, which still served him well in bad weather even though he had recently given up that particular trade. The third member of the party still wore a heavy dark overcoat, which remained buttoned up to his throat.

The venue for the meeting had been carefully chosen. The buffet was a long narrow room between platforms. There was a long line of square tables, each with four chairs along one wall. At a table in a far corner they could pass for three lone travellers sheltering from the rain while waiting for their various trains without attracting attention from other rail passengers, not that there were many of those around at this time on a rainy mid-week afternoon. In a pub or cafe they would have been the object of some probably idle but unwelcome curiosity. Here on the British mainland there were no sympathisers to provide more secure meeting accommodation, as there had been in Beaufort just over a month ago.

"Do you know Sean Conlon, Liam?" asked The Man by way of introducing the man in the dark coat.

"No, but I've heard a bit about him," replied Daly as the pair shook hands.

"What news have you for us Liam?" asked The Man.

Daly lit a cigarette and cast a wary eye at the man in the overcoat. "Sure it's only a week since I landed and that's no time at all to see what's going on."

"It's all right Liam, we can be quite candid in front of Sean here, he knows the score. Wasn't it the happy day for us when their worships up in Armagh got fed up with him at home and sent him over here as shepherd to the flock of good Irish Catholics coming over for the money."

In the humid atmosphere of the room, Conlon undid the top button of his coat to reveal a stiff white Roman collar.

Daly was surprised to hear that the priest, well-known for his sermons unashamedly supporting the Republican cause, and which provided so much embarrassment to the hierarchy of The Church in Ireland, had been sent here of all places. But it would be, as The Man from Dublin had intimated, extremely useful to have an ally who would undoubtedly wield some influence over the thousands of the Catholic Irish navvies employed at Gretna.

"So now Liam, you have surely seen something that I can take back to our leaders at home."

"I'll tell you this," said Daly, "you never saw the like before in your life. This is nothing like any building site I ever came across before. There must be thousands of Irishmen over there in Gretna, building roads and railways as well as the factory itself. They are in digs all over the place, you'll see train loads of them coming into Carlisle here in a couple of hours and it's the same in every town for miles around. I haven't been here long enough to see for myself yet but I bet there are some lively times to be had here on a Saturday night. The site itself must be as big as ten Irish townslands, it starts up near the town of Annan and they say it will stretch over the English border to Longtown up the road from here. It would take a good few hours walk to get from one end to the other, which I suppose, is why they need all the roads and railways. There are whole towns of huts for the workers already built and there are more going up every day. I hear that they will soon be building houses for the bosses and hostels for a whole army of women workers, and maybe even churches for yourself and other ministers Father."

He looked at Conlon who was nodding in agreement with the description of what was happening in the peat bogs and farmland along the nearby north shore of the Solway Firth.

Anticipating the next question Daly carried on: "From what I hear, The Brits are so desperate for ammunition they will start making it here even before the factory is finished, and that will definitely be sometime soon."

"And what is your part in all this Liam?"

"Now isn't that the funny thing," said Daly. "I'm not working for anyone, all I have to do is walk around looking like a navvy and nobody bothers me. Yesterday I was with a gang building three or four massive earth banks between the different parts of the factory."

At this The Man from Dublin looked up sharply. "Well now is that a fact. From what the experts tell us that definitely means this place will be making and handling explosives. Those banks are to make sure that if there is an accidental explosion in one place it won't set off another one down the line. I tell you Liam you will have to report every little thing you see and hear because any of it could be important to the men over in Dublin. That goes for you too Sean."

"And important to the Germans?" asked the priest.

"That depends on whether we tell them anything," said The Man. "And that's another thing, keep an eye open for anyone who you think might be a German spy. I know that won't be easy because they're clever buggers, but we think they're sure to try and check the place out themselves."

He leaned across the table and handed Daly a small piece of paper. "There's one of the lads coming over to give you a hand, he'll be told how to contact you, but what's in that note will tell you how to check that he is who he says he is. Between you we want you to find out as much as you can. If you can, try to persuade a few more lads to help you, although you have to be careful, we can't trust everyone, but here must be a few good loyal Irishmen among all these fellas here." He sat up. "You can give him a hand there Sean, you might come across some lads you know and can trust."

"And you might hear if someone finds out something he shouldn't and has a mind to tell on us," said Daly.

Conlon looked directly at The Man from Dublin. "I'll do what I can for The Cause" he said, "but I won't betray the sanctity of the confession box."

51

Daly raised his eyes in a gesture of disgusted resignation but the Man said, "Ah sure God knows we wouldn't ask you to do that Father Sean. Right I'm off now back over the water. I'll be back again in a couple of weeks when you should have a bit more to tell me, I'll let you know when and where. If they tighten things up and you can't come yourself Liam – and we don't want you getting the sack for sloping off work now do we? – pass on what you know to Sean. His job gives him more scope to move around."

With that he closed the meeting. "*Slan go Foill,*" he said in a low voice as he left the buffet.

. . .

As The Man from Dublin was enjoying a relatively calm westward crossing from Holyhead to Dun Laoghaire, further north the Irish Sea was up to its usual winter tricks and tossed the eastbound steamer from Larne to Stranraer about like a cork. As a result both Michael and James were suffering from seasickness. Rather than go below to the third class passengers saloon, where many of their fellow passengers were also suffering, and the smell of vomit from the toilets was overpowering, they found what shelter they could at the stern of the ship in the lee of the superstructure. The journey from Dublin to Larne had been completed almost entirely in darkness and by now, even for James, the excitement of travel had waned. Michael too was beginning to wonder if it would not have been better to wait for more favourable conditions before setting out from home. He was feeling the cold more than he usually did and there was a slight pain across his chest. But he was reminded of his responsibility to his family and the thought soon passed.

He looked at the unhappy James and had to raise his voice against the howling of the wind: "It's a wild night for sure Jim but it won't be long now before we see land. God knows how Jack was able to stand weeks of this on his way to Mesopotamia."

His son remained silent and so he went back to fingering the cold pipe in his pocket and wished that the chance to light it would soon arrive. The steamer continued to corkscrew its way towards

Scotland. Other unhappy travellers came out on deck preferring the cold damp air to the nauseous conditions below. To one side of where they stood a group of half a dozen men, plainly Irish labourers, stood drinking stout from bottles and trying unsuccessfully to light cigarettes in the wind. One went below for a minute and to light up and returned to ignite the others from the glowing end of his Woodbine.

Eventually, as a grey dawn broke, they steamed into the shelter of Finnart's Bay and crossed Loch Ryan to the harbour of Stranraer. They gratefully disembarked and set out to find the station and the train for the last leg of the journey. Michael noticed that many of the men getting off with them were obviously Irish labourers, the smokers from the steamer among them, and he guessed that they would be making for the same destination as themselves.

He was right. Michael and James had joined the vast army of Irish navvies employed to build the world's largest munitions factory at Gretna in Scotland.

Chapter 9

A construction site nine miles long by two miles wide – the biggest in the world at the time – this was what greeted Michael and James in the cold January drizzle as they got off the train at Gretna, a small Scottish town on the Solway Firth. By now (January 1916) the groundwork was nearing completion and buildings were being erected at an unprecedented rate, but the overall impression was one of utter chaos. Out of the chaos would soon emerge His Majesty's Factory, Gretna. The factory was needed for the production of cordite, the dangerous material which propelled high explosive shells from the barrels of British guns at the enemy on the Western Front and other theatres of war. By the end of the war more cordite would be made at Gretna than all of the other British factories combined. But for the moment there was the mud and the noise which, when combined with the skeletons of the half-finished buildings painted a picture not dissimilar to that of the battlefields it was designed to serve.

The army of engineers, builders and labourers had grown to well over twenty thousand and more were arriving every day. On entering the, as yet unfinished, administrative buildings to where they had been directed on leaving the train they joined a disorganised queue of other prospective employees in an unpainted corridor, still smelling of wood, brick and cement leading to an open door. Applicants were made to wait and were called into the inner room at regular intervals, none came back out, as having been accepted for employment they left by another way. Few if any seemed to be rejected. There was a distinct lack of any supervision resulting in much disorderly pushing and jostling for position; 'first come, first served' being the obvious order of the day. Eventually Michael and James managed to get to the front and were called forward into a middle-sized room furnished with a single table at which sat an interviewing panel of two. James, standing in front of one bored looking interviewer stated that his previous employment had been that of a farm hand. He was given a cursory visual once over and informed that he had been accepted. The interviewer wrote on a card, stamped it and handed it to James. He was told he would be employed as a labourer by the firm of Noble and Thomson, to report to their foreman at the Dornock site at 7.00a.m. the following morning, and the next applicant was called forward.

Michael's obvious age drew a more searching examination, and although he tried hard to hide it, he was still a little out of breath as a result of the walk from the station. Fatigue from the journey showed on his face. His mode of dress and general appearance were hardly in keeping with those of the joiner he had claimed to be and both interviewers carefully looked him over. One went through a door behind the table and on return asked him to move to one side and wait. James, who had been directed to leave by a third door, waited with his father and even if this was noticed there were no objections raised.

"What's up Da? Do you think there's a danger they won't take you?"

"I don't know Jim but I think we'll find out in a minute," replied Michael, as a woman, plainly a secretary, came and motioned him to accompany her. As James moved to follow he was told to remain where he was.

Michael found himself in a small office as yet undecorated in keeping with the general unfinished appearance of the rest of the building. Stacks of folders stood on the floor awaiting filing in the single cabinet on which stood a telephone. The only other furniture was a table on which rested a large blotter covered with papers, pens and pencils. A slight balding man, roughly of Michael's age whose dress pointed him out as someone above the rank of clerk, sat at the desk.

"Now then," he said in a businesslike but not entirely unfriendly manner, and with a distinct English accent. "I see that you are Michael Quinlan and you are applying to be taken on as a joiner?"

"Yes," replied Michael, and added, "sir."

"I must say that I agree with the men outside that you do not look like a man who has spent his life in the building trade. I by the way am a member of the factory personnel staff. I work for the Ministry of Munitions and not for any of the building firms here."

Michael, whose conscience had been bothering him for having compromised his principles by lying, decided to revert to the truth: "I'm sorry sir, I only said I was a joiner because I didn't think you would be taking on a coachman, I haven't seen one single horse since I came here, and I need the work."

"You're right," said the personnel man, "there are very few horses here, and we certainly have no need of a coachman. But tell me who you worked for and where."

Michael told him about Beaufort House and about being laid off because of the war. At the mention of the owner's name the man raised his eyebrows.

"Can you verify any of this?"

From his pocket Michael took the letter of dismissal he had received just a matter of weeks before and handed it over.

The man looked closely at the crest at the top of the page and read the letter. He looked directly at Michael: "You do realise that I can easily check this out?"

"Yes sir."

The man spent a few minutes in thought then said, "All right, Quinlan, we can't take you on as a coachman but the factory administration is looking for some men to fulfil a special purpose and I think you could be suitable. I do not have time to give you all the details now but come back here tomorrow morning at" – he consulted a diary – "ten thirty. You are to ask for Mr Wilson, and he'll tell you more about it. Are you prepared to accept that for the moment?"

"Yes sir."

"I've already told you that you will be working for the Ministry of Munitions. I'm afraid that it is something of an open secret that we intend to produce munitions here, but I must warn you that we expect all our employees to exercise discretion and not to talk about their work to anyone outside. Is that understood?"

"Yes sir."

"In the meantime have you anywhere to stay?"

"No sir."

"I fear that there is very little accommodation left in the area, but we have just completed some huts over at Durnock for factory employees and you will be able to stay there, look for Hill Farm." He wrote on a piece of paper and gave it to Michael, "We'll see you tomorrow then."

"Thanks sir," said Michael and left.

Back in the interview room he collected a curious James. "Did you get a job Da?"

"I think so," said the confused Michael. "I'll tell you all about it on the train. We have to go to somewhere called Dornock. The man said we could stay the night there."

For the first time he looked at the paper he had been given. Scribbled beneath the heading 'Ministry of Munitions' was a note to the effect that Michael Quinlan was an employee of HM Factory Gretna. The signature was illegible. James showed him his card. "Well it looks like the two of us are in," he said as they made their muddy way back to the station.

As they collected their bags and waited for the train it was impossible for the two newcomers to grasp exactly what was happening to Gretna. A mere village six months ago, known only for the runaway marriages performed at nearby Gretna Green, it had been transformed into a bustling boomtown. The station, which six months ago had merely served a branch line linking the North British and Caledonian Railway lines, was now one of the busiest in southern Scotland. A new line was being built from Mossband near Longtown in England to Dornock near Annan in Scotland to serve the factory.

Having spent the greater part of the last thirty or so hours travelling, and most of that by rail, Michael relaxed on the short six mile ride to Dornock but James was much too fascinated by what he was experiencing to be tired. The line ran along the northern edge of the site and so even through the mist he was afforded a good view over the entire area. In some places there was just a sea of mud through which roads and the railway were being driven; in other parts large earthen banks were being built; elsewhere several large buildings were under construction. Men worked in gangs often up to their knees in mud. Where roads had been completed, heavy lorries sped loads of building materials to the various sites, where there were no roads they progressed slowly up to their axles in mud. The whole area was being surrounded by miles of high wire fencing topped with barbed wire. At Eastriggs, a whole new township was being created. James Quinlan wondered at how it was possible for anyone to make sense of it all.

Chapter 10

They arrived at Dornock and were directed to Hill Farm. This turned out to be a collection of wooden huts laid out with military precision and bore no resemblance whatsoever to its agricultural name. They were met by a short old man wearing an ancient khaki greatcoat, and whose pronounced limp did nothing to detract from his military bearing.

"Good afternoon, what can I do for ye?" The matter of fact question delivered confidently in a Scottish accent reinforced the impression of a soldierly background.

"We were sent over by the people in Gretna, they told us we could find somewhere to stay here," said Michael.

"All right, let's see your chits, I'm sergeant McGregor, I'm in charge here."

They handed over the letter and the card.

"Ah," he looked at Michael. "I can accept you but" – turning to James – "I'm afraid you won't be able to stay here. These billets are for the Ministry of Munitions employees only. The navvies have to find their own lodgings."

The news stopped them in their tracks. They had always assumed, quite wrongly Michael now realised, that they would be able to lodge together. The thought of being separated had not occurred, and for the first time since they left home Michael had a feeling that things here would not be as straightforward as he had hoped. His first reaction was to argue but his short acquaintance with the sergeant made him realise that he would be wasting his time. To cover his uncertainty he said:, "I'll have to think about this. Young James here is my son and it's his first time away from home."

McGregor looked at James and said in a not unkindly manner, "I'm sorry about this laddie, but that's the rule, only factory people can be billeted here."

Michael was about to say something when James, who was feeling hurt at being treated like a child, spoke up: "It's all right Da, you stay here I'll be all right on my own. Sure I'll easy find somewhere else to stay."

Michael felt that he was losing control of the situation. It had been his idea to come to Scotland and it was he who had decided to bring James with him. He thought that he had carefully planned the move, but at a stroke his plans were falling apart and he found himself in an uncomfortable position. While he knew that he would have to release James from under his wing at some stage he did not like the idea of having to do it under the current circumstances and, although he would not have admitted the fact, having this decision foisted upon him went against the grain. Then there was the question of how to explain it to Annie who was sure to worry about James being left to fend for himself.

He turned back to McGregor. "Is there any chance of finding lodgings for the two of us around here?"

"You might find somewhere in Annan or Gretna or even Carlisle, but it won't be up to much. What sort of post did they assign you to over at the HQ?"

"I'm not sure yet" said Michael. "I have to see a Mr Wilson tomorrow."

The sergeant looked Michael up and down and nodded his head knowingly. "Och well now if you're going to be working for His Majesty's Factory and doing what I think you might be doing, the powers that be won't like you billeting with the navvies."

Michael was frustrated and not a little annoyed at the old man's disparaging attitude towards his son and at the fact that he seemed to know more than he did himself about what was happening. But before he could say anything James spoke up again: "Where would I go to find out about lodgings?"

"The best bet," said the McGregor, "is to go to the Noble and Thomson site office up the road there, you'll need to know where that is anyway before you start work for them. Why don't you leave your kit here with me and your father and go over to see if they can fix you up. When you come back we'll be in hut number 2."

Michael was getting worried. If what the old man said was true, and he had no reason to think that it wasn't, it meant that he and his son would have to part company anyway. It was galling but he was beginning to fear he might have bitten off more than he could chew.

"Sure it'll be fine Da," said James. "Like your man here says I have to go over there tomorrow anyway and if I go now I'll get the lie of the land."

Without waiting for an answer he set off in the direction indicated and Michael reluctantly but without comment let him go. James followed a muddy road to where the former farming hamlet of Eastriggs was rapidly being transformed into a sizeable new town. There were the same lines of huts, not in the same state of completion as those he had just left and plainly there would be more of them, but unlike the neighbouring Dornock site there were streets of solid brick-built houses in various stages of construction. All around was a scene of high activity as foundations were dug, bricks were laid, doors and windows were fitted, roofs were tiled, and labourers served the tradesmen. Building materials were brought up on lorries to central dumps and then carried or wheeled in barrows to where they were needed. James took it all in and was impatient to become involved. He was directed by a strong County Cork accent to a fenced off area where his new employer's site office proved to be yet another wooden hut.

A self-important young lad not much older than James himself took his card and gazed at him with some distain. "You are not supposed to start until tomorrow. You can't just turn up here this late and expect to get paid for today."

The accent was unfamiliar but the manner was decidedly officious. "I know that" said James, he was tempted to add 'sir' but decided not to. "Sure I only arrived today and I was told you might be able to help me find a billet." He hoped the term he had picked up from McGregor was the accepted one.

The clerk was not impressed, "Only soldiers have billets, navvies have lodgings, if you can call it that." He went to a cabinet, retrieved a file, opened it and wrote something on the top sheet of a pad, tore it off and handed it over as if it physically hurt to do so. "You could try there, and don't be late in the morning."

Outside James was addressed by the same Cork accent he had met before who waved a grubby thumb at the office. "How did you get on with himself in the office, the Prince of Wales?"

The speaker, a man possibly in his late twenties and of medium height and build with a cheerful face, removed the two heavy scaffolding planks from his shoulder and rested them on the ground.

James warmed to the friendly tone: "Is he the big fella around here?"

"Jesus no, he thinks he is but sure he's only a little shite, take no notice of him. When do you start?"

"Tomorrow morning, he gave me a place to stay do you know where it is?"

He showed the Corkman the address. "Sure that's where I am myself." But then, while hastily crossing himself with his finger, he added with more than a touch of sadness, "You'll be taking poor Joe Riordan's place, Lord have mercy on his soul."

From this James knew someone had died. "What happened to him?" he said.

"He got drunk over in England and fell off the viaduct taking the short cut on the way back."

James was mystified. "The viaduct, what's that?

"Ah sure it's only an old railway bridge over the Firth. These days it's only used for goods trains to bring stuff here. But some of the boys use it as a shortcut into England, the pub opening hours are better over there."

"Are you sure this poor fella is dead?" asked James.

"Oh he's dead all right, if the fall didn't kill him the tide washed him out into the Irish Sea. No one could fall in the Solway at high tide and come out alive. Ah sure a grand Kilkenny man he was too."

James crossed himself as well. "I'm sorry about that, will I look for somewhere else."

"No," said the navvy, "it's not your trouble. Joe knew the score, and anyway you might as well have the bed, before someone else, maybe an Englishman or some other heathen does." His cheerful attitude returned as he held out his hand. "Pete Casey from Macroom in the County Cork."

"Jim Quinlan from Killarney," said James as they shook.

"Oh God save us from all Kerrymen," said Casey with a grin. "Look Jim I've got a brickie the size of a horse waiting for these planks so I'll be off before he comes looking for me. We knock off at six, if you are down at the station then we'll go down to Gretna together and I'll take you to your fine new mansion where we live an eat as well as parish priests."

"Thanks Pete," said James as the other staggered off under the weight of the planks.

.   .   .

As James left to find the site office, McGregor showed Michael into one of the long wooden huts. The building was divided into ten six-by-four foot four cubicles separated by thin plywood partitions. There were no doors but the cubicle openings were covered by curtains made from rough blanket material. Two round coke-burning stoves stood in the central aisle. The one nearest the door by which they entered was alight and went some way towards warming the chill January air. Michael was conducted to the far corner and MacGregor pulled back the blanket to reveal a space containing an army-style made-up cot, a small bedside table and a wooden chair.

"This is your bunk," said the sergeant. "It's up to you to do the best you can with it, there are no strict standing orders about what you can add to make it more like home, but be careful not to drive nails into the plywood or they'll come through the other side. I stay here myself and my bunk is at the bottom end. My duty is to look after the general state of the barracks and to keep the fires going, you are responsible for keeping your own bunk tidy."

The unexpected parting with James had been hard on Michael and was causing him to feel the effects of the journey. Without thinking he sat wearily down on the hard chair and breathed a sigh of relief. McGregor carried on issuing orders:

"The ablutions are in the hut to the right out that door. You eat in the cookhouse over at Eastriggs at the moment, but they are supposed to be building one here soon. The meal times are posted on the notice board over there, but if you are on funny shifts they will make special arrangements. You'll be stopped fifteen shillings a week out of your wages for room and board. If there's anything else you need to know you ask me."

Having finished his lecture he reverted to his more amiable civilian manner. "How do you fancy a cup of char, I always make one about this time, and I'll light this stove as well." Michael was getting used to MacGregor's military turn of phrase, so he nodded his thanks. There was nothing he would rather have at that moment than a cup of tea and a pipe of tobacco.

Soon they were seated by the fire smoking and drinking tea from chipped enamel mugs. "That's a good looking laddie of yours, is he your only one?" said McGregor.

"No there are two younger ones at home and the eldest is in the army in Mesopotamia." Michael told him briefly about his family and felt proud to tell the old soldier about Jack's enlistment.

"Mesopotamia," said McGregor, "now there's a godforsaken hole if ever there was one."

"Have you been there?"

"No but I have known a few who have. I was in the Sudan myself when we went out to avenge General Gordon's murder at Khartoum."

"Is that where you got the limp?" Michael was unsure if he had asked something rather too personal.

"Oh this? No." McGregor rapped his leg with his knuckles and it gave off a hollow wooden sound. "No this was a present from the Boers up on Spion Kop. Those were real battles," he added with a wistful sigh, "not like the stupid butchery of this new trench warfare."

"Do you have any family of your own?" said Michael.

"The missus died many years ago," said McGregor sadly. "We had two sons, one is with The Royal Scots in basic training. But I'm afraid the other one died in the train crash a few miles from here at Quintinshill."

"God knows I'm sorry to hear that."

"Two hundred and twenty-seven fine young Royal Scots killed and another two hundred and forty-six injured when their troop train ran into a stationary locomotive," said McGregor quietly. "Dead before they got anywhere near the front."

Michael crossed himself. "I'll remember them at Mass on Sunday."

"I'm not of your faith, but I'm grateful for that. What regiment is your lad in?"

"The Royal Field Artillery."

"There's been times when I was glad they were around. I've known some good men in that mob. It must be great to know that what we are doing here will be of use to him, from what I hear they're awful short of the stuff at the minute."

Before Michael could reply James returned to tell him about finding lodgings in Gretna and about his meeting with Pete Casey. He omitted to tell his father the sad circumstances under which he had managed to procure the lodgings.

"You're lucky to find a billet at all," said McGregor. "I've heard that some navvies are sleeping rough."

James picked up his bag and, as Michael got up to accompany him out, he said: "Don't stir yourself Da, I'll be fine. Pete Casey is going to show me the ropes. You stay here and I'll come over to-morrow after work and we'll take it from there."

Michael was surprised to find that he felt a growing confidence in James' ability to fend for himself. He decided that it was time to see if that confidence was well founded.

After James had left McGregor resumed the conversation:

"My given name is Alistair, what about yourself?"

"I was christened Michael."

"Have you seen any service Michael? You have the cut of a military man."

"No," said Michael and went on to tell his new friend about his life as a coachman to the aristocracy in Ireland.

"Och well," said the sergeant, "that's two of us who had to take a step down in the world."

Chapter 11

James met Pete Casey as arranged and they travelled to Gretna together. On arrival he was surprised to be led through a somewhat neglected front garden and up some steps to the main entrance of a large detached house. The street had a prosperous feel to it, probably the homes of professional people, but the house itself had seen better days. At the door Pete removed his muddy boots and motioned to James to do the same.

"Say three 'Hail Mary's' quick," said Casey, "and I'll take you in to meet Our Blessed Lady herself."

'Our Lady' turned out to be the owner of the house, Mrs Mary McBain. A local doctor's widow, she had struggled for several years to keep the house in a reasonable state of repair and had been about to give up and move to somewhere smaller when the war began. Now both she and the house had been given a new lease of life. She let the empty bedrooms to managers and other administrative staff at the factory and had turned the attic into accommodation for (carefully vetted) navvies.

James was looked over from all possible angles and told that being a friend of Casey's was no recommendation whatsoever, but he would, strictly on a trial basis, be given the bed so tragically made vacant by the death of that poor Reardon boy. Board and lodging would be seventeen shillings and sixpence per week, laundry should he require it – and he had better if he expected to sleep in her beds – would be one shilling and sixpence extra, and as it was obviously waste of time expecting payment in advance he had better watch his step until payday. Dinner would soon be ready and they had twenty minutes to make themselves presentable. Be on time or go without. Welcome to 'Solway View'.

Pete led him upstairs to the landing and then via a ladder to the loft area under the roof where five army surplus beds, covered with blankets of similar origin, were arranged, three along one side and two on the other to make room for the trapdoor. There was a skylight let into the slate roof, but the only artificial light was provided by candles, which residents were expected to supply themselves.

"That'll be your bunk," said Casey pointing to the bed nearest the trapdoor. "If it eases your mind it used to be mine but I moved next door into Joe Reardon's to stop myself falling down the trapdoor when I go to water the horses in the middle of the night."

There was no one else in the room but all the bed spaces showed signs of occupation. Items of clothing and other belongings were strewn over beds or hanging on the rafters which criss-crossed the loft.

"The two there are the McCarthy brothers and the one in the corner belongs to the holy Saint Patrick himself." Pete pointed to the bed in the corner which had a crucifix pinned to the rafter over bed-head.

"Saint Patrick?" said James.

"Ay," said Pete. "Holy Pat Murphy, he spends more time on his knees than he does on his feet or his arse and he'd be in the church more than at work if he could get away with it, and we'd have meat instead of fish on Fridays if it wasn't for him." But he relented. "Ah sure he's not that bad, you can trust him not to steal the shirt off your back and to tell on anyone else that tries it."

"The lads will be out the back washing behind their ears for dinner, and we could do worse than do the same." Pete explained that there was a washroom and conveniences outside in the back garden for the navvies use. There was a bathroom on the second floor for the 'guests' but any navvy caught using it would face immediate excommunication. Guests ate in the dining room, navvies ate in the kitchen.

"It's not up to what your darling mother lays on for you, but I'll tell you this Jim, it's a whole lot better than some of the cowsheds a lot of the boys have to live in."

Over a plain but substantial supper supervised by the aging cook, James met his new room mates. The McCarthy brothers proved to be heavily built middle-aged men, whose puffed shiny and sweaty faces showed every sign of having seen the inside of numerous public bars. They were Irish but from nowhere in particular, being jobbing building workers who followed the best paid jobs and were not particular where they happened to be. Their home was where they laid their caps and, having no family to send money home to, their earnings usually ended up in the pockets of barmen and bookmakers. They were the attic's longest serving residents but often, as Pete told James later, they would not come in at night, especially at weekends. 'Our Lady' would not tolerate drunkenness and rather than face her wrath they would sleep rough.

'Saint' Patrick Murphy was reportedly from Dublin and kept himself very much to himself except when saying his morning and evening prayers. Because he was obviously a man with more than a basic education rumours circulated. He was either a failed applicant for the priesthood, a teacher who had turned to drink and lost his job but was now reformed, and it was even said that he was in fact an Englishman who was a conscientious objector to the war. Nobody really knew and, in truth, nobody really cared. The navvies at Solway View were a fairly representative cross section of the men who built HM Factory Gretna.

After dinner, Pete Casey went out for a walk and said he might drop in for a glass of stout. The McCarthy brothers sat on one of their beds in quiet conversation and passed a bottle between them.

'St' Patrick sat on his bed and read a book.

James lay on his bed, alone with his thoughts. He was dead tired and had declined an invitation to go out with Casey, but he was too excited to sleep. He wondered how his father was getting on but did not worry about him. For as long as he could remember Michael Quinlan had been the steadying influence in the family and it did not occur to James that there could possibly be any situation his father would not be able to cope with; although he had been surprised at the ease with which he had been released to come to Gretna on his own. He thought about the rest of the family at home and wished that he could tell them all that had happened. In particular he longed to let Jack know that he was not the only one of the Quinlan brothers who had left home to make his own way in the world.

Eventually the brothers finished their bottle, stretched out fully clothed and began to snore. Patrick in the space next to him fervently and audibly said his prayers and James felt compelled to silently join in. He was asleep when Pete Casey returned and, having always had to share a room with his brothers, the presence of the other sleepers did not disturb him.

Next morning they were given a breakfast of strong tea and thick porridge. Casey expressed a difficulty in distinguishing between the porridge and the concrete he had to mix at work and received a clip around the ear from the cook. They picked up the rough sandwiches pre-prepared for their lunch and set off.

James was met by the site foreman, a small man in a heavy coat and a bowler hat.

"So you are Quinlan are you?" he said. "From the look of you I'd say they've sent me another Irish farmer. And I don't need an opinion from you Casey so you just get on with your own job. On second thoughts as you're both farmers you have had plenty of experience at shovelling shit so you're just the blokes they need over there on the road gang."

Casey groaned but held his tongue.

So James spent his first day at Gretna digging, shovelling, barrowing and sweating even in the bitterly northerly cold wind on a road laying gang. It was the hardest day's work he had ever done and by the end of it he was exhausted. After dinner he just wanted to sleep but he knew he had to go to Dornock and see how his father was getting on. Pete Casey offered to go with him and he was glad of the company.

Having exchanged news, they sat in Michael's cubicle and carefully composed a letter home while Casey and McGregor sat and exchanged tall tales by the stove. Once the letter was finished to their joint satisfaction McGregor offered to post it, James and Casey set off back to Gretna.

"Your man McGregor was telling me what your father told him about your family. I'd say you were a lucky man Jim," said Casey, who for some minutes had been unusually quiet.

"I suppose in a way I am," said James. "But families can hold you back at times. What about yourself Pete, have you any family?"

"The old ones are gone," said Casey sadly. "I have a sister working as a nurse down in London, she keeps in touch and I might go down and see her one of these days. There is an uncle over in America, I have a mind to go there myself after the war. Maybe you'll do that yourself someday Jim."

"Maybe I will," said James.

Chapter 12

While James Quinlan sweated over a shovel in Gretna, The Man from Dublin had returned to the Irish Capital. He was seated with a cup of tea in the kitchen of a comfortable home in Rathmines, a middle class area of Dublin, waiting for the meeting in the parlour to end. The meeting between representatives of the principal organisations engaged in the struggle for Irish Independence had gone on for several hours, but he knew he would be expected to wait until it was over before being called in to make his report and receive new instructions. In the meantime he was being well looked after by the aged maid who served the owner of the house. She wondered at his presence here but knew better than to question him.

"So, to sum up:" The speaker, and elected chairman of the meeting was Padraig Pearse, a member of several Irish nationalist organisations and leader of the Irish Republican Brotherhood.

"We have formed an Alliance between The Irish Republican Brotherhood and The Irish Citizen Army for the purpose of mounting an armed rebellion aimed at the overthrow of British Rule in Ireland."

"We are agreed that in order to take advantage of the war, action must be taken this year and that we should plan for armed resistance to begin at Easter, if possible on Good Friday April 21st. The assumption is that a rising during Easter Week will come as a surprise to the British authorities who will not expect us to mount a rebellion during the Holy Season."

"We will begin the action by issuing a proclamation to the effect that we are the Provisional Government of the Irish Republic."

"We have received assurances of adequate finances from our 'Clan na Gael' friends in America."

"We have been promised a consignment of arms and

ammunition by the Germans under the agreement brokered by Roger Casement."

"We regret that while we do not have the full active support of The Irish Volunteers, we are confident that many individual members of that organisation will join us. Several thousand have already left the main body to form a breakaway Irish Volunteer Force dedicated to the policy of armed resistance."

"To conclude then, are we agreed that the Military Council should immediately begin detailed planning on the basis of what we have discussed?"

There were expressions of agreement from around the table.

"Thank you gentlemen, that concludes the business for today. I suggest that we keep in touch informally through our usual contacts and the Military Council will call a further meeting at an appropriate time."

The security arrangements for the meeting called for delegates to leave the house one at a time on signals from watchers in the street and neighbouring houses. As the last man was about to depart he was quietly called back by Pearse. "Can you wait behind James, our friend is back from Scotland and I think you should hear at first hand what he has to say."

James Connolly was the founder of The Irish Citizen Army. Connolly, a confirmed socialist, had founded the organisation to provide protection for the Irish Transport and General Workers Union following the attacks made on union members by the authorities during the strikes and subsequent employers' lockout in Dublin in 1913. Although never numbering more than a few hundred men, by 1916 it was a highly disciplined paramilitary force openly holding regular military style manoeuvres. Their alliance with Pearse's Irish Republican Brotherhood, a much older revolutionary group descended from the Fenians, formed the backbone of the Irish armed resistance movement.

The Man from Dublin was called into the room and welcomed by Pearse and Connolly both of whom he knew well. Pearse, who trusted him implicitly, outlined what had been agreed at the meeting, and The Man nodded his satisfaction. His host made special mention of the fact that they could not count on the full support of the Irish Volunteers.

Many members of this, numerically the largest of the organisations involved with some 180,000 members and originally earmarked as the main strike force, were against mounting an armed rising in wartime and felt that they should instead join the British forces in the struggle against Germany. Their leader, Eoin MacNeill, was among those who were against a rising during wartime on grounds of principle. The resulting split left the revolutionaries with a total of about 10,000 IVF extremists they could rely on to join them.

"So," said Pearse, "be very careful in your dealings with Eoin's people. Make sure you can trust your contacts there. Now what news have you brought us from over the water?"

The only positive thing that The Man had to report following his meeting in Carlisle with Liam Daly and the priest, Sean Conlon, was an assumption that the factory was designed to produce explosives only, and not ammunition ready for use in battle. He explained that this opinion was based on what he had been able to learn so far about the layout of the site being built at Gretna, but he was confident that confirmation would soon be forthcoming.

Connolly expressed some disappointment: "So there is no possibility of us being able to lay our hands on any ammunition for our men from there?" he said.

"I doubt it," was the answer.

"Don't worry too much about that James," said Pearse, "we'll be getting enough for our needs from Casement."

"I still believe," said Connolly, "that we are missing an opportunity by having all those Irishmen gathered together in one place over there and not using them to help The Cause."

"I agree James," said Pearse. He turned to The Man, "Is there any way we can make use of this situation.

"At this stage I would have to say that the sheer size of the place would make it the devil of a job to put it out of commission entirely, and we would have to do just that to cause any real material damage to the Brit's war effort. We would never be able to recruit enough men from the workforce over there and, even if we did, we will need every Irish patriot we can scrape up for the rising here at home if all the Volunteers aren't with us. So what we are left with is mounting an operation with a few good men against one small but important part of the factory. They're building the place so fast it must be hard for even them to keep track of progress, and I think that they will be pushed to get it finished by Easter. But that narrows down the number of possible targets and we should be able to do something to give them a kick up the backside, and with luck, time it to coincide with the rising here. I've already started the ball rolling but it's too early yet to say what the best target would be."

Connolly thought for a minute before commenting. "I think we should squeeze what we can out of this Padraig," he said to Pearse. "At least it should create a few more martyrs to help in waking up the whole Irish nation."

"All right," said Pearse, "we'll go ahead on the assumption that you can identify a worthwhile action."

With that The Man from Dublin was dismissed and the two senior revolutionaries went on with other important Nationalist business.

Chapter 13

Michael went back to Gretna next morning and was ushered into Mr Wilson's office. Wilson turned out to be yet another man with a military air about him, although much younger and obviously fitter than McGregor. Even though he was addressed as 'Mr' he gave Michael the impression that he was in fact a serving officer.

"Ah, Quinlan," he said without any form of introduction as Michael entered still another partly finished office. "You have been sent here as someone who might possibly be of use to me. I'm told that you have a rather impressive reference, could I see it please."

Michael, now more thankful than ever that the letter of dismissal included the character reference, handed it over.

Wilson glanced through it and looked up. "Are you aware that His Lordship is currently engaged in highly sensitive war work for the government? No, I thought not, so I think we had better keep this in your file here for the time being, we don't want it getting into the wrong hands. Now as to your duties, have you been given any indication about what will be expected of you here at HM Factory Gretna?"

It occurred to Michael that he had not so far been asked if he actually wanted the job whatever it was, but all he could think to say was, "No sir."

"Right well here is a broad outline, you will be given more information later – to be honest we have not worked out all the fine details ourselves yet. But the present situation is this: I have been placed in charge of the internal security arrangements here at the factory. Most of the men under my command should be members of the Ministry of Munitions Police. That is a newly formed organisation and, as it is still very short of fully trained officers, I am having to recruit members here. Outside the perimeter fence all security is in the hands of the civilian police and of course the War

Office, but internally The Ministry of Munitions, to whom I have been seconded, has sole responsibility. Am I making myself clear?"

Michael nodded.

"The obvious threat to security comes from the Germans. The likelihood of the Germans mounting an all out attack here is nil, but they may well try to insert some agents to collect intelligence and perhaps sabotage the operation. Should you come across anyone or anything that arouses suspicion you are to report the matter immediately. But that is not the only threat we face. This factory will be producing high explosives from some very volatile raw materials so there is a grave danger of serious accidents if the stuff is not treated with extreme care. There will be a strict code of practice introduced for handling and transporting materials as well as for the manufacturing processes, and it will be our job to see that they are properly enforced. Any lapses in discipline could get people killed; I cannot emphasise this point too strongly. So you can see now why I like to personally hand pick my staff."

Much of Michael's confidence, and the self-esteem, which had suffered such a blow over the last few days, was beginning to return as Wilson spoke.

"Then there is the usual problem associated with an enterprise as large as this one: theft, there is a lot of material and equipment around which could easily be sold on the open market. I'm afraid that many of your countrymen are not noted for their sobriety and this leads to fighting and rowdy behaviour. Generally the contractors who employ them are expected to deal with it, but there will soon be more and more factory workers arriving as the factory goes into production and they will be our problem."

He looked closely at Michael to see if there was any adverse reaction to what he had just said, and finding none, he continued: "I think that the best thing for you to do now is to get over to the storage area where you will be based at the Dornock site and introduce yourself to your immediate superior officer. His name is Brown and he will fill you in with the details. I will telephone ahead to tell him to expect you."

Believing that the interview was over Michael began to rise

but Wilson carried on:

"There is one thing more you must understand. The force you have joined is called the Ministry of Munitions Police but that title only applies on Ministry property, off-site you have no authority whatsoever. However, should you happen to notice anything suspicious on the outside you must report it, directly to us if you can but if not then to the civilian police. And I must warn you that if you mention anything about what you see or hear during the course of your duties you will face instant dismissal. Is that understood?"

"Yes sir," said Michael.

"Good then off you go. I shall come and see how you are getting on later but at the moment I have other people to see. Oh and you had better have one of these." He gave Michael an armband bearing the words 'Ministry of Munitions Police'. "We have been promised that some more uniforms will be available within a few weeks."

So Michael went back to Dornock by train, a journey he was getting used to. There seemed to be several main line trains making the fifteen minute trip, but he guessed that the site's own internal railway would be in operation before long and he would soon be using that. It took him the entire journey to collect his thoughts and, although there was much he did not yet understand about his new career, it was a relief to know that he would be in a job which did not seem to entail hard labour. It was not that he considered himself to be above labouring, but he had to admit that the rigours of the journey from home had taught him that he was no longer physically suited to it. He asked a navvy where he could find 'the stories' and was directed to a large cavernous building still under construction.

Brown turned out to be a man of similar age to Michael but of much slighter build. He had a pleasant face and wore the uniform of the Ministry of Munitions Police.

"Hello you must be Michael Quinlan, I'm Robert Brown." The accent was North Country English. "I'm glad to see that they have sent me some help at last." He held out his hand and Michael took it.

"There were only three of us now but you make four, come on over to the office."

He conducted Michael to the partitioned office space and invited him to sit. "The three of us Bill Williams, Jim Coughlan, a countryman of yours by the way, and myself have been covering the whole twenty-four hour day by ourselves; now that you are here we should get some time off."

Michael thought that the most appropriate thing to say was: "Sure I'm glad to be here. What is it we have to do?"

"Good question," was the reply. "At present there is not a lot we can do. As you can see the place is still being built, but as soon as it's finished they will be storing some very dodgy stuff here and our job will basically be to guard it. But on top of that we will be responsible for seeing that all the safety rules are obeyed. People are still working on a set of rules and regulations for doing that, but in the meantime I believe that the best thing we can do is to let everyone know we are around, which is why I want someone here around the clock wearing that armband. God knows when your uniform will arrive. For the next couple of days you can have the early shift, six am to two pm starting tomorrow morning, and for the rest of today you might as well stay here to get the feel of the place ok?"

Michael was not at all sure that it was ok, and this concerned him, but he said, "That's grand."

"There is a desk of sorts over there by the door. I want you to stand there as if you are watching everyone who goes in and out, and make sure they see that armband. Yes I know it's all for show at present, but it will get all too real before long. You could also take an occasional walk around to orientate yourself, soon you will need to be familiar with every nook and cranny, I'll come and relieve you later so that you can do that."

So Michael went to work as a member of the internal police of HM Factory Gretna. He was happy to be there even though he felt somewhat ashamed to admit that he took some pride in being given a post of some seeming importance. He put his good fortune down to the reference from his former employer, which seemed to carry a great deal of weight. He stood behind a makeshift desk just inside an open doorway wide enough to accommodate the trucks, which would soon begin to deliver the raw materials required for the manufacture of cordite propellant. Just outside the door he could see the finishing touches being made to the rails which ran parallel to it. Much of the material to be stored here would arrive by train, and narrow gauge tracks ran through the building to facilitate its movement internally. He gazed around the interior of the massive structure, now in the final stages of construction, where workmen were installing specialist storage facilities.

Glad to be indoors out of the bitter north wind, which had replaced the misty rain and brought with it flurries of snow, he still felt the chill, mainly because he had to keep his warm coachman's cloak thrown off his shoulder. By wrapping the cloak around him he would have obscured the armband bearing the legend 'HM Ministry of Munitions Police' he wore in lieu of the uniform he had been told would be issued later. For the moment he had little to do except to 'get the feel of the place' as instructed and keep his eyes open for anyone who did not have a legitimate reason for being in the area. Across the concrete floor in an enclosed office his immediate superior, the Englishman called Brown, was making tea. Michael hoped that Brown, who seemed a decent sort and who already wore the navy blue uniform of the Ministry Police, would bring him a cup. In the meantime he could only try to come to terms with what had happened to his life in the space of three short days since leaving home.

Although dead tired from his journey he had a disturbed night in his strange surroundings. He had dinner with McGregor in the canteen but with little appetite as he found the mass produced food did not reach the high standard of Annie's home cooking. Still he thought he would have to get used to it. Later he considered adding to the letter he and James had written but gave up the effort when he found that he had no definite news. It would be better, he thought, to wait until after he found out more about what his new job actually entailed, and he felt he must be able to reassure her that James was being well looked after. News that he had been obliged to leave James to fend for himself would worry her, and any mere speculation about her son's living conditions would make things worse. She would want hard facts, and even so she would still worry. He tossed and turned in the unfamiliar bed and listened to the sounds coming from the few other cubicles that were occupied. McGregor had told him that it would not be long before the hut was fully occupied and that most of the residents would be on shifts once the factory went into production, so there would be comings and goings at all hours. So he tossed and turned and thought of the cottage by the river Laune and worried about Annie and the others at home.

Would William be able to manage all the chores as well as holding down his farm job? Was James settled in decent lodgings? He should never have let him go off on his own. And what about Jack, had he been involved in the fighting? His last letter seemed to indicate that he would soon be embroiled in the war. The sight of those wounded soldiers on the station in Dublin came back to haunt Michael. The slight pain in his chest helped to keep him awake. Finally he dropped off but in a few short hours he was woken by McGregor with the most welcome mug of tea he had ever tasted. The old soldier brushed off his thanks by saying that when Michael was properly settled in he would be expected to reciprocate and he would show him where the brew-up kit was stored. He had never been a man to accept favours easily, but this simple demonstration of comradeship served to brighten Michael's mood.

Chapter 14

In spite of what he had told Michael, Wilson did not have any more interviews that morning. He tidied up some overdue paperwork then went out to a prearranged meeting. As he left the factory compound he wondered why his visitor from Whitehall had decided to hold this particular meeting in the back room of a public house in Gretna rather than in his office. When he got to the pub, virtually deserted at that time of day, he found to his surprise that the man from Whitehall was not alone. It was an even bigger surprise to find him in the company of a man who to all intents and purposes was a navvy.

The Man from Whitehall was the senior officer in the British Security Services. He was Commander Wilson's superior officer and was known only as the director of one of the branches responsible for home security. Before they were seated he introduced the two men.

"Ah Wilson, this is one of my operatives. He has been fully briefed on what is happening here at Gretna and for the purposes of identification let's just call him 'Patrick'. It fits well with the part he must play."

"Patrick, this is the man I told you about, Commander Wilson of the Royal Navy, who is in charge of all security matters here at Gretna. Yes I know it is unusual to have a navy man in a post like this but Wilson has a good deal of experience in intelligence so you two should get along quite well."

He turned to Wilson. "How is the recruiting for the police coming along?"

"Quite slowly I'm afraid," was the reply. "It's difficult to find exactly the right men for the job, and we must have men we can trust. I could do with a few more experienced hands."

"Not a chance at the moment I'm afraid, we are stretched to the limit. You may have to lower your standards somewhat because time is of the essence. And don't forget that you will soon be getting a large number of female officers from the newly formed Ministry of Munitions Women's Police Service, as most of the factory workers will be women. I spoke to His Lordship only yesterday and he impressed on me the necessity of getting this factory operational as quickly as possible, even if that means cutting a few corners. He was at great pains to point out that without a steady supply of cordite from here we could easily lose this war, and I'm afraid that I have to agree with him."

There was silence for a few minutes while he let this sink in.

Wilson eventually spoke up: "It's funny you should mention His Lordship. I recruited a former employee of his this morning, his old coachman from his estate in Ireland, he seems like a reliable sort of chap."

"He might prove useful," said 'Patrick'.

"I'll leave that to you," said The Man from Whitehall, "but on no account are you to reveal to anyone that you are working for us."

Wilson was beginning to feel that there was something going on here that he was not a part of. He was getting a little irritated and it showed. "If 'Patrick' is to be working here perhaps I should know exactly what his brief is."

"Yes, I'm sorry Wilson I should have explained earlier. 'Patricks' job is to pose as a navvy and keep his ear to the ground. Now listen carefully both of you. You will have to work closely together, one out in the open and one undercover. There is obviously a possibility that the Germans will try to plant some agents here to gather intelligence and cause some mischief if we don't weed them out. But in my view there is a much greater threat coming from nearer home, by that I mean our friends from across the Irish Sea. We know that something's brewing over there and we must think that they will take advantage of our involvement in the war to further their own ends. With all these Irish navvies in the area HM Factory Gretna must be an obvious target. We already know that one Irish Nationalist sympathiser, the priest Sean Conlon, has been sent here. Unless there is a dire emergency you must keep actual meetings to an absolute minimum. You had better work out some secure method of keeping in touch with each other. You both have access to me at any time and please keep me fully in the picture."

"I believe I've heard of him," said Wilson "isn't he some sort of rabble-rouser? Does this mean that the Catholic Church in Ireland is in league with the rebels?"

"I doubt that very much," said The Man from Whitehall. "I rather think that they sent him here simply to get rid of him, he was becoming something of an embarrassment, but in doing so I'm afraid that they have inadvertently passed the problem over to us."

"Do you think that we should get rid of him then?" said 'Patrick'.

"No," said The Man from Whitehall. "He is the only one we have identified as yet. So I suggest that we keep a close eye on him and see if he leads us to any others, I'm certain they will want to make use of him, if only as a means of communication between themselves. That is your job 'Patrick', watch him closely and see where he goes and who he meets. But be careful, while the vast majority of the Irishmen here do not support the nationalist cause they would not take kindly to our harassing one of their priests."

Again he let his words sink in before continuing, "That is all for now gentlemen we will not meet as a group again unless we have something of national importance to discuss. I will continue to visit you at regular intervals Wilson but 'Patrick's' cover must remain intact. So you had better leave now by the back way 'Patrick' and we will follow later."

After 'Patrick' had left, Wilson said, "Why was I not told about him before now?"

"I had my reasons," said his superior officer, "but you know about him now and you are the only one here, other than myself, who does know and I want it kept that way. If you use him properly he will prove to be the best tool you could possibly have for dealing with anything nasty that may come up, and something of that nature undoubtedly will."

Chapter 15

January 6th 1916, the Feast of the Epiphany, was a 'Holy Day of Obligation' when all Catholics were bound to attend Mass. In common with other church holy days it was also to a public holiday, the traditional 'Women's Christmas', in Ireland and was celebrated like a Sunday.

William had harnessed the pony to the trap and those members of the Quinlan family who remained at home went to Mass for the first time since Michael and James had left for Scotland. After the service the priest came to Annie with a few kind words as she waited for William to prepare the pony and trap for the journey home. Annie had expected as much from the man, she thanked him and assured him that if she needed his help at any time she would not be afraid to ask. As soon as the priest had moved away she was approached by another acquaintance, an approach she had also fully expected and was equally well prepared for.

Mrs Connor was the postmaster's wife and it was said locally that by far the most efficient method of passing information was not by telephone or telegram but by 'telling Mrs Connor'. For years she had regarded Annie Quinlan as a special 'friend' mainly because she believed the coachman's wife would have a direct line of communication to the aristocratic owners of Beaufort House, but since the house had been closed that 'nice Mrs Quinlan' had become 'the old coachman's wife'. Annie was of course fully aware of this and while she was Christian enough to tolerate Mrs Connor, she had been upset by the fact that the whole village knew that there had been a letter from Jack before it had even been delivered. Still it was not letters that caused Annie Quinlan concern but, in common with mothers all over the British Isles and indeed the British Empire, what really worried her was the thought of receiving a telegram. It was not only her son who had gone off to the war, several other local boys had also joined up, and thank God no telegrams had as yet arrived at the local post office. But she had seen and heard enough to know of the increasing frequency with which they were being sent out and she feared that it would only be a matter of time before one reached Beaufort. She prayed that it would not be addressed to her.

So she listened politely to Mrs Connor's concerns for her and her family's welfare and assured her that poor Mr Quinlan had not been reduced to labouring but had a good position in a munitions factory where he was helping their son Jack to win the war.

. . .

At HM Factory Gretna the feast of Epiphany was just another working day. Michael went off to work at six where he relieved one of his new colleagues, an amiable Welsh ex-policeman drafted in to the factory force. His other colleague, a Dubliner who had lived in England for several years and worked at a variety of trades, would relieve him at two o'clock. Brown – he was not yet sure what his superior's official title was – would come in at eight. The night shift of fitters installing the storage equipment would knock off at eight when the day shift would take over. All of this went on while the contractors were still putting the finishing touches to the building itself. It was all still very new to Michael but he was gradually settling in.

James too was getting used to life at the Gretna site. It was only a few short days since they had arrived but it was long enough to convince him that road building was not something he would wish to make a career of, at least not if it was carried out with the same level of urgency that was applied here. But it was plain that the internal roads and railways at the site were nearing completion. He had heard some of the more experienced men grumbling that on a normal site the roads would have been laid first so that materials for the building work could be moved more easily. But such was the need to get the production started at HM Factory Gretna such niceties were put to one side.

"Ah sure what would they want with roads when they have

me an' a wheelbarra," was Pete Casey's solution to the problem.

At the Catholic church Father Conlon said the Holy Day Mass. The congregation was sparse: a smattering of off-shift workers, some local women and children and a few pensioners. The only obvious navvies were 'Saint Patrick' Murphy who had somehow managed to get away from work to take care of more pressing matters, and Liam Daly. After Mass, Daly hung around until he could approach the priest unobserved.

"Have you heard anything Sean?" he asked.

"He'll be over next week, same time and place," said Conlon.

"Right," said Daly as he sauntered off.

· · ·

The feast of the Epiphany was not celebrated in Mesopotamia. Nothing could have been further from Jack Quinlan's thoughts. He was wet, hot, sweaty, tired and not a little dispirited, and the only comfort available to him was prayer.

The march to relieve Kut-al-Amara had begun and in weather that was unbelievably bad: humid and misty with frequent downpours by day followed by temperatures well below freezing at night. Jack was part of a makeshift force called the Tigris Corps advancing up the river of that name from Basra. The force had passed Amara and was approaching Sheik Sa'ad when they came up against Turkish forces dug in on both banks of the Tigris. A frontal assault was ordered, but without adequate and properly coordinated artillery support the attacking troops were cut down by the entrenched Turks and suffered heavy losses. Jack and his gun crew had manhandled the 18 pounder field gun into their designated firing position with the other guns of the battery, but because of a shortage of high explosive shells they could not fire for any real effect. It soon became obvious that the assault had failed and the attacking troops were ordered to dig in.

Next day, January 7th, a second assault was ordered but again ran directly into a murderous small arms fire from the Turkish trenches. As the attacking British troops were being cut down the Turks mounted a counter-attack in an effort to encircle them, and finally the field artillery came into its own. Firing shrapnel rounds, virtually the only type of shells they had and totally ineffective against deeply entrenched positions, they were at last able to provide effective covering fire and the Turkish counter-attack was repelled. After two days of savage fighting the situation remained stalemate.

The Tigris Corps had suffered 4,000 casualties and their available medical supplies, trained staff, equipment and field ambulances would have been hard pressed to cope with half that number. Jack, together with the rest of his battery stood and watched morosely as hundreds of wounded men lay unattended in terrible conditions out in the open ground. Like most of his comrades he had volunteered to go and help but had been ordered to stand fast in anticipation of a second Turkish attack; an attack which in the event never materialised. In fact the Turks, for some unknown reason, abandoned their positions and withdrew up river during the night.

So all that was left was for the artillerymen, young officers, experienced senior NCOs and gunners alike, was to suffer in silence as they listened to the sounds of men dying. They spoke little but in their minds they played games of 'if only': If only the order to attack had been delayed until the guns were properly in position; if only they had been supplied with an adequate number of high explosive shells; if only there were more medical facilities; if only some of the infantrymen would not look so accusingly at them. 'If only' the mind game played by frustrated soldiers since men first went to war.

The 18 pounders of the field artillery could have gone some way towards redressing the balance if they had been supplied with suitable ammunition. Low-bursting shrapnel acted like shotgun blasts and was designed to give close support to the infantry using 'fire and movement tactics' but had little effect against trench positions where high explosive shells were needed. Even if the artillerymen of the Tigris Corps had known that the failure at Sheik Sa'ad was not their fault it would have given them little consolation.

Along with the thoughts he shared with the rest of the force,

Jack was also struggling with a feeling of personal guilt. On his only home leave since joining up he had played the part of the gallant soldier to the full. With uncharacteristic pride he had swanked in his uniform and tried to look every inch the conquering hero. His parents had not been impressed, but the younger children had lapped it up so they had not intervened. William had been anxious to learn all about the technical details of modern artillery, but it was James' reaction which came back to bother him now. The restless James had taken it all in and had on several occasions pleaded with his brother to take him when he left so that he too might join up. As he thought of it now Jack hoped and prayed that his father's influence, which had prevented James from enlisting at that time, was still holding strong. Two short days of the reality of war had made him realise how wrong he had been, and he deeply regretted having deliberately set out to impress his younger brother.

He had not as yet had a reply to his last letter home, and did not know exactly when, if ever, he would receive one, but he resolved that at the first opportunity he would write to James in the hope of making him see sense before it was too late.

. . .

On the feast of the Epiphany in Dublin, members of The Irish Citizen Army went on parade. They assembled openly in Croyden Park and were virtually ignored by the British authorities. They drilled under the supervision of their officers and were inspected by their commander, James Connolly. In their dark uniforms criss-crossed by bandoliers, and Australian style slouch hats with the brims turned up on left side, they looked every inch a well trained fighting unit.

Chapter 16

For the second time in its long history the city of Carlisle was playing host to an army of workers engaged in a monumental construction project. In the second century AD the Roman emperor Hadrian, established a garrison there, and Carlisle became the western base for the thousands of soldiers and slaves building his famous wall. The Romans had driven out the Celtic warlords who had once ruled the area, but now the Celts were back in the shape of the army of Irish navvies building the great munitions factory at Gretna just a few miles away over the Scottish border.

On their first Saturday payday, Michael came off duty at two o'clock so he and James caught the train from Dornock to Carlisle, principally to visit the post office and send some money home. There was a perfectly good post office in Gretna but both were anxious to see the city they were constantly hearing about. Michael had decided that while he would not dictate to James about how he should spend his wages, but he was determined that they would jointly send a substantial weekly sum home to Annie. Most of the Irish at Gretna sent some money home, but most also retained enough to satisfy their thirst. The question of drink among the navvies was something Michael had thought of before leaving the hut at Dornock. He first heard of it from the old sergeant McGregor who owned up to being partial to an occasional 'dram' himself, but admitted that he was totally outgunned by the Irish. The extent of the problem surprised Michael and he could see that he would have to keep a wary eye on James. He was grateful that the lad had made friends with Pete Casey who, in spite of his irreverent easy going attitude, gave the impression of being of sober character.

As James was getting ready to leave for Carlisle, Pete had offered some advice. "If I was you I wouldn't go into town in my Sunday Mass suit Jim, it pays better to go there looking like an

Irish navvy."

James thought he was joking. "And why would that be?"

"You'll have the girls after you in those togs," said Pete.

"Sure I hope you're right," said James. "Anyway I have to meet me Da so I'm off, I'll see you for a pint later."

Pete was about to say something but let it go, he liked young James Quinlan but decided there were some things the lad should find out for himself.

So Michael and James paid their first visit to Carlisle. As they had not had dinner they went in search of something to eat before going to the post office. Michael introduced James to a dish which would prove to be a major attraction for the younger man every time he came into Carlisle; fish and chips. He had heard about English fish n' chips but had never before tasted them, but from that moment on they became a firm favourite with James. It was only a little incident but it gave Michael a lift to know that there were still a few things he could teach his son. At the post office they bought postal orders to send home. Michael also placed a couple of pound notes in the envelope with them, and added a note to Annie advising her to try and cash the orders in Killarney rather than Beaufort. In spite of the recent upheavals in his life he retained enough pride to baulk at the thought of Mrs Connor, and consequentially the whole neighbourhood, knowing how much money they were sending home.

As they stepped out of the post office they were approached by a group of three laughing girls walking along arm in arm. Seeing James, the girl's attitude abruptly changed and they moved in unison to block his path.

"Why aren't you in uniform?" demanded the one in the centre of the trio, standing squarely in front of him and looking him directly in the eye.

James was totally taken aback by the unexpectedly aggressive approach by three seemingly normal girls, and not understanding what was happening he was completely at a loss for something to say. Michael vaguely remembered having heard or read something about how patriotic young girls on the British mainland often resorted to shaming young men into joining the armed forces, but he had never really considered that he would see it actually happen to James. He tried to step in and rescue his son, but before he could intervene one of the girls shouted "Coward" in James' face and shoved something into his hand. With that they marched off and resumed their happy conversation leaving him standing there. Still in a quandary James opened his hand and found a small white feather nestled in his palm. He looked at his father in the hope of some form of explanation. Michael had no option but to tell him what he knew about young women handing out white feathers, a sign of cowardice, to young men they thought should be serving at the front. James was mortified. The thought that he might somehow be branded a coward stung him deeply. He moved to go after the girls to explain that he was in fact helping to build the munitions factory at Gretna but by then they were well out of reach. Michael could see that his son had been badly affected, yet he had to admit that under similar circumstances his own pride would have been equally damaged. But that was the least of his problems. His reason for bringing James to Scotland with him had been to prevent him from joining the army like his brother Jack, now he sensed a danger that a much stronger motivation would compel the lad to enlist. He knew that he would have to handle the situation with some care.

All he could immediately think to say, however, was, "Ah take no notice of them Jim, they don't mean anything by it."

James remembered what Pete Casey had told him about wearing his best clothes and knew now what his friend had meant. "But if they think I'm a coward, I'll have to join up to prove I'm no such thing Da."

Michael had now been given a little time to think. His reply came as yet another surprise to James. "Don't do anything yet awhile Jim," he said. "God knows I might need you here."

He paused for a minute or two and then with some reluctance he told James about the shortness of breath and of the occasional pains in his chest. "I'm all right now but if it got too bad for me to work I might have to go home. But I can't go until we make sure your mother and the young ones are well fixed up first. So all I'm asking is for you to hang on until she has enough in the bank to see them over the war. Then you can do what you like."

It was the second time within the space of one afternoon that a bombshell had dropped on James. His mind was in a whirl but there was nothing he could say but, "All right Da."

When he had gathered his thoughts and accepted the fact that the army would have to wait he resolved that he would know better in future and come to Carlisle dressed in his work clothes. From what Pete had said it seemed that the girls didn't bother the navvies, he supposed they thought it was good enough to be engaged in essential war work like munitions. He was all for going back to Gretna to change his clothes when Michael came up with a solution; the next time they were approached by a group of girls he took the armband of the Ministry of Munitions Police from his pocket and waved it at the girls who left them in peace.

James brightened up a little. "I'll have a loan of that the next time I come to town Da."

"No you won't," said Michael. "And make sure you keep quiet about this or I'll lose my job."

James had been mulling over the problem of breaking the news to his father that he intended to stay on in Carlisle for the evening rather that accompanying him back to Dornock, however, the unexpected news of the older man's health worries forced him to consider changing his mind. But much to James' relief when they got back to the station they found Pete Casey waiting. Michael did not raise any objections. The fact that his son would be in Casey's company eased Michael's mind, but he gave James a hard look.

"I'll see you at Mass in the morning," he said.

"Ah sure I'll bring him there myself," said Pete, "and with his neck washed and his hair combed and his rosary beads in his hand."

After Michael left, James told Pete about the girls with the white feathers. "Didn't I try to tip you the wink," said Pete, "but you were gone like a hare before I could say a word."

"Why do the girls here do that?"

"God knows," said Pete. "I think some of them do it just to take a rise out of us, but I suppose a lot of them have brothers or fathers or sweethearts fighting in the war and don't like the idea of other men being safe here at home."

"Have they ever called you a coward Pete?"

"Oh ay they've been on at all of us," said Pete. "That's why we come to town looking like what they expect us to look like, drunken Irish navvies. I think they know their men can't win the war without what comes out of the factory so they leave us alone."

"I'll take your word for it the next time you tell me something," said James

Pete changed the subject. "I heard tell that they will be giving the factory workers a badge to wear to keep them safe from the girls."

"When will we get them things," said James.

"You don't think they will give them to the navvies do you?" Pete replied. "Our only badge of office is mud and shit up to our oxters. Come on I have a terrible need for a pint."

On Saturday nights the Irish took over Carlisle. The public houses did a good trade virtually every night catering for the navvies who lodged in the city, but on Saturdays these were joined by their fellows from all over the area; all of them having their wages in their pockets and all of them eager to spend it on drink. A few may have gone to the local cinemas and dances, but for the vast majority it was the public bars which beckoned.

James and Pete wandered around for a while as James savoured the atmosphere. They looked into the smoke filled public bar of a pub on a street corner, but it was packed to overflowing and Pete decided that they should move on. In the next pub there was a little more room and as they pushed their way up to the bar, James noticed that it already had a line of whiskies poured, and which constantly needed to be replenished by two busy barmen. They were offered two of the glasses but Pete declined on behalf of both of them and ordered two pints of stout, for which he received a vexed look from the barman who would now have to find clean pint glasses, pour the stout, calculate the cost and give change, rather than just hand out the whiskies and take whatever money was offered – often without giving change unless the customer demanded it.

It pleased James to find that Pete had not asked whether he wanted a pint but had taken it for granted that he was a drinking man. As they turned from the bar James heard a familiar voice.

"Well now boys, would you look at that, Jim Quinlan with a pint of porter in his hand."

James looked up and spotted Liam Daly in a corner by the door leaning against the wall and in the company of another navvy. As he and Pete made their way across, Daly went on:

"So you finally made it Jim, and what about your old man, bad luck to him, how has the grand coachman taken to labouring for a living, what will he do without his lovely coach and darling horses?"

James was stung by Daly's attitude towards his father just as he had been back in Beaufort. "Da's not laboring," he blurted. "He's in the Ministry of Munitions Police at Gretna."

"Jesus Christ," said Daly, "wouldn't you know it. You could put good money on having that clever old bastard walking into a nice easy job in the dry. Is it any wonder Ireland is in ruins with the likes of him around."

He saw James tense up and modified his tone. "Anyway forget about him, what about yourself Jim? Are you still ready to fight for Ireland."

With everything that he had been obliged to deal with since leaving home, James had forgotten about The Cause until now. He remembered how he had felt about it back in Beaufort but realised how much things had changed since then. It was now very unlikely that he would be able, or indeed want, to join in armed resistance to British rule in Ireland. Pride, however, made him decide that he would not admit it to Casey.

He took a long swallow of porter and thought before answering. "Sure I don't know Liam, I'm still thinking about it."

"Well don't keep thinking for too long, things might happen any day now and you'll be left out of it. And what about your friend here, he looks like he might be a loyal Irishman."

"This is Pete Casey from Macroom," said James.

"Holy Mother," said Daly. "Don't tell me you're associating with Corkmen now Jim, is it any wonder you can't make your mind up." But he held out his hand to Pete, "Liam Daly from the County Kerry."

Pete shook hands but said nothing.

Daly's companion looked on with an expressionless face and continued smoking in silence. By now the bar was becoming crowded, and drinkers were spilling out into the cold and dimly lit street. James and Pete were gradually edged away from Daly who eventually turned and resumed his conversation in the corner. They finished their drinks and James, feeling himself to be at last a man in a man's world, and with money of his own in his pocket for once, took Pete's glass and shouldered his way to the bar for refills. When he returned, Pete gave him a puzzled look.

"I wouldn't have put you down for a rebel Jim," he said.

"Oh I'm not," said James, "I thought a bit about it though." He told Pete about the meeting in the pub back kitchen in Beaufort and about Daly and The Man from Dublin. He omitted to mention about Roger Casement and the German guns as he felt that would be tantamount to 'informing'.

"So you thought you might take up arms in the great fight for Irish freedom and drive out the British with Daly and his crew over there" said Pete.

"It's hard for me," said James. "I believe that the cause is right but my Da is totally against it and I have my brother Jack fighting in Mesopotamia. What do you think Pete, do you believe in fighting for Irish freedom?"

"No," said Pete. "Oh I believe in the idea of an independent Ireland right enough, and I think Home Rule will come sometime soon, but to my mind an armed uprising is a lost cause, it would be beaten before it started."

"Why's that?" said James.

"Well look around you Jim, most of these eejits would be so drunk they'd be more of a danger to themselves than to the British," said Pete with a grin. "But seriously now think about the amount of work being done and the money being spent up at Gretna, and that's just on the ammunition. What chance would a bunch of poor Irish farmers sons have against a country that can afford something like that."

The second pint of stout was beginning to take its effect on James.

"What about the Germans, they're not doing too badly against the British," he argued.

"Germans my arse," said Pete. "I wouldn't trust them any farther than I'd trust your man Daly in the corner over there. The last time I was down in London to see my sister she was telling me about the wounded soldiers she has to nurse and the things the Germans did to some of them."

"I saw some of them myself on the station in Dublin," said James, somewhat sobered by the memory.

"Ay that's bad enough," said Pete. "But I don't want to see Irishmen left lying dying in the streets and the fields or being buried in the bogs."

Before James could reply he was interrupted by the return of Daly. "Drink up lads," he said reaching for their glasses.

James, by now definitely feeling the effects of the two pints he had downed felt that the manly thing to do was to accept. But Pete got in first. "Sure another pint would go down fine Liam but I missed my dinner and my stomach thinks my throat is cut. I'm for a feed of fish and chips before they shut. Are you coming or stopping Jim?"

The thought of another meal like the one he had enjoyed earlier was enough for James. "I'll come with you Pete."

As they left, Daly shouted after them. "Come back when you have a full belly Jim and we'll walk home over the viaduct like real Irishmen."

For the second time that day James felt his courage being called into question. He was about to say something but Pete pushed him out of the door. "Don't take any notice of that blowhole," he said. "You won't see me doing anything stupid like trying to walk over that bloody viaduct, Joe Riorden thought he could do that and where is he now?"

Later they sat on a bench at the station and ate their supper out of newspapers. Pete was unusually quiet on the train back to Gretna but by the time they got back to the lodging house he was back to his old self. As they approached the house he saw a second story curtain move and remarked:

"Tis Hail Mary time Jim, Our Blessed Lady is looking down on us."

Behind them in the Carlisle pub Daly's companion was questioning him about James and Pete.

"Can you trust them two," he asked. "It might be safer not to tell them anything at all."

"Oh I'll tell them nothing," said Daly. "But if young Quinlan's old man is in the factory police we might be able to use them."

. . .

Next morning at Sunday Mass, Michael was comforted by the familiarity of the service. True to his word he remembered McGregor's son in his prayers along with his own family. He looked round the crowded church and couldn't spot James, but thought it was unlikely after what had happened yesterday, that his son would not come this morning. He knew that the church was too small to hold all the Irish, plus the few local Catholics, who congregated there on Sundays and so many of them knelt or stood outside the building. He guessed that James would be among these and sure enough when he came out at the end of Mass his son was waiting for him with Pete Casey.

"How are you feeling this morning Da," said James.

"Not too bad," said Michael. "I slept well. How were things in Carlisle last night?"

"Great. We had a couple of pints and fish and chips."

"You'll have to open a chip shop in Killarney when you go home Michael," said Pete, "or your man here will starve."

Michael enjoyed the light-hearted banter, it gave some relief from worrying about his family and wondering how they were. He left James and Pete talking with some other navvies and went off to have a pre-dinner cup of tea and a pipe with McGregor back at the Dornock huts. At two he was due to go on duty on the second shift. By now other people were moving off and the crowd was thinning. He looked round and was disturbed to see a familiar but unexpected and indeed unwelcome face; Liam Daly was in conversation with the priest Father Conlon. Michael had heard of a priest called Conlon who was reported to preach nationalist views but did not know if this was the same man. Certainly in his sermon today the priest had confined himself to matters of religion, but the sight of Conlon and Daly together concerned him. He wondered if he should mention the fact to his superior, Mr Brown, but decided that it would be better to wait. Jumping to conclusions and perhaps accusing the wrong man, in this case an innocent priest would not, he reasoned, serve any useful purpose and might even cause a great deal of harm.

But he was resolved to keep a close eye on the situation and at the first indication of possible trouble he would inform Brown.

Chapter 17

"Nitroglycerine," said The Man from Dublin.

Liam Daly winked at Father Conlon. "God bless you," he said.

They were once again seated at a far corner of the buffet at Carlisle railway station and, as on the occasion of their previous meeting, the station was sparsely populated on a rainy midweek afternoon. The Man from Dublin was the last member of the trio to arrive. Before entering the buffet he had wandered around the station to satisfy himself that there was nobody in evidence who had been there on his previous visit. He discounted porters and other railway staff believing that they saw so many travellers they were unlikely to distinguish one from another.

"Nitroglycerine," he said again. "It's made from glycerine mixed with nitric and disulphuric acids."

"He was at school with the Christian Brothers," said Daly to Conlon, "and grew up to be a schoolmaster himself."

The Man gave him a hard look, but went on: "The nitro is then mixed with gun-cotton to produce cordite. That's what is known as a propellant, the stuff that explodes and sends the bullet or the shell out of the barrel of a gun."

"Now you're talking," said Daly.

"It sounds impressive," said Conlon, "and I suppose there is a reason for telling us all this."

"There is," said The Man. "We had a chat with some brainy fellas that we can trust at Trinity College in Dublin. In their opinion it's odds on that the factory at Gretna is going to produce cordite and they told us how it's made. Without it the British artillery would be useless, so you can see how important it is."

He paused for effect then went on. "Now what I want you lads to do is to keep your eyes and ears open and find out if any of these materials are to be found around here. If you spot any of them try to find out where they are stored. It's mainly down to you Liam but you might hear someone talking about it as well Sean."

"You won't be hearing about them in the confessional Father, so you needn't worry about breaking any confidences." Daly's sarcasm got him another hard look from The Man, which he ignored.

"What is it we have to look out for again?" he said.

"Glycerine – that's something left over from making soap, which you might have heard of somewhere Liam – Nitric acid, sulphuric acid and cotton waste. There are a lot of other chemicals involved in smaller quantities but these are the main ones. You should also look out for any large lead-lined vats, oh and rubber bags. This is highly dangerous stuff and they need these special containers for mixing it in, and for moving it around."

"Does this mean we are going to see some action at long bloody last?" said Daly.

"Maybe," said The Man. "You told me the last time I was here that the factory wouldn't be ready before Easter, so at present it's just a case of us being ready."

Daly thought for a moment. "At the speed they're building the place I wouldn't bet on that anymore," he said. "The roads and railway are about finished and they're able to move things around the site quicker. I heard that the factory workers are starting to arrive too."

"Shit, begging your pardon Father Sean," said The Man crossly. "I told the boys at home that nothing would happen before Easter." But he immediately brightened up, "that could be a good thing though, it might mean we will be able to work on a definite plan for approval at home."

"What's so special about Easter?" said Conlon.

"It's the Resurrection of Our Lord. I thought you'd know that Father," said Daly with a grin. "But why do we need the go ahead from the boys in Dublin?"

"Because we are all working for the same thing, an Irish Republic, and unless we all pull together we'll never achieve it," said The Man. "Now shut up the pair of you, we might need to move fast, has the lad I sent over arrived Liam?"

"Oh he's here all right, working hard like a good Irish navvy even if he's not too happy to be helping the Brits, but he's making good money, which is more than can be said for some of us. I'm without the price of a pint and if there's no money to be had soon I'll have to raid Father Sean's collection."

The Man from Dublin handed him an envelope. "That should see you all right for a while Liam but don't blow it all on gargle. Are you still sure you are free to wander about without a real job?"

"Sure as long as I look like a navvy," said Daly, "nobody takes any notice and I have the new fella to cover for me now. The pubs are good places to pick up information and they'll be even better if the factory workers get thirsty. Just think of them as my confessional Father," he said.

The Man ignored the remarks. "Have either of you seen anyone you know, or who might know you?" he asked.

Conlon shook his head, but Daly said: "The only one I know of is young Quinlan, you might remember him from the night in Beaufort, his father was laid off from Beaufort House because of the war."

"Is he likely to say anything about it," said The Man.

"No," said Daly, "He's like the rest of them, he won't join The Cause but he won't inform on us either. It's his father, the bloody coachman, I'm more interested in. That old bugger has landed a job on the factory police and he's sure to know all about what's going on."

"Do you think he might tell you something of use to us?"

"Jesus no," replied Daly. "He wouldn't give me the time of day, but he might tell his son things and it wouldn't be hard to get young Jim drunk enough, and vexed enough, to talk."

The Man from Dublin thought about this. "Maybe you could help there Sean," he said to Conlon. "If either of them won't talk to Liam they might not be too worried about talking to you. So try to get friendly with them and see what happens."

The priest, who had been feeling left out of things and was getting fed up with Daly's sarcastic remarks, was glad to have been included at last. "Right," he said. "I'll see what I can do."

"Ok," said The Man. "If you have nothing else for me that's

it. We'll leave one at a time, you first Sean."

When the priest had left Daly turned to The Man: "What's all this about Easter?"

"Things are planned to happen at home on Good Friday, but that's between you and me. If the factory is up and running before then you should have the chance of having a hooley over here as well. But for Christ's sake don't tell him." He turned his head in the direction that Conlon had just taken.

Daly nodded. "Fine, and with things the way they are I'd be happier if I had something for my personal protection if you get my drift."

"I'll see what I can do," said The Man from Dublin as he left the buffet.

. . .

Daly had been right about the factory soon being ready. It was reaching the point where raw materials could be delivered in anticipation of beginning production. The internal roads were finished and the railway was nearing completion. Storage facilities were in place.

James and Pete Casey were, much to their relief, taken off the road gang and moved into an almost completed building, one of the largest on the site, where they were directed to serve as labourers for the engineers installing masses of very technical looking equipment.

Pete's first reaction on viewing the masses of pipes, containers, and valves was to nudge James and state: "Jesus Jim, we're made for life, sure this is not a munitions factory at all, what we're building here is a brewery. The plan is to get the Germans too drunk to fight."

Pete was not far off the mark, what was being installed were the still and condensers for refining crude glycerine, the first process involved in the manufacture of cordite. Before they could begin work however, the man in charge of the installation informed them in no uncertain terms that they were not to discuss what they saw here with anyone. The chargehand suspected that he was wasting his breath but he was obliged to go through the motions. He then broke the news that from now on they would be expected to work shifts along with the engineers and fitters. Round the clock working was rapidly becoming the norm as work on the factory progressed. The unwelcome news was that James and Pete would not be on the same shift. They were allowed to toss a coin to determine who should start on the day shift, James won and Pete wandered off back to Gretna to rest before coming back for the night shift. He reluctantly agreed that it was up to him to inform 'Our Lady', Mrs McBain, of the situation. "I wouldn't put it past her to raise the rent," he muttered as he left.

James missed working with Pete at first but became so fascinated by what he was being asked to do that he soon forgot about his friend. His new job was to fetch and carry pieces of equipment with names that were totally alien to him, some of it requiring the combined strength of several men; he held pipes, struts, containers and valves in place for the fitters to weld, screw and hammer into position and he received instructions in half-a-dozen different accents, some even in broken English. There were specialists here from all over the British Empire and beyond. As well as the four Home Countries there were Australians and New Zealanders, Canadians and Indians, and even a few Americans. Several, including the chief engineer, were South Africans. To the coachman's son, whose previous work experience had been confined to farming, and latterly road building, it was a different universe, but he loved it and soon got the hang of things. And it was 'a job in the dry' out of the wind and rain. He hoped he would have the chance see Pete before his friend came on shift and let him know what to expect, and he looked forward to giving his father the news.

Chapter 18

When it wasn't raining heavily in Mesopotamia that January the days were as usual, hot and humid and the nights were, as always, freezing. The rivers were in flood and turned the land for miles around into a sea of mud. In spite of the conditions the Tigris Corps were under pressure to press on with the attempt to relieve the troops bottled up in Kut-al-Amara, before Turkish reinforcements were brought down from Baghdad. Blocking their path was a Turkish force well dug in around a position known as The Wadi. This was a stream running through a deep valley into the river Tigris from the north, about six miles upstream from Sheikh Sa'ad. Behind The Wadi was a strip of land called the Hannah Defile, which lay between the Tigris and the Suwaikiya Marshes. British troops would have to pass through the marshes in order to reach Kut.

January 13th and Jack Quinlan was as usual wet through. His clothes were wet from the outside by the mist and humidity and wet from the inside by the sweat generated by the effort involved in man-handling the 18 pounder and its limber into position. Jack's battery had been ordered to take up a flanking position designed to cut the Turks off from the Tigris. The heavy mist had caused a delay in getting the move started and it was midday before the attack on the Turkish defences could be launched. The artillery again did what they could with inadequate supplies of high explosive shells and the infantry attack was pressed home with great determination. By the end of an afternoon's fierce fighting, with heavy casualties on both sides The Wadi was in British hands, but the flanking move in which Jack's battery were involved failed, and no British forces got around the Turkish flank to reach the river. Occupation of The Wadi constituted some progress but the Hannah Defile was still held, and strongly fortified by the Turks. British casualties were in excess of 1,500 and as at Sheikh

Sa'ad, there was a lack of medical facilities and many of the wounded lay for days in the open waiting for attention.

The besieged troops in Kut were running short of rations for the men and the situation was even more desperate for the horses. Eight days after the battle of The Wadi the Tigris Corps attacked the Hannah Defile.

The artillery bombarded the Turkish positions on the day before the attack but were restricted to firing for less than half an hour. Next day they were in action again from both banks of the Tigris and were supported by some gunboats on the river itself. It was, however, a bombardment that would have been thought totally inadequate preparation for such an attack on the Western Front. The infantry attacked half an hour after the guns ceased firing. The Turkish defenders rose up to man the trenches and the attackers were cut to pieces. Turkish artillery came into action and the British gunners suffered their first serious casualties. Being back from the front line troops the wounded artillerymen could be treated quickly, but the wounded infantrymen were again left in terrible conditions. Next morning the British commander called for a truce so that they could be taken into shelter and tended as well as the meagre medical supplies would allow. But no sooner had the truce begun than bands of Arabs came out from the Turkish lines to rob the dead and wounded of anything they could lay their hands on, especially rifles and ammunition. Many of the wounded were killed out of hand, and it was some time before a few Turkish officers were able to stop the carnage. It was the worst example of this kind of deplorable treatment suffered by British troops since the Crimean War, and nothing could have done more to instil a loathing for the enemy in the hearts of the Tigris Corps.

Following the defeat at the Hannah Defile it was clear that the current attempt to relieve the siege of Kut had failed. Having suffered some 7,500 dead and wounded for very little ground gained the Tigris Corps badly needed to re-group and re-equip before a second attempt to get through to the besieged troops could be mounted. The Turks seemed content to dig in and strengthen their defences around the defile rather than go on the offensive so the British commanders decided to build up their forces to a point where they could attack in strength with a reasonable chance of success. The garrison at Kut would therefore, be obliged to hold out in extremely difficult circumstances until an effective relief force could be properly organised, and any attempt to break through would also have to wait until there was a significant improvement in the weather. In the meantime attempts would be made to supply them by gunboats on the river and by air, which given the types of aircraft available at the time would constitute no more than a morale boosting gesture.

For the officers and men of the Tigris Corps, bitterly disheartened by their failure to break through to Kut and still haunted by the horrors suffered by their wounded comrades, the gloom was partially lifted by the arrival of mail from home.

Jack Quinlan finally learned of his father and brother's departure for the munitions factory in Scotland. The news triggered off a variety of emotions: worry about how his father would cope with such an upheaval to his life; relief because he felt it unlikely that James would now follow him into the army; a little pride in the fact that other members of his family were now involved in the war; a war, which for members of the Tigris Corps had taken on elements of a personal crusade.

He wrote a letter to his mother to let her know he was well, being careful not to mention the experiences of his first taste of battle. The thought of telling her the truth about his experiences did not enter his mind. After having impressed on her that he was not in any great danger and, having reminded her that she and the others at home were constantly in his prayers, he asked her to send an address so that he could write personally to his father and James. With them he felt he could be more open about the real situation, and even if the letter fell foul of the censor and arrived with large portions obliterated he thought that enough of the message would get through.

Aware of their mood, the Battery Commander called his men together in an attempt to assure them that the failure to relieve Kut was not their fault. He added: "You were not responsible for the shoddy planning of this ill-conceived enterprise, and you are certainly not to blame for the supply shortages, particularly the lack of ammunition."

"Ah well we won't have to wait long for that to be put right sir," said Jack, "sure aren't my father and my brother on the job now."

. . .

Annie received the first letter from her husband and son. The whole family gathered round to read it. She was disturbed to learn that Michael and James had been obliged to find separate lodgings but William, whom she was already coming to rely on, was able to convince her that everything would be all right. She did not reply immediately, for Michael had told her that a second letter would soon follow with some money.

As soon as she realised that there had been a letter, Mrs Connor found an excuse to visit Annie. She was politely received and assured that all was well but given absolutely no further information. In the event she was forced to try and obtain some fuel for her gossip from the younger children who excitedly supplied her with several widely differing versions of what the letter had contained. She knew she would have got no more from William than she had from Annie and so had to be content with what little knowledge she had. A few days later the second letter arrived with the money enclosed.

Annie heeded Michael's advice and on the following Saturday William harnessed the pony to drive her and the children into Killarney. He took the children off to buy sweets while his mother went to the post office to cash the postal orders. There was more than enough money for her immediate needs so she opened a post office savings account. It would give her enormous pleasure to tell Michael that for the first time in their lives they had money in the bank.

Chapter 19

The month of January 1916 gave way to February but the Solway weather took no notice. A chill wind off the Firth was bringing flurries of sleet, which further inland would turn to snow.

Michael was getting used to the routine of shift working and to life in the Dornock huts. The strange hours didn't bother him because as a coachman he had been required to make himself available at any time day or night 365 days of the year. It was the living and sleeping arrangements in the hut that he found more difficult to come to terms with. The hut was by now fully occupied by a variety of men from different parts of the world and with a wide range of jobs and responsibilities in the factory. Michael found that he was the only member of the factory police in that particular hut, had he thought about it he would have realised that the living arrangements for his colleagues were deliberately scattered throughout the site. All the men in 'his' hut were working on a shift system of one sort or another so there were comings and goings at all hours. Most were conscious of the need for quiet when their fellow occupants were sleeping, but the bare floorboards and thin walls made complete silence impossible. It was an unwritten law of the hut that the stoves were kept going during the cold Scottish winter and anyone coming off or going on shift was expected to stoke them up. Then there was the food. It depended on which shift you were on whether you got hot, warmed up or cold meals.

The factory police had been issued with their dark blue uniforms and, while Michael had felt rather conspicuous in his at first, he was getting used to that too. Shift working made it difficult to keep in touch with James, but he found that the uniform allowed him the freedom of the entire site and so he could visit the glycerine still where his son was currently working when coming off or going on shift.

The one saving grace as far as Michael was concerned was Alastair McGregor. He had struck up a real friendship with the old soldier who acted as a sort of janitor for several of the huts. They often shared a mug of tea, a pipe of tobacco and a yarn, and both were surprised that although they came from widely different backgrounds, they had much in common and plenty to talk about. So although Michael sorely missed his wife and family, and he still suffered from shortage of breath and the occasional pain in his chest, he reasoned that life could have been much worse.

The store complex where he still worked – he was required to be ready to move to another post should the necessity arise – was now completed and supplies of raw materials were being stored. Carboys of nitric and sulphuric acid, containers of crude glycerine and other chemicals, and bales of cotton waste for processing into gun-cotton were being delivered daily by the lorry load to be carefully stored on special racks. Before long they would be transported to the different manufacturing processes in special wagons on the factory's internal railway. At this stage it was not strictly necessary to shift the materials by rail but as they went through the various stages of cordite production the mixtures became dangerously unstable and it was decided that well sprung trucks rails would provide the safest possible method of transport.

The number of factory police force was increasing significantly and during the day shift when materials were being brought in two men were on duty. Michael was standing by the open doors booking in the lorries while a colleague was keeping an eye on the storage operation to ensure that all safety requirements were being adhered to. Wilson, the factory security chief, who Michael now knew to be a commander in the Royal Navy, could be seen through the windows of the office on the other side of the doorway talking to Brown, the senior policeman in the stores complex. Since delivery of the materials had begun Commander Wilson's visits had become more frequent.

Michael had just checked a load of cotton waste through when he noticed two figures approaching out of the murky sleet. He recognised the jarvey's cape before the wearer was fully visible. As Liam Daly came through the door he spotted Michael in his new uniform.

"Jesus Christ Mick," he said loudly to his companion. "For a minute there I thought I saw Michael bloody Quinlan. Will you look at the cut of him in his gorgeous new peeler suit."

He sneered at Michael. "Look at yourself Quinlan you can't wear decent togs like an honest working Irishman. If you're not in your fancy coachman's outfit you have to dress up and pretend to be a copper. And by the way where's your beautiful carriage and horses, did you have to leave them at home?"

Michael immediately became angry. "What do you think you're doing here Daly?"

"If it's anything to do with you Quinlan we only came in out of the weather for a fag."

"Well you can't do that here, did you not see the 'no smoking' sign, its big enough, and even if smoking was allowed you have no business here so be off with you."

Daly made a threatening move forward but Michael stood his ground and the jarvey's companion held his arm, "Easy now Liam," he said. "Come on there's nothing here for us."

As they left the store Daly turned: "You still think you can lord it over a poor old jarvey Quinlan, well I'll fix you one of these days Mr high and mighty coachman."

Even when they were away from the store, Daly was still seething. He said to his companion, "I swear to God Mick, when I get the chance I'll do for that old bastard."

"That's between yourself and him Liam, but don't let it come between you and what we have to do," said Mick."Did you get a look inside that big shed?"

"I did," said Daly. "I'd say that's the place we're after. We'll have to find a way of getting a closer look when that bloody coachman is off shift."

Michael was standing watching them leave when there was a tap on his shoulder. His colleague pointed towards the office where Brown was beckoning him to come over. He entered the office. "What was all that about Quinlan?" said Brown.

"A couple of navvies tried to come in out of the rain for a smoke sir, so I got rid of them." Michael thought for a moment and realised that this was an opportunity to say something about Daly, and he could also mention the priest, Father Conlon, without having to worry about accusing the wrong man.

"I know one of them from home sir, his name is Liam Daly and I had a row with him once. I wouldn't trust him out of my sight."

"Why is that?" Brown asked.

"Well sir when I was the coachman at Beaufort House he was a local jarvey, what you would call a cabman sir, and he used to be hired sometimes to take people from the house to the station in Killarney. One day I caught him nosing around the stables, I'd swear he was thieving and I reported him to His Lordship. Daly got no more work from us and he's had it in for me since."

Wilson spoke for the first time. "Have you seen him around here before?"

"I have sir, I saw him talking to the priest, Father Conlon, after Mass a couple of Sundays back. If you don't mind me saying so sir I thought that was funny because he was never a great one for going to Mass at home. He spent more time in the public houses blathering about Home Rule and Irish independence."

"Did he now?" said the commander. "Do you think he is a member of one of the rebel factions we've been hearing about?"

"I don't know for sure sir, he might only be all talk, but I wouldn't put it past him."

Wilson thought for a moment then said: "All right Quinlan, thank you for letting us know, you did the right thing."

After Michael had left Wilson said, "He seems like a good sort."

"Yes," said Brown, "he's doing a good job."

"Perhaps better than you realise," said Wilson as he left the office.

Michael felt better for having had the opportunity of passing on to a higher authority his suspicions regarding Daly and the priest Conlon. Later that evening while he was enjoying a pipe and mug of tea with Alistair McGregor he told his friend about the incident. The old soldier looked up when Michael mentioned that he suspected Daly of being a nationalist rebel.

"I served in Ireland many years ago, up in Belfast it was. As I recall there was no' a lot of support for independence there at the time. What's the feeling over there now?"

"I'd say," said Michael, "that there never was much support in the north. There was a lot more in the south before the war, but now there's more support for the war against Germany. A lot of lads have joined up and their people are behind them, like we are with my son Jack. Mind you there are still a good few hotheads like Daly around, but then again I think he has it in for me and his Lordship more than he has for the British."

"How do you feel about it yourself?"

"Well," said Michael. "I always made my living by working for the British gentry with big houses in Ireland. A good living it was too after I was made the head coachman, so I was always dead against home rule of any kind. But now anybody with eyes in his head can see that the day of the coach and horses are over and I'm too old to learn to drive a motor car. I don't know what I'll do after the war, so maybe home rule would be a good thing some day. But I'll tell you one thing Alistair; I'll have no truck with armed rebellion or anybody that wants it."

"You're right there," said McGregor. "I fought for the British Empire against people who were fighting for their independence. You might think it a strange thing for a British soldier to say, but I always thought better of them for doing it. But if there's one thing I learned from nearly forty years a soldier it's that war never settled anything in the long run. We cheer our victories, and we honour the dead. But we never ask them if it was worth it."

. . .

Commander Wilson went straight back to his own office and contacted his superior in Whitehall who immediately decided to come up to Gretna. He arranged to meet with Commander Wilson and the agent known as 'Patrick' in the buffet on Carlisle station from where he could make a quick return to London.

When all three had arrived and were seated Commander Wilson reported in detail what had happened at the raw material stores. At the mention of Daly's name 'Patrick' interrupted.

"Was he wearing a sort of cabman's cape?"

"Yes," said Wilson testily, as if fearing that he was again being left out of things. "Why, did you already know about him?"

"No not really," replied 'Patrick', "but I've seen him around the pubs here in Carlisle and he certainly has a lot to say for himself regarding Irish politics." In an attempt to pacify Wilson he turned to The Man from Whitehall. "I think the commander is on to something here sir, particularly if Daly has been seen with Father Conlon."

The Man from Whitehall turned to Wilson. "Do you think that your man, Quinlan, is telling the whole truth, or is he merely exaggerating things in order to settle an old score, and I shudder to think of the consequences of His Lordship's former coachman turning out to be a rebel. There's no danger of that is there?"

"In my opinion, no sir, I believe Quinlan was telling us the truth, I got the impression that he was already thinking of saying something about this fellow Daly and the priest but didn't quite know how to bring it up."

"Thank you, that sounds definite enough," said The Man from Whitehall. "All right we must assume that there is an Irish rebel cell established here at Gretna and plan accordingly. For a start you will need some help and, although we are short handed, I propose sending someone else up here. We ought to have someone inside the factory work force while 'Patrick' concentrates on the navvies. If we have someone ostensibly working inside the factory they can act as liaison between the two of you."

"I don't see why 'Patrick' and I can't communicate directly," said Wilson. "I can understand that you have to consider your operative's safety but surely in this situation that is not an issue."

His superior looked directly at him. "I realise that our methods are different to those of the Royal Navy commander. But you must understand that while the operative's safety is certainly a consideration the safety and integrity of the operation takes precedent."

Wilson looked at 'Patrick' but the 'operative's' face gave nothing away.

Chapter 20

The first of the expected 30,000 factory workers from all over the British Empire had arrived at Gretna. At the Dornock site the glycerine distillery was to all intents and purposes ready. Stills, condensers, pumps and presses were all in place. The electricity supply from the factory's own brand new power station, constructed on the banks of the river Sark, had been connected; the equally new pumping station was ready to start supplying water, and the massive boilers were ready for firing up. All that remained was to carry out a test run before the work of producing nitro-glycerine in unprecedented quantities could begin.

The installation engineers handed the facility over to the operators and moved on to putting the equipment for the next stage of the cordite manufacture in place. Because he had shown such aptitude in learning the skills required to fetch and carry for them they asked for James Quinlan to continue working with them. As a result he was transferred from the contract builders to the factory staff.

Like his father, James had by now got used to shift working. Now that he was a Ministry of Munitions employee he could have moved into one of the accommodation huts in what had become known as 'Timbertown'. But he had opted to remain at Solway View where he had also settled into a routine. With time he had become accustomed to 'Our Lady's' – Mrs McBain's – strict, but in reality, quite kindly ways. By staying at the Gretna lodging he could keep in touch with Pete Casey, and leaving there would not have brought him any closer to his father as the Dornock huts were now full, which meant that his only option would be a move to the new township at Gretna. He had discussed it with Michael who had agreed that he was probably as comfortable in the house at Gretna as he would have been in a wooden hut, and Michael was pleased to have something positive to tell Annie who would see James' transfer to the factory staff as a promotion. James could see how the news would be welcomed at home, but he still harboured a niggling worry about his father's health, he could not help but notice that, although he tried to hide the fact, Michael had obviously been short of breath when he visited him at the glycerine still. He wondered if he should tell his mother but decided that there was no point in causing her further worry, and he did not want to go to her behind his father's back.

Shift working meant that they were rarely able to go to Carlisle together. Michael went to send the money home as often as he could but, as he insisted that it should be sent on a weekly basis, there were times when the responsibility fell to James. On the Saturday afternoon following Michael's argument with Liam Daly, James was preparing to take the money to the Carlisle post office. He dressed in his Sunday best. Now officially a factory employee he was the proud owner of one of the little silver badges, which identified him as a 'War Munitions Volunteer' and this would be his first opportunity to wear it in public. He had been to Carlisle with Pete Casey since he had been issued with the badge but had decided to go as a navvy on that occasion because Pete, for reasons of his own which James failed to fathom, had declined a move to the factory staff in order to remain in the employ of the builders.

This would be the first occasion he had ventured into town on his own.

He reached Carlisle in time to get to the post office before it closed, purchased the postal orders, sealed them in the envelope together with some notes and a letter, and went to get his favourite meal of fish and chips. To his surprise he found that they did not taste quite as good when eating them by himself. He wandered around the city for an hour or so and was extremely disappointed not to run into any of the local girls in town on the lookout for unsuspecting young men to shame with their white feathers. He had been looking forward to showing them his badge, which he fully expected would have met with their enthusiastic approval.

Being on his own he found, caused Carlisle to lose some of its glamour. Having failed to show off his new badge to any purpose he considered his options, he could return to Gretna but with Pete working until about ten, and with the MacCarthy brothers sure to be going out drinking, he would be left with only 'St Patrick', and that individual would undoubtedly be too engrossed in a book to be of any worthwhile company. He could go to the cinema but that did not appeal. So for the first time since he had left home he ventured into a public house alone. It was still relatively early so the pub contained only a few navvies. James tried to strike up a conversation with them but was surprised to find that they didn't seem interested, which was most unusual for the naturally friendly Irish. Although he did not realise it at the time this was his first experience of the strict social demarcation line between the builders and the munitions workers. Eventually he went back to drinking alone.

He had finished his first pint and was about to leave when he was thumped on the back. As he turned around, Liam Daly looked at him aghast.

"Jesus Wept! Will you look at Jim Quinlan, in his best Sundays and Holy Days suit and wearing the sacred badge of a British munitions worker. Where the hell did you steal that thing Jim, or did your old man steal it for you?"

James, who was getting fed up with Daly's sarcasm about his father, retorted: "Nobody stole it, I was issued with it because I'm working for the factory now."

"Sure and what else would a Quinlan be doing. Was it the old fella that got you the job." He turned to his companion. "It was Jim's father that stopped us going in out of the rain for a fag a couple of days back Mick."

"He couldn't let anybody in there," snapped James. "There's a whole load of dangerous stuff stored there."

"That's no reason to leave two of his hard working countrymen standing in the rain," said Daly. "I suppose he still thinks he's the great bloody coachman lording it over the poor jarvey. It's a miracle that he lets you out to drink with honest Irish navvies."

"I'll drink where I like," retorted James. Before Daly could reply, his friend, Mick, intervened. "Easy now Liam, sure being at odds with his father is no reason to come down on young Jim here."

Daly stood for a minute then turned on his heel. "I'm off for a piss," he said.

When Daly left, Mick said to James, "Ah take no notice of him, he has a thorn in his arse about something. Come on have a drink, I'd like to know how you got a job with the factory, the truth of it is I'd like to have one of them badges myself and bugger what your man Liam thinks about it."

When they had pints in their hands, James, feeling that he was with a friend, said, "I was working with the engineers fitting out the glycerine still and they wanted me to stay on with them when they went to do the next job. My Da had nothing to do with it."

"Sure I never thought for a minute that he did, that was just Daly talking. What is the new job?"

"I don't know all that much about it yet." The strong porter was beginning to have its effect on James. "We're shifting in some massive big vats, they're like great big basins, but the funny thing is they're lined with lead."

"Is that out at Dornock too?"

"No this place is just up the road from Gretna."

They drank their porter in silence for a while. James was feeling the effects of the alcohol and, although two pints had been the maximum he had previously managed, he confidently ordered another round.

"This new job you have," said Mick, "it sounds to me like you have to have to be some sort of an engineer to work at it. Is that how you got into it?"

"Not at all, I picked it up a bit at a time," said James proudly.

"Ah sure it's fine for a smart young fella like yourself, but how would a thick navvy like me get on. Tell me now what is it you have to do."

Unsuspecting and, by now well on his way to being drunk, James proceeded to explain to Mick as best he could about the pipes, pumps, condensers and other equipment he had helped to install. Although he found that trying to talk about it in technical terms, even if he entirely understood them, was not quite as easy as actually doing the work under the supervision of the engineers. But Mick proved to be a good listener and seemed satisfied.

"If you hear of any jobs going where you are now would you let me know? God knows it's more in my line than pushing a barrow."

"Sure I will," said James. "What about Liam, is he looking for work too?"

"Ah don't be worrying about him. Sure all he wants to do is talk about fighting for Ireland."

At that juncture Daly returned. "Now there's a grand pair of conspirators if ever I saw one," he said. "Is there no danger one of you might make a friend the offer of a pint."

"Jim was telling me all about building the glycerine distillery, and it's better than listening to you blathering about Irish freedom, and you have enough drink in you for one night," said Mick.

"Building a distillery is it," said Daly, "sure he wouldn't know where to start. The only still his old man ever heard of was a poteen still. And if he found one of them he'd go straight to his precious British boss to get the peelers to shut it down."

James was by now ready to go for Daly but Mick stepped between the two.

"Easy now the pair of you." He turned to James. "I'll take him off out of your way Jim before a fight starts and we all get run in, are you all right for the train back."

"Sure I am," said James. He was about to say more but Mick held up his hand.

"We'll leave it there," he said and winked at James. "And don't forget about what we talked about."

After James had left Daly said, "How did it go Mick, did he tell you anything at all?"

"The young eejit couldn't stop talking," said Mick. "We could do worse than take a look at that stores where his old man works. And that glycerine still would be worth a visit too".

"Right," said Daly. "Come on we'll strike while the iron is hot and have a look tonight."

Chapter 21

When James left the warmth of the bar the combination of strong porter and the cold air began to take effect. The walk to the station was accomplished with some difficulty and was accompanied by amused, sympathetic or disapproving glances depending upon the various beliefs and standards of those casting them. But the exercise had worked in his favour so that when he finally reached the station there was a distinct improvement, and he had recovered some of his poise if not his pride. He considered going to the buffet for a cup of tea but thought better of it and sat on one of the wooden benches to wait for the train. But once the train began to move the motion caused him to feel nauseous and he spent the bulk of the short journey in the toilet. By the time they reached Gretna he was again feeling decidedly under the weather.

On the platform at Gretna, James had to look twice to make certain that the man standing talking to the extremely pretty young woman was indeed his friend Pete Casey. She was of medium height and figure and her coat and hat had obviously been chosen for comfort rather than extravagance, but she wore them well and carried herself with elegance. But she seemed quite happy to chat with Pete in his navvy's clothing. By her feet was a large suitcase.

Pete spotted James, beckoned him over and said to the girl: "This disreputable looking tinker is the one and only Jim Quinlan from the County Kerry and I'm ashamed to admit that I have the misfortune to be lodging with him. Jim this is Miss... er?"

"Birks," said the girl laughing.

"Birks," said Pete. "Will you look now at the cut of him Miss Birks, he must have smelled the cork out of a Guinness bottle. I'll have to take him back to our room at the Savoy or Our Lady is likely to skin the both of us alive."

Miss Birks looked bemused but smiled and said nothing.

"Miss Birks," said Pete. "You were asking me if I knew the

way to the ladies' hostel. Now if you would permit two perfect gentlemen to walk you there we would be happy to oblige, and carry your case for you into the bargain."

"Why thank you both Mister... er?" said the girl, her north of England accent more pronounced.

"Casey, Peter Casey at your service," said Pete.

"Thank you Mr Casey," she said.

They walked her into Gretna, or to be more accurate, Pete walked her into Gretna while an embarrassed James stumbled along behind with the heavy suitcase. They conducted her to the door of the brand new hostel specially built to accommodate some of the thousands of women and girls who would form the majority of the munitions workforce when the factory was in full production. She explained that she was one of the first to arrive but hundreds of others were coming in daily.

At the door, Pete took off his cap and bowed. "Good night Miss Birks, I sincerely hope we meet again."

She laughed, curtseyed and replied: "Good night and thank you Mr Casey, I'm sure we will. And thank you also Mr Quinlan." With that she was gone.

The befuddled James was by now completely at a loss. "Who was that girl?" was all he could manage to say.

"That was no girl Jim," said Pete. "That was an angel from heaven sent down to Gretna by way of Yorkshire to comfort some poor lonely navvy, and I'm the first in the queue. I think I'm in love."

He became more serious. "And what about yourself, I'd say you had a few drinks with the rest of the good Catholic Irishmen in Carlisle tonight and it got the better of you. Why don't you tell your old uncle Pete all about it?"

In slurred tones James related to Pete all he could remember about his encounter with Liam Daly. On hearing about the conversation over pints of porter with Daly's friend Mick, whom James thought was a 'grand fella', Pete remarked: "And I suppose you told him all about what you are doing over there in the factory."

James looked sheepishly at his friend. "I'm afraid that I did

Pete."

"Jim, oh Jimmy boy, what am I going to do with you. Didn't I tell you not to trust that Daly an inch, and that goes for his pals as well."

"Ah sure Mick's all right," said James

"Maybe so," said Pete. "But if I was you I'd stay sober around him and keep my mouth shut."

They made their way back in silence and Pete managed to get James past 'Our Lady's' covert inspection without incident. Back in the loft they found that only 'St Patrick' Murphy was at home. The MacCarthy brothers had, as was usual on weekends, opted to stay out rather than attempt a late night return. They had often voiced the opinion that no amount of whiskey could instill enough courage to face the music from Mrs McBain, and they were loath to be evicted from the relative comfort of Solway View.

When James' head hit the pillow the whole loft began to go around in circles. As he made a dash for the outhouse 'St Patrick' stirred and muttered, "What's wrong with him?"

"He's in love," said Pete.

. . .

Michael and his fellow policeman went off duty at ten and one of the new men took their place. There were no deliveries that Saturday night and only one policeman was required to be on duty. A gang of men were, however, busy at the back of the stores selecting and loading materials onto one of the special rail wagons to be transported to the glycerine distillery for the first test run scheduled for the Sunday morning. The guard was alone by the entrance which remained wide open for the wagon to be moved through in the morning.

In the early hours the peace was shattered by the sound of a drunken Irish voice rendering 'The Rose of Tralee'. As the inexperienced policeman left his post and went out to move the singer on, a shadow slipped through the door behind his back and into the building. The intruder went unnoticed through the well lit building, keeping to the shadows yet making careful notes of the contents of the various containers and their locations. In less than an hour he had all he needed to enable him to produce a comprehensive report on the stores and what was stored there. When the men working on loading the wagon stopped for a break they were joined by the bored policeman and the uninvited visitor was able to slip quietly away.

His exit from the building did not, however, escape the notice of an alert watcher hidden behind a stack of building materials.

At the glycerine distillery things were easier for the intruders. The place was a hive of activity preparing for the test run. All that was required to escape notice was to look busy. An hour before dawn two men arrived and sauntered into the building, one dressed in an engineer's overalls and pretending to be issuing instructions to the other who was dressed as a workman. For an hour they moved purposefully and unchallenged around the installation not looking at all out of place. When they left they were not missed. Daly retrieved his jarvey's cape and they left the site as the cold dawn was breaking.

But as had happened at the stores their exit was observed and they were stealthily shadowed at a discreet distance. They were then watched until they had left the factory site for the awakening streets of Gretna, where it would have been difficult to tail them without being discovered.

· · ·

Next morning James was noticeably bleary eyed when he arrived just in time for Mass. He was met at the door of the church by an impatient Michael who was wide awake and had some exciting news for his son; news which would now have to wait until the service was over. When they emerged after Mass, James found that his father was more concerned with showing him the letter, which had come direct from Jack rather than being relayed via Annie, than he was with learning about his son's escapades of the night before.

"It's not a bit like the letters he sent home before," said James when he had read Jack's account of the war in Mesopotamia. The letter was heavily censored with several passages obliterated with black ink.

"You're right there Jim," said Michael. "They don't want people to know the full story and you have to read between the lines. But, knowing Jack, the message is clear. It's a bit like seeing all those poor suffering wounded men at the station in Dublin. It shows what war is really like, it's nothing at all to do with what we hear from the politicians or read in the papers."

"Do you think we're doing any good at all here Da? Will this place make things better for Jack and the other soldiers once it's finished?"

"They have a terrible shortage of ammunition all right," said Michael, "and Jack says he's glad that we're working here. Anyway I'd rather be doing this than sitting at home doing nothing, to my way of thinking it kind of keeps us all together. And the only other thing we can do for Jack is pray for him."

James' hangover had miraculously disappeared. "You're right Da we can always do that."

"And what would that be you can always do?" They looked round and found Pete Casey standing there.

"Pray for Jack," said James. He looked at his father who nodded so he showed Pete the letter.

When Pete had finished reading James asked: "What do you think, Pete, are we doing any good working here?"

"I think," said Pete, "that your brother is glad you're working here, in a way you're backing him up. And I'll tell you this much for sure, he'd rather you were working here than getting your handsome head blown off in Mesopotamia or France or somewhere."

"You're a grand philosopher Pete," said Michael. "I thought you were working today."

"Oh I am," said Pete, "but at this very minute we're hanging around waiting for a load of bricks. So I came over here on the chance that the gorgeous Miss Birks might be a Catholic and was at Mass."

"What's he talking about?" said Michael.

"Sure isn't the great philosopher in love," said James.

Before they could continue with the conversation they were approached by the priest, Father Conlon. "Good morning gentlemen," he said. "I've seen you all here fairly regularly on Sunday so I thought I'd come and introduce myself, I'm Father Sean Conlon." He held out his hand.

Pete Casey was the first to react. He took the priest's hand. "Pete Casey, Father, and this is Michael Quinlan and his son James".

James immediately shook the offered hand, Michael hesitated but followed suit.

"I suppose you're all working up at the factory," said the priest.

"That's right Father," said James. "Pete is on the building, I'm working with the engineers and Da here is on the factory police."

Pete looked at Michael and shook his head.

"Well now that's great," said Conlon. "You must see a whole lot of interesting things. But tell me Michael is there much crime up there? I know a lot goes on in Gretna and Carlisle of a night, even in the church you can't help hearing about it, but I didn't think there was much for a policeman to do at the factory itself."

Michael thought back to the talk he'd had with Commander Wilson regarding Liam Daly, and however reluctant he was to even consider that a priest might be involved in some ungodly scheme, his niggling suspicions were more pronounced. Neither could he escape the worrying possibility that if the rebels were up to something at Gretna it might have a direct effect on Jack's chances of surviving the war. But he couldn't very well tell Father Conlon to mind his own business.

"Well Father," he said. "There's more than one kind of crime, I suppose you'd say they're all covered by the Ten Commandments but I think the people I work for have made up a few new ones."

"Is that right," said the priest, "and what would they be?"

As Michael was pondering what to say next an altar boy came running up to the priest. "There's a man in the sacristy that wants to see you father, he said it's urgent."

"Oh, I'm sorry gentlemen please excuse me. It might be

someone who wants me to hear his confession," said the priest. "Maybe we can go on with this chat later Michael."

"Sure we can Father," was all Michael could think to say.

He chatted for a few minutes more with James and Pete. As they were about to split up a figure came out of the sacristy and walked off without looking in their direction.

"That was a quick confession," said Pete.

"I know him," said Michael. "He's a friend of that blackguard Liam Daly, what would he be doing going to confession?"

"His name is Mick," said James without thinking. Pete took one look at Michael's face and decided it was time he went back to work.

"How do you know the likes of him," said Michael with visible restraint.

James was forced to tell his father about his trip to Carlisle the night before. He confessed that he had spoken with Mick and told him about his job, but he omitted to tell his father that he had been drunk. He tried to make light of the incident by relating the story about Pete and the girl Miss Birks, but could see that his father was still deeply concerned.

A few short months previously Michael would have torn a strip off James, now in this new world all he did was issue a mild rebuke. "You stay away from that gang Jim, they're out for trouble and you won't be doing Jack or any of us one bit of good if you get mixed up in it."

He was gratified to see that this approach was at least as effective as shouting, and all a contrite James could say was: "Yes Da."

It was not confession but the delivery of a sheaf of papers, the results of the previous night's activities, which had brought Mick to the church that Sunday morning. Father Conlon took the rough notes and placed them in a preaddressed registered envelope. Next morning he took the package into Carlisle and sent it on its way to Dublin.

Chapter 22

Commander Wilson was not happy about what he was being asked to do, but he was a serving officer in wartime and would carry out his orders to the best of his ability. Over the telephone to the Man from Whitehall he had made his objections to 'Patrick's' scheme quite forcibly but had been overruled. He had though, been forced to admit that the plan put in place following the previous meeting had worked well enough. The new 'operative' sent to Gretna to assist 'Patrick' and act as liaison was in place and proving to be a useful contact. It was via this route that he learned of the visit by 'Mick' to the priest.

He had immediately telephoned his superior at Whitehall with a strong recommendation that Daly and his accomplice should be apprehended, by himself and his men if they were discovered on ministry property or by the civilian police should they be found off-site. Wilson had carried out a thorough investigation to establish who had initially employed Daly at Gretna with the disturbing result that the man was apparently not employed by either the ministry or any of the contractors. This was in his opinion, sufficient evidence to have Daly arrested. Much to the commander's annoyance the Man from Whitehall was adamant that nothing was to be done until after he himself came to Gretna to discuss the matter with Wilson and 'Patrick'.

In the Royal Navy, Commander Wilson's intelligence duties had involved predicting possible enemy strengths and movements, and devising ways of disguising his own fleet's intentions in order to confuse the enemy. Undercover operations of any kind had not formed part of his duties. In fact he harboured a profound dislike for what he referred to as 'cloak and dagger' operations. When he had accepted the post of Head of Security at Gretna he had expected a straightforward approach with a clear set of rules in place, and anyone found breaking them would suffer the consequences. Now he found himself immersed in an unfamiliar world of undercover plots and counter plots. It was not to his liking but he was stuck with it.

To be fair, the Man from Whitehall had put forward sound reasons for not immediately placing Daly and co. under close arrest; it was extremely unlikely that they had identified all the members of the gang and the arrest of Daly would only drive the others further underground. The best way to discover the full extent of the rebel intentions was to allow them to go on with their scheme unaware that they had been discovered, while keeping a close eye on them; as long as the rebel leadership were convinced that their men in Gretna were undiscovered they would not change their plans. Then there was the wider picture to consider; it was known that the vast majority of Irish people were opposed to any kind of rebellion in wartime, but this situation could easily change if the rebel propaganda machine was presented with an opportunity to create martyrs.

"The Irish love a good martyr," said The Man from Whitehall, "and we have to be particularly careful not to provide them with a holy one in the form of the good Father Conlon. This is definitely not the time for gunboat diplomacy commander."

Wilson could see the logic behind the decision to allow Daly and his accomplices a carefully monitored degree of freedom, although he suspected that it was he who was likely to bear responsibility if the surveillance were to fail. It was when 'Patrick' proposed that some action should be taken to bring the matter to a head, and especially when he outlined a plan for such action, that the commander raised his most strident objections. It was not so much the plan itself that he objected to, it was the part he would personally have to play that he found particularly distasteful. The Man from Whitehall listened politely to Wilson's objections then made his decision:

"I realise that this is not how things are done in the Royal Navy commander, and I sympathise that this goes against your professional integrity as a serving officer, but I believe that Patrick's approach is sound and I should like you to put it into effect."

Before he rang off he added: "I believe that to be on the safe side, we should introduce this in stages. I leave it to you to work out the details between you, but I want this plan implemented and I want it done within a few days so I suggest that you get on with it."

They had been left in no doubt what was expected of them so they had little choice but to put aside any personal differences and work together. In the event Wilson was relieved to find that 'Patrick' was quite ready to listen to suggestions and a way forward was agreed. In spite of this the sour taste persisted.

So now he sat in his office going over in his mind for the umpteenth time how he was going to approach this disagreeable task. Eventually he picked up the telephone and rang the stores complex.

. . .

The package from Gretna arrived at an accommodation address in Dublin where it was passed on to The Man. He studied the notes and collated them into a comprehensive report, added some recommendations of his own and took them to the small group of men charged with planning the Easter Uprising. Having read the report the planners contacted their scientific friends at Trinity College and arranged a consultation.

Having delivered his report The Man from Dublin made his way by a circuitous route to the house in Rathmines where he presented a second copy to Padraig Pearse in person. It came as no surprise that Pearse wanted a personal copy. The Man knew that as yet only a handful of people knew the details of the planned uprising and Pearse wanted to keep it that way until the last possible minute. He also wanted to keep complete personal control of events. Even Roger Casement, who was currently arranging for the 20,000 captured rifles donated by the Germans to be delivered by sea to a point in south-west Ireland, had not been informed of the date of the uprising. And The Man was one of the very few who knew the reason for this. Pearse believed that one consignment of obsolete rifles and a few out-dated machine guns would make little or no difference to the eventual outcome of the rebellion. The rebels could not, in his view, ever succeed in an armed struggle with the British Empire. Even senior members of the Nationalist organisations involved did not know that the real object of the exercise was to create enough martyrs to arouse the sympathy of the Irish people.

Pearse was resigned to the fact that he himself would be one of them.

Chapter 23

On his way to answer the summons to Commander Wilson's office Michael felt some apprehension at the unusual nature of the order, but as soon as he entered Wilson put him at ease.

"Ah there you are Quinlan, please come in and sit down." His manner was as usual businesslike but without any sign of annoyance, so Michael relaxed.

When Michael was seated Wilson said, "First of all Quinlan I want to thank you for tipping me off about the man Daly. I've done some checking and I cannot find a single contractor on the site who has actually employed him. So I must assume that he has to be up to no good, there is no other explanation for his being here posing as a worker."

"I'm not a bit sorry if he's been put in the jail sir," said Michael. "While he's in there he won't be able to bother me or my son anymore."

Wilson was surprised at the mention of Michael's son but he had more serious business on his mind. "I'm sorry to disappoint you Quinlan but Daly has not been arrested yet. Oh he will be I can promise you but not yet. We don't know how many accomplices he has or who they are, but he is obviously not acting alone so we are letting him run free for the moment but keeping a close watch on him in the hope that he will lead us to the rest of his gang."

Michael did not notice the subtle change from 'I' to 'we' as the commander continued: "The only one of Daly's friends we have identified for certain is the man who was with Daly when they ran into you at the stores the other day. I don't suppose you have seen him again since?"

"Yes sir," said Michael. "He went to see the priest after Mass on Sunday, he's called Mick by the way."

Although Wilson already knew this all he said was: "Did he now? well that seems to confirm something else."

There was silence for several minutes. Michael was beginning to think the meeting was over and was about to get up when Wilson said, "Look Quinlan there is another matter of a more delicate nature I want to discuss with you, but first I want you to tell me honestly how you personally feel about the Irish Nationalist situation."

This did not come as a complete surprise to Michael. In view of what had happened recently he was surprised that he had not been asked the question before. He repeated to Wilson what he had told Alistair McGregor. He had always been employed by British aristocracy and had never been in favour of a split from the 'mother country' as he had heard it called, because he feared it would make it difficult for him to support his family in the way he wanted to. But as he could no longer see any future for himself as a coachman he might have to consider whether Home Rule might someday be to his family's advantage. He would not, however, support armed resistance under any circumstances and especially not now in wartime.

Wilson nodded but Michael went on: "There is another thing sir. I have a son serving in the field artillery in Mesopotamia."

He told Wilson about the letter from Jack and his son's frustration at how he felt that the lack of ammunition meant that there were so many casualties.

Wilson wondered how that had managed to escape notice by the wartime censor but kept the thought to himself. "I'm afraid your son is quite right. You can see why it is essential that we get this facility operating at full capacity as soon as possible and without any interruptions whether it be from the Irish or anyone else."

"Now, what I am about to say must remain strictly between you and me. Is that clear?"

"Yes sir," said Michael.

Commander Wilson cleared his throat. "All right Quinlan" he said, "do you know the local Catholic priest Father Conlon, or do you know anything at all about him?"

"Well sir," answered Michael, "apart from seeing him at Mass I only met him the once. That was last Sunday morning when he came over to meet me and my son when we were talking to a friend of James', Pete Casey. He was asking about my job with the factory police."

"What did you tell him?"

"Nothing at all sir, he was called away to the sacristy before I had a chance to tell him anything. I think it was that fella Mick that he went to see." Michael thought that as things had gone this far he might as well ask the question that had been bothering him. "Tell me sir is he the same Father Conlon I heard about at home that was preaching rebellion from the pulpit?"

"Yes, I'm afraid it is," said Wilson. "Have you heard him do anything like that here?"

"No sir, not when I was at Mass," said Michael.

"Look Quinlan I don't like doing this, and I stress that what I am about to ask you to do is not an order. I'll quite understand if you refuse, but I have no choice in the matter. We have to assume that the priest is in league with Daly, it would be totally irresponsible not to, and so we have to keep an eye on him as well. But as you know we have no authority outside Ministry property and I don't want to go to the civilian authorities without definite proof, so that's where you come in." The commander had decided that he should take full responsibility and reverted to 'I'.

"What do you want me to do sir?"

Wilson cleared his throat once more and Michael was aware of his embarrassment. "I should like you to keep an eye on the man and see if he lets anything slip about what kind of mischief he and Daly are actually up to. I really have no right to put you in this position Quinlan, but I really don't know what else to do."

Michael thought it over for a minute then said: "I want to help out sir for my son's sake, but I wouldn't know how to go about drawing him out."

"I'm not suggesting that you approach him directly," said Wilson "he obviously knows you are with the ministry police so let him come to you. If he does, just be friendly and answer his questions as best you can. Don't be afraid to tell him a few things, God knows there are no real secrets around here, and he may let something slip in return. If he doesn't come to you then I won't ask you to go any further. Do you think you would be able to do that?"

"It's not my way of going about things," said a thoughtful Michael, "but I'll take a shot at it."

"Thank you Quinlan," said Wilson. "If it is any consolation I can assure you that this is not my usual way of doing things either."

After Michael left, Wilson leaned back in his chair and sighed with relief. But although the first phase of the plan had gone well he was not looking forward to putting the second part of 'Patrick's' plan into operation should it prove necessary.

For the remainder of the week and particularly while preparing to go to Mass the following Sunday morning, Michael thought long and hard about what he had to do. Acting as a spy, and he admitted to himself that what he was doing constituted spying, did not rest easy on his mind. But he did not regret having agreed to Wilson's request, and he was satisfied that it was a request and not a direct order. He had already made up his mind about Daly, Conlon, and those who advocated armed rebellion, and he held a genuine fear that any Irish Nationalist disruption at Gretna would have dire consequences, not only for Jack, but also for himself and the rest of his family. There was a danger, he reasoned, that if the rebels caused severe damage or delays to the factory it might go hard for all the Irish working there. At the very least there would be stringent security checks carried out on all the Irish workers and it might come out that James had been seen talking to Daly and his friends.

But agreeing to become friendly with the priest was one thing. Carrying out the exercise with any degree of competence was something else entirely.

After Mass, Michael was chatting with Pete Casey – James was working – when they were again approached by the priest. "Good morning gentlemen, only two of you at mass today I see, where is your son Mr Quinlan, not ill I hope."

"Not at all Father, he's grand thanks," said Michael. "He's working today." As an afterthought he added: "And the name is Michael by the way."

"Ah this shift working," said Conlon. "It makes it very

difficult for Catholics to fulfil their duty of Sunday Mass. What exactly does your son work at up there Michael?"

"Now you have me there Father. He tells me that he's helping some engineers and tries to explain the work, but it's well past the understanding of an old coachmen like me," said Michael.

There were a few more general questions about the family which Michael answered without difficulty, but when he told the priest about Jack fighting in Mesopotamia there was a definite, if only momentary, cooling in Conlon's friendly demeanour.

"I'm afraid that too many of our young Irishmen have been persuaded to fight in a war they know nothing about," he said crossly. "Will they never listen to those of us who know better." But he quickly recovered his easy going approach. "Ah sure I suppose we were all the same when we were young."

"To be sure there was no holding us either Father," said Michael.

An awkward silence followed, which was eventually broken by the priest asking Pete: "Have you never thought about joining up yourself Peter?"

"No Father, I got enough fighting to last me out playing hurley at home in county Cork," said Pete.

"Good man yourself," said Conlon. "Tell me now are you working with the engineers as well?"

"The only engine I could tell you about Father is the engine of a wheelbarra'," said Pete. "And I'm sticking to what I know. Now if you don't mind I'm for my dinner and maybe a trip to Carlisle for the pictures."

Michael wondered what was coming next and when the priest said nothing he decided to take the initiative. "How are you liking it here in Gretna Father, I'd say it's a whole lot different from your last parish at home."

"It is that Michael, but I'm not complaining. The church is full to the door and beyond every Sunday. Thank God that Irishmen are always conscientious about going to mass of a Sunday even if they are up to all kinds of devilment for the rest of the week."

"They're far from home and earning good money, there's a great temptation to spend it," said Michael.

"You don't have the look of a drinking man Michael," said Conlon. "What do you do when you're not working?"

"Not much Father, at my age I'm content with a pipe of baccy and a cup of tea with an old soldier I know over in Dornock."

"Well," said the priest. "I suppose that he spends all his time boasting about the great victories won by the brave British army over the downtrodden people of the Empire who only want their freedom. But I think they've met their match in this war, these Germans are the boys to put them in their place."

Again Conlon soon regained his composure. "Anyway if you get fed up listening to him come over to my place here and have a cup of tea with me and we'll talk about home instead."

"I'd like to do that Father," said Michael, and felt that this was the point to take his leave. He held out his hand and said: "I'd better be going or I'll miss my dinner, but I'll see you again next week Father."

"Ah well I won't hold you up, and I have a few things to do myself. But don't forget about that cup of tea."

As Michael left he felt that he had done quite well. The priest's reaction at the mention of Jack being in Mesopotamia, and his remarks about the British army was enough to convince him that Conlon was indeed a rebel sympathiser. The thought made him feel much better about what he was doing.

. . .

After Mass in Beaufort that Sunday, William Quinlan looked up from harnessing the pony for the drive home to see his mother being approached by Mrs Connor. He was getting fed up with the regular Sunday inquisitions by the postmaster's nosey wife, and wondered how his mother managed to put up with the woman's constant questioning. He was particularly concerned that his mother should not be upset today in view of what had happened in Killarney the day before.

They had taken their weekly trip into the post office to cash the postal orders and add any spare cash to the growing post office saving account. By now the little girls were used to the Saturday trips and could be left in the charge of young Michael who was entrusted with some money for sweets. William went to the post office and stood in the queue with Annie. The counter was today being manned by the post master himself, but as he was about to serve Annie he was called to one side by an assistant holding a telegram. William had a clear view of the postmaster looking at the telegram and instead of calling a telegraph boy to make the delivery he said that he would take it personally. The assistant took over from him and began to serve Annie. William watched as the postmaster picked up the telephone and he distinctly heard him ask if Father O'Donovan was available. When the priest answered, the postmaster told him that a War Office telegram had come in for a local family, he would deliver it in person and suggested that the priest stand by in case he was needed.

On the way home and for the rest of the day he noticed that his mother seemed unusually subdued.

William had heard about these dreaded telegrams and it was obvious that the significance of what was happening had not escaped Annie. He could only hope that if ever a similar telegram arrived for them it would be treated in a similar sensitive manner and their local priest contacted in case he was needed, but knowing Mrs Connor he very much doubted that it would.

Chapter 24

In early March the weather in Mesopotamia was beginning to show some sign of improvement.

Having abandoned the disastrous Gallipoli campaign the British army were busy pulling troops out of there and sending them to Mesopotamia. Reports from agents in Constantinople indicated that the Turks were engaged in a similar exercise.

Following the defeat at the Hanna Defile and the resulting failure to relieve the besieged Indian troops in Kut-al-Amara, reinforcements began pouring into Basra. At one point there were more troops there that at the front. There was a shortage of river transport to ferry them to the forward areas and spring flooding rendered the movement of large numbers of troops and material overland all but impossible. At the beginning of March of the 63,000 men in the theatre only 14,000 were at the front, while at least another 8,000 were in hospital. But by March 7th, the date set for the next attack on the Turkish positions in the Hanna Defile, the Tigris Corps had been increased to some 37,000 including a cavalry brigade and 66 field guns. Bombardier Jack Quinlan was again about to go into action with the 18 pounders.

The Turkish position at Es Sinn was in sight of Kut-Al-Amara. It was reasoned that if this stronghold could be taken enemy communications would be cut and they would be forced to abandon their siege positions. The main objective of the planned attack was to take two Turkish strong-points or redoubts by frontal assault, one at Sinn Abtar and the other in a deep gully to the south known as the Dujaila Depression.

The Hanna Defile was bombarded with all the ammunition available from the Corps' meagre supply and a diversionary attack, supported by 24 field guns, was mounted there to divert the enemy's attention from the main effort at Es Sinn.

The advance began at dawn and soon reached the point where

the force split into two to attack the separate redoubts. At the Dujalia redoubt patrols found the Turkish trenches empty and could have easily occupied them but, in a supreme example of lack of initiative, they were ordered to wait in order to comply with the rigidly planned timetable, and the opportunity was lost. This timetable called for the artillery to be brought up and registered on target before the infantry went in, an operation which took several hours to complete. By the time the attack went in some 6,000 Turks were back in the trenches waiting to cut the British soldiers down with machine gun and rifle fire.

The troops detailed to attack the northern redoubt at Sinn Abtar were also ordered to adhere to the timetable and could not begin their assault until the southern attack was under way. Here some of the infantry got into the enemy trenches, but once the Dujalia attack had been repulsed the Turks were able to send up reinforcements and the British were driven out again. The cavalry brigade spent the entire day totally ineffectively behind the lines. A planned breakout from Kut was called off when it became clear that the attack on the redoubts had failed.

British casualties on the day numbered over 4,000 dead and wounded and many of these were lost without even seeing the enemy. Again due to inadequate medical facilities many of the casualties were left in the open, and at night gangs of Arabs came out to rob the dead and kill the wounded, without any interference whatsoever from the Turks.

While their woefully incompetent commanders concentrated on shifting the blame for the fiasco, Jack Quinlan and hundreds of his colleagues were unashamedly reduced to tears of frustration.

. . .

While Jack was struggling to come to terms with the events of the day his father was in the office at the stores complex with Commander Wilson reporting on his encounter with Father Conlon.

Wilson had come to the stores after dark ostensibly to see Brown whom he knew very well had already gone off shift, because he thought it best that Michael should not be noticed coming regularly to his own office. This, he reasoned would arouse suspicion if spotted by Daly or his associates, and indeed would probably arouse the curiosity of many others on the site. The commander was beginning to grasp some of the finer points of undercover working even if he still found them not to his liking. He had called Michael into the office on the pretext of leaving a message for Brown.

He nodded as Michael recounted Conlon's reaction to the news of Jack serving in the army, his disparaging remarks about the British army in general, and his high opinion of the Germans.

"Well," said Wilson. "He doesn't seem to worry about airing such views in public. Did anyone else hear what he said?"

"My son's friend, Pete Casey, heard some of it sir," said Michael.

"Thank you Quinlan, I must say you've done extremely well so far," said Wilson. "The problem is of course that you only come into contact with the priest on Sundays. I'll have to try and find someone who can go in and out of Gretna without attracting attention during the week."

Michael thought about this and decided to take the plunge. "If you don't mind my saying so sir I think I might know someone who could do that. My friend Alistair McGregor would fit the bill just fine, and I'd say for certain that he would like to have a shot at it."

He explained who McGregor was and what he did at the huts at Dornock. "Alistair is an old British soldier and proud of it. Like me he has a son in the war and he lost another in the train crash here a couple of years back. I'd put my life on him."

"Well I'll certainly bear that in mind," said Wilson.

Chapter 25

The test at the glycerine still had been carried out successfully and preparations were in hand for the next stage in the process. This involved the production of the dangerously combustible active ingredient of cordite, nitroglycerine.

Nitroglycerine was produced by reacting the pure glycerine with a concentrated mixture of nitric and disulphuric acids. The glycerine and acids were gently mixed in lead cylinders and then left to settle. The nitroglycerine rose to the surface and was skimmed off. It was then washed in a mixture of water and chalk to remove any excess acid. Nitroglycerine was much too volatile to be pumped so it had to be moved under gravity along lead lined troughs to the next stage, the production of 'gun-cotton'.

The successful distillation of glycerine and the production of nitroglycerine meant that intensive on-the-job training programmes could be instituted for the growing number of, mainly female, munitions workers arriving at Gretna. Safety was a major concern and as all procedures would be monitored by the ministry police, Michael Quinlan and his colleagues were included in many of the training sessions. These courses included practical demonstrations to leave nobody in any doubt about just how dangerous the materials they were handling really were. The factory was designed on the principle that all the processes would be continuous and materials would flow smoothly through the system. But it was recognised that bottlenecks were inevitable and in some cases these highly dangerous materials would have to be stored.

. . .

There was a woman traveller sitting drinking tea at one of small tables by the door of the Carlisle station buffet, so The Man from Dublin waited until she was finished and had left the room before he entered. He was concerned that they were more conspicuous than usual because they had been joined by Daly's colleague Mick. But he had asked for him to be there because, although not by any means a scientist, Mick had a much greater understanding of technical matters than either Conlon or Daly.

As he greeted the trio he placed the small carpet bag he was carrying on the floor by his chair. "Right boys," he began, "we don't want to be here too long or we'll be noticed, so here's the gist of it. The lads at Trinity College over in Dublin had a look at the notes you sent me and to cut a long story short they think that it is possible to cause some ructions here. The top men know this and have given their blessing."

"About bloody time and all, begging your pardon Father," said Daly. "When do we start?"

"Now hold your horses there Liam." The Man made a slowing down signal with his hand, "we need a bit more information before we can come up with anything definite."

"From what I can see of it," said Mick, "the Brits are all set to blow themselves sky high without any help at all from us."

"According to the brains at Trinity you're not far off the mark there," said The Man, "and that's one of the problems. An accident could happen at any time and it would be easy to arrange one, but an accident is no good at all to us. We have to leave them in no doubt whatsoever that what happened was no accident, and on top of that we don't want to give them the chance to claim that it was one."

"A couple of their top men with bullets in their heads would leave them in no doubt about anything." Daly was obviously excited by the prospect.

"That's one way," said The Man, "but they could soon be replaced and people getting killed all over the place is nothing strange in this war. They'd give them a medal, bury them with full military honours and bring in somebody else without anybody taking a bit of notice. And they'd probably blame the Germans if anybody started asking questions. So we'll have to be a bit smarter than that."

He got up and walked out to have a look around on the pretext of going to the toilet but there were as usual very few people about the station and no one on that particular platform.

When he returned he resumed. "Now here's what we do next. The boys at Trinity are working on a way of causing trouble with the production here but you lads will have to help them out with the latest news from the factory. They want to know what stage of production the factory is up to and what tests they have carried out, things like that. And they definitely want to know if any nitroglycerine has been made yet and where it's kept. They say that stuff is dangerous enough on its own without us having to bring anything else in."

"So you and me will have to go on another poaching trip Liam," said Mick.

"How will we know this nitro stuff if we come across it?" asked Daly.

"Sure all you have to do is strike a match and it'll introduce itself." Mick laughed at his own joke.

"He's right there," The Man said. "Look lads, if that's the only way to get the information we want you'll have to go in again. But for Christ's sake be careful we don't want you to get caught and bollocks up the whole deal." If the priest was expecting an apology for the language one was not forthcoming, The Man was more concerned that Daly got the message. He went on. "But I was hoping we might be able to find out what we want another way. Have you got anything out of this fella Quinlan yet Sean?"

"Not much yet," said Conlon. "But I'm working at it. He's a smart one and he doesn't give much away."

"Well hurry up." The Man turned to Daly. "What about the pubs Liam, have you picked up anything useful there?"

"Bugger all," said Daly. "Except what young Jim Quinlan told Mick. The most of them are having too good a time to talk about work and the rest are too drunk to be any good at all. But listen here, why don't you leave Quinlan to me, Give me ten minutes alone with him and I'll get everything he knows out of him. I'll teach him to go running to the boss and doing me out of an easy way of making good money."

"When this is over you can settle up with him any way you

like. But it won't do The Cause any good at all if one of the factory police turns up missing, and you'd have to shut him up permanently because his pals would start asking questions." The Man was adamant about it.

Mick had another suggestion. "What about the old fella that looks after the huts at Dornock. To my way of thinking Quinlan tells him everything. We could easy make him tell us what he knows."

"I'd prefer to have Sean here to handle this side of it," replied The Man. "We don't want any rough stuff yet. Is there any way we can get a load of these Irishmen together in one place without a load of drink in them?"

He was met with some blank looks until Conlon, who was not happy with all the talk of killing, suddenly had an idea. "If I was at home I'd be busy organising a Saint Patrick's night dance in a couple of week's time. I thought about doing it here but I didn't think it would be much of a dance without any women. But we could hold a do of some sort to mark the great Irish saint's day."

Mick was again first to pick up the point. "You could still have a real dance Father if you were to invite some of them nice factory girls that are coming in by the hundred. I heard they're being trained up to start work any day now. They are sure to have learned something and they might be persuaded to talk about what they have to do."

"Now you're talking," said The Man from Dublin."That's a fine idea. It'll give you every chance to talk to a lot of people in the know Sean. They'll think it's safe to tell things to a priest they wouldn't tell anyone else. So set it up, I might even come myself."

The Priest in Conlon was regretting what the Nationalist had suggested. The thought of a lot of factory girls being turned loose on his good Catholic Irish boys and leading to all sorts of shenanigans was too much to bear. But the Nationalist won the day and he agreed to go ahead with plans for the dance.

The Man from Dublin was beginning to feel apprehensive about how long the meeting was taking. Again he got up and went to check for any signs of prying eyes. Finding nothing suspicious he came back to the buffet, sat down and said. "Unless anybody has anything else to say I think we'll leave it there. You go out first Sean."

When Conlon had left, The Man nudged the bag by his feet and pushed it under the table until it rested against Daly's leg. "What you said about knocking off a couple of people here was something I had in mind myself Liam. But I didn't say anything in front of your man Father Sean, no matter what he says about armed rebellion he's still a priest, and when the real trouble starts he might just remember it. Anyway, after we do whatever the brainy boys at the college have in mind that's how we're going to leave our calling card. There might be some bodies lying around after the nitro goes up, but if you add a couple more with bullets in them there will be no doubts about whether it was an accident or not. And it doesn't make any difference whose bodies they happen to be either. You'll find the tools for the job in the bag."

"Well I'll tell you who'll be the first to go," said Daly. "I'll put that bloody coachman under the ground before I leave here."

"Only after the main job is done Liam. Until then keep your personal arguments out of it, this is too important. Now the other thing I didn't tell you in front of Sean is that the date is set. The priest in him might not like the idea of the rising starting over Easter." With that he got up and left.

After The Man was on his way back to Dublin, and they were alone back in their lodgings, they opened the bag to find a pair of brand new Webley MkV .445 calibre British military revolvers with a supply of ammunition.

. . .

"'Patrick' tends to agree with you Commander." The Man from Whitehall was speaking to Wilson on the telephone from his office in London. "And, having had a look at this man McGregor's military record, I must concur. Your man did well to pick up on this second rebel suspect and this is what I think you should do." He explained what he wanted done and rang off.

For once Wilson was reasonably happy with what he had been asked to do. Immediately after he had finished on the telephone he contacted the stores asking Brown to send someone to find McGregor and bring him to his office. He suggested that Brown send Quinlan if he was available because he knew the old soldier.

"Is this anything to do with your job in the police?" asked a mystified McGregor as they made their way via the factory internal railway to the administrative offices at Gretna.

An equally mystified Michael had decided that he would not lie to his friend. "I think it must be Alistair, I know there's something up with that blackguard Liam Daly I was telling you about and Father Conlon might be part of it. But that's between you and me and the gatepost."

"Right you are." McGregor touched his nose with his finger and nodded knowingly. "What like is he, this Commander Wilson?"

"All I can say is that he has every sign of being a gentleman if you see what I mean. But I think he's doing a job that he's not altogether happy about. He's a serving officer in the Royal Navy so I suppose he would rather be spending the war on a ship at sea."

They reached the administrative centre and Michael led McGregor to Wilson's office. When they entered the old soldier snapped to attention and saluted smartly. "Sergeant McGregor reporting as ordered sir."

The commander rose and acknowledged the salute. "Stand easy sergeant."

Michael turned to go but Wilson gestured for him to stay. "I'd like you to stay Quinlan, what I have to say concerns you too. Now sergeant McGregor, I expect you are wondering why I asked you to report here, but before I go on I must stress that what I tell you must remain in strict confidence. Is that clear?"

"Yes sir."

So Wilson went on, "I'll be frank with you sergeant I've had your military record checked and I am satisfied that you know how to keep your mouth shut. Now then, thanks to Quinlan here we may have uncovered an Irish nationalist plot to cause some form of disruption here at Gretna involving a man called Liam Daly and a priest called Father Conlon among others, some of whom have yet to be identified. Any questions so far?"

"No sir, I'm still with you." Wilson had no doubt that the old soldier was in fact 'with him'.

"Good. Now the crux of the matter is this. We have to keep a close watch on these people, but I don't have enough men to cover even half of the factory and its support service areas so I need to recruit some more personnel. The problem is finding the right people, but I believe that you could fit the bill and I wonder if you would be willing to help out sergeant."

The old sergeant snapped to attention and visibly grew in stature. "Yes sir, of course I'd be only too pleased to do anything I can to help. What do you want me to do sir?"

"Thank you sergeant," said Wilson. "There are two things I should like you to do at present: Firstly I want you to keep your eyes open for any strangers hanging around the huts asking questions. I'm aware that you do this already, but from now on I want you to spread your area of responsibility to take in the whole of the Dornock factory site. You will have to familiarise yourself with the whole area up there. But more importantly I should like you to act as our eyes and ears on the outside. My uniformed staff don't have any official authority anywhere other than on Ministry property, but you can move around Gretna, and in particular the new township, without raising comment. Should you see or hear anything in the least suspicious I want to be immediately informed. Is that clear?"

"Clear as day sir," said the sergeant.

The Commander felt more comfortable issuing orders to someone with a military background than he was with his civilian staff. "The second thing I want from you is to act as liaison between myself and Quinlan here. He is carrying out a particular duty for me on the quiet and it will look odd if he is seen coming here regularly to report. You, on the other hand can come and go at will without anybody thinking anything of it, and so you can bring both your own and his reports. Now this will mean extra work for you I'm afraid because you will still have to carry on with your normal duties at the huts. Do you think you can manage that?"

"Yes sir," was the reply. "I'm sure I can manage that. To be honest I'd like to have more to do, I'm on duty twenty-four a day but a lot of the time I'm left hanging around with time on my hands. But if you don't mind me asking sir, what will my official position be?"

"Good question sergeant. I intend to quietly enlist you into the Ministry of Munitions Police, but for the moment nobody is to know about it except for myself and Quinlan here." He shook his head in frustration. "God I do hate these underhand methods! I prefer my men to be in uniform when on duty. But I'm sure you understand sergeant that desperate times mean we have to make compromises and adopt desperate measures. I will issue you with an official armband but I must insist that it should only be used in cases of absolute necessity. You will also be given passes to use the internal transport system, and to get you into the various restricted areas; and of course you will be paid as one of my men. You will of course have to learn the standing orders for the factory police and sign a form agreeing to the rules regarding secrecy. Are you sure you are happy about that?"

"Yes sir," said an extremely happy McGregor. "It's a bit like being back in the mob."

"Very well sergeant. In theory your immediate superior will be Mr Brown who is also Quinlan's supervisor at the stores complex. He will be fully briefed to explain the relevant procedures to you in detail, but he will not know the real purpose behind it. Quinlan will also be on hand to help and advise you. I want you up to speed and effective as soon as possible so take every opportunity to get around the Dornock site and the Gretna Township; and of course, here at the administrative centre. Make yourself a familiar figure so that people don't question your presence. This is in effect what the man Daly is doing and I leave it to Quinlan to describe him and if possible point him out to you."

The Commander cast a glance at Michael. "You should pay particular attention to the comings and goings at the Catholic church, but please be careful not to make it obvious that you are nosing around. I suggest you adopt the excuse that you are running errands for the people at the huts, some real errands would of course be excellent cover." He had determined not to use words such as 'cover' but could not find an alternative.

He stood and looked at both men. "I cannot stress too strongly the importance of discovering what the enemy is up to and nipping his plans in the bud. Right then, I want you to go back to work Quinlan and ask Brown to come over to see me. In the meantime I will complete the formalities with McGregor."

Later that evening, while Michael and Alistair discussed the situation over their mugs of tea and pipes of tobacco, McGregor expressed his thanks to Michael for getting him the post with the factory police.

"Ah sure I did nothing Alistair," he said.

"Och, laddie I'm sure you put in a good word for me with Commander Wilson, it's a great thing to be doing something to help the war effort at last."

. . .

Next Sunday after Mass Michael and James were, as usual, talking to Pete Casey when, as Michael had expected, they were again approached by Father Conlon. "Good morning men, I hope you will all be coming to the St. Patrick's night dance."

The remark was met with silence until Michael surprised everyone by saying: "I think you're on to something there Father. Sure I'm a great one for the dancing and I'll come if I'm not working."

James couldn't believe his ears. "I never once heard you talking about dancing before Da."

"Ah sure where did you think I met your mother Jim?"

James was still thinking about this when Pete spoke up: "Will there be many women of the opposite sex there, Father?"

"Well, as I said at Mass I'm sending an invitation to the factory workers. I'm hoping that a lot of them might come because it'll be the first do to be held at the new Central Hall at Gretna Township. I suppose some of them will be women, but I don't want this to degenerate into something of a sinful nature in the eyes of God." The priest was still feeling unhappy about the presence of the factory girls and announcing it from the pulpit did nothing to ease his conscience.

"Why don't you ask Miss Birks to come Pete?" said James.

"Good man yourself Jim Quinlan," said Pete "that's a grand notion. And I'll ask her to bring one of her friends for you."

James blushed, Michael laughed and Father Conlon frowned.

"Will there be drink there, Father?" asked Michael.

"No Michael the powers that be won't give us permission, and when I hear about what goes on of a night in Gretna and Carlisle I can't say I blame them." This was true, but it was also where the priest had already drawn the line knowing the navvy's love of drink, but he was happy to be able to blame someone else.

"I don't think that will stop some of these boys bringing in a supply of their own Father." Pete voiced a thought that was already worrying the priest.

"I'm afraid you might be right Pete. Anyway I must be off, duty calls I have someone waiting to see me."

On the train back to Dornock Michael was joined by McGregor. "Did you spot your man Alistair? Daly wasn't at Mass but he was hanging around after, talking to his pal Mick and Father Conlon."

"Yes," said Alistair. "They went into the room at the back of the church with the padre when he left you. I'll remember him when I see him again."

Chapter 26

Thursday, March 17th 1916 – Saint Patrick's Day. At Mass, Michael and James wore the sprigs of Irish shamrock sent by Annie on their lapels to mark the occasion. They had more than they needed and gave some to Pete Casey and a few others who seemed not to have any of their own. In her latest letter, Annie had written that she had also sent some to Jack, and Michael prayed that it would reach their son in time. The church was full to overflowing and many worshippers were obliged to stand or kneel outside the open doors. Although a working day many of the Irish had been given, or had taken, time off to mark this, the most important of the many Irish saint's days, by going to Mass. Many of the congregation were in their working garb.

In his homily, Father Sean Conlon reminded his congregation of the significance of the little three leafed plant, which it was said would grow only in the Holy Ground of Ireland. He spoke about how the Saint had used the shamrock to explain the mystery of the Holy Trinity by demonstrating that just as the three leaves made up a single flower, the three persons Father, Son and Holy Ghost constituted but one God. But on this of all days Father Conlon could not resist going further.

"I can tell you that the great Saint must be delighted to look down and see all of us good God fearing Irishmen wearing the shamrock in his honour. But what is he thinking about the dire situation over there in his beloved Ireland itself. If he was here to-day what would he say about the country he won for Jesus being still under the heavy boot of the British Empire. When will Irishmen wake up and stop believing everything their foreign masters tell them to believe. When will we begin to think for ourselves and realise that the only way for us to become the great Catholic nation Saint Patrick meant us to be is to throw the invaders out."

While he was letting this sink in and looking around the church he spotted the grinning face of Liam Daly leaning casually against the wall by the open doorway. He disliked Daly and his irreverent attitude, but the sight of that insolent smile was enough to make him remember where he was. He realised that he could not preach here as he would have at home in Ireland and, with some reluctance, he returned to the subject he had opened with.

"But that is another story for another time and place. Let us now humbly ask Saint Patrick to pray for all of us here, our families at home and our poor country."

The Mass passed without further incident. Before the final blessing Father Conlon reminded the congregation that he expected to see them at the Saint Patrick's dance and they filed out.

Michael, James and Pete all had to return to work and did not have time to discuss the priest's disjointed sermon. They parted after having planned to meet again that evening.

When Michael got back to work he found McGregor in the office talking to Brown. After he emerged, Alistair told him that Brown had given him a run down on the safety regulations. As Michael looked up he could not help but notice the puzzled look on the senior policeman's face.

. . .

Following High Mass at Dublin's Pro Cathedral in Marlborough Street, Padraig Pearse met with James Connolly and they went together to watch the Irish Citizen Army parading in Phoenix Park. The uniformed branches of the various rebel factions were becoming ever and ever bolder and, even if the authorities were aware of what was happening, they did not seem to be taking any kind of counter-action. The general opinion was that the British military were too occupied with the war, and their civilian counterparts felt secure in the belief that nothing would happen in Ireland at least until after the Germans had been defeated. Irrespective of the fact that any representatives of the British authorities were conspicuous by their absence the two rebel leaders preferred to mingle with the public holiday crowds rather than risk arousing interest by showing themselves openly. They were recognised, and ignored, by their own agents moving through the groups of onlookers handing out Nationalist literature. Leaflets which were for the most part stuffed unread into pockets or handbags to be largely discarded later.

Today's parade was intended for the benefit of the citizens of Dublin. It was designed to demonstrate that the Irish could march and drill and put on a military display just as competently as the British soldiers the people of the capital were accustomed to seeing. It might even attract a few new recruits, hopefully from among those young Irishmen with ambitions to join the British army. After an hour of watching the show, Pearse and Connolly slipped away. They caught a tram out to the seaside suburb of Clontarf where a lunch had been prepared for them in a house situated in a quiet back street. They were joined by the Man from Dublin. Lunch over, the three gathered in the front parlour to review progress and plan future actions.

Although it had not been chosen for any specific reason, Pearse was aware of the significance of the venue for the meeting. It was at the Battle of Clontarf fought in 1014, some nine hundred years before, that the High King of Ireland, Brian Boru who had unified the various Irish clans and kingdoms, had defeated the Danes and driven the Norsemen out of Ireland. In the battle both Brian and his son Murchard had lost their lives.

The rebel leader opened the meeting by reminding his colleagues of this most momentous event in Irish history and added:

"It strikes me that between the defeat of the Danes and the conquest by the Normans, Ireland enjoyed less than a century of real freedom. Since then we have suffered under the yoke of foreign rule. I pray that the enterprise we are embarking on will at last lead to a free and independent nation."

The others muttered their 'amen' in agreement and Pearse, who had by now emerged as the undisputed leader of the insurgents, went on to outline the latest situation regarding the proposed uprising. They had seen for themselves the readiness of the volunteers. There could never be any suggestion that these men were anything other than regular soldiers. Any propaganda put out by the British branding them as terrorists, anarchists or criminals of any kind would be immediately rejected by the world at large. When the uprising ended in defeat, as it inevitably must, then the survivors would have to be treated as prisoners of war, the wounded properly treated and the dead buried with honour. But Pearse believed that Britain would not recognise the Brotherhood as the legitimate government of an Irish Republic. And to those present at the meeting on this St. Patrick's Day he could voice his secret hope that the insurgents would be subjected to some form of summary justice and treated harshly. This would arouse the sympathy of all Irish people not only at home but abroad, and particularly in America.

They turned to the rising itself. Action was originally scheduled for early on Good Friday morning April 23rd but Pearse and Connolly were agreed that Easter Sunday would be a more appropriate date. Easter Day was traditionally a day of celebration when all kinds of parades took place, and they would avoid suspicion by holding some of their own as a way of assembling their forces for the rising. Several important buildings in the city would be occupied including the General Post Office from where the declaration announcing the establishment of the Irish Republic would be made. It was estimated that several hours would elapse before the authorities could react and it would take even longer for a military response to be organised. This would give time for the occupied locations to be supplied and fortified.

Pearse then raised the subject of Roger Casement and the German arms. "The real significance of the arms lies not in their actual usefulness to the military action, although they will obviously be of assistance, but in the fact that by supporting us in this way, Germany will in effect be recognising the Irish Republic. In my view it is very unlikely that there will be an outright winner in this war, but in any case German recognition should allow the Irish Republican movement to have a voice at any post-war peace negotiations."

As to the guns themselves? They were currently being prepared for loading onto a German cargo vessel, the *Libau*, which would be disguised as a Norwegian fishing vessel and renamed *Aud Norge*.

"Casement will be put ashore in County Kerry from a German submarine a few days before the rising and the *Aud* will land the guns soon afterwards. They will be met by the Volunteers and transported directly to Dublin."

Connolly, who already knew this, nodded in agreement and The Man from Dublin expressed his satisfaction.

"So now," said Connolly. "What is the position at the Scottish munitions factory?"

The Man explained that he would shortly be receiving from Gretna the information needed to formalise the final plan. He suggested that at this stage of the game it would help if he were given permission to use the telephone to contact his agents. Although he still intended to keep a personal eye on things 'over there'.

Connolly, who seemed to have taken overall charge of this operation, agreed. He went on to say: "This is not the only 'event' we are organising to take place in conjunction with the rising. There are several more planned but because of all those Irishmen working at the factory yours will be the most important. It will not really matter what kind of disruption you are planning, a fire or an explosion, etc, we leave that up to you. But that will no longer be the main objective of the exercise. We now believe that we can make use of the situation over there to much greater effect. Once the rebellion has begun here in Dublin we want you to distribute as many leaflets as you possibly can among the Irish navvies, and indeed anyone else who happens to be around. These leaflets will include the Declaration of the Irish Republic, and carry a message to all Irishmen to join in the rebellion. Hopefully some will actually do so, but if you can circulate enough leaflets before the authorities catch on then the rebellion will be public knowledge and the workers at Gretna will know all about it before even the British government are fully aware of the situation. This news will spread like wildfire and they will not have time to suppress the story or distort the facts. Not only will this cause them maximum embarrassment but it will also force them to spend a great deal of time and effort on looking for the culprits and tightening up security at the site."

Pearse rejoined the conversation. "Timing is of the utmost importance. We will notify you by telephone immediately after we issue the proclamation and you must do nothing before then, nobody on the British side must suspect a thing before it actually happens. But you must also be ready to act immediately you hear from us. To that end I want you to be over there to supervise the operation in person."

The Man from Dublin expressed some disappointment. "I'd rather be here," he said. "The lads over there can handle this on their own."

"No," said Connolly. "I know Liam Daly, he's too much of a hothead to be trusted with something as important as this. And although Sean Conlon is a fine speaker he's no man of action. Anyway if you plan your escape properly you will be back here in plenty of time to join us."

This seemed to satisfy The Man who could see the logic of the argument and was in fact quite excited about the role 'his' team in Gretna had now been chosen to play. He estimated that he would need at least several thousand leaflets and Connolly agreed that these could be printed in time.

"But you'll have to take them over there yourself. We can't risk them falling into the wrong hands. And you will have to find somewhere to store them."

"Sure that will be easy," said The Man. "I'll get Father Sean to keep them in the church sacristy; nobody will look for them there. It would be great if the ructions started around about Mass time; that would make distribution dead easy."

"What do you think of our Father Conlon?" asked Connolly.

"Like you said yourself, he's no man of action," came the reply. "We don't tell him anything that might help him to remember the collar he wears and the vows he had to take to get it."

"Very wise," said Pearse and closed the meeting.

• • •

There was no Mass in Mesopotamia that St. Patrick's Day albeit there was no lack of sacrifice. The Tigris Corps was licking its wounds after three bloody defeats and men were still dying as a result of the woeful lack of medical facilities.

Like many of the Irish soldiers in the various regiments involved, Jack Quinlan wore a sprig of shamrock sent from home. The shamrock from home brought with it thoughts of home.

'Patrick's Day' always fell in the middle of lent and it was traditional for the Irish to grant themselves a dispensation from the Lenten observance on that day so that they could properly honour their great patron saint. They took a day off from 'giving it up for Lent'. The season of Lent meant little at the battlefront in Mesopotamia, but it was not through a lack of religion. A few days after the failure of the latest attempt to relieve Kut-Al-Amara a Catholic chaplain had visited Jack's unit to comfort the wounded, which in far too many cases meant performing the Last Rites. He said Mass in the open using empty ammunition boxes as an altar base, and the service was attended not only by the Catholics among the troops, but also by members of many other Christian denominations. Recent experiences led many men who had previously ignored him to turn their thoughts to God.

It required no effort whatsoever for Jack to imagine what was happening back in Beaufort on that' Great Day for the Irish'. The whole family would be dressed in their very best for Mass. His mother, William and young Michael would be sporting sprigs of shamrock and the little girls would wear bright badges made up of golden harps and green ribbons. He would have bet that his father and James were also wearing shamrock sent from home. After Mass, Annie would prepare the midday meal while William would entertain the youngsters, a task that both he and James would have joined in while their father smoked by the fire, had they all been at home. His mother would have got 'something special' for dinner today but Jack guessed that her heart would not be in it. She would be missing her husband and sons. When the meal was finished and everything cleared away he could picture her sitting quietly with her rosary beads while the children did their school homework – even though their father was not there he knew that his mother would not vary from this established routine. And what of his brother William? Bill would be walking by the river in the spring sunshine looking for signs. Jack guessed that he would have already caught his first brown trout of the year using the most rudimentary equipment and would be looking out for signs of a salmon. The war meant that gamekeepers and water bailiffs were laid off and Bill would see this as his opportunity to catch a few of the famous Laune salmon, if he could only lay his hands on the right tackle. Jack was currently catching up on his letter writing and he resolved to add a note to his father suggesting that they set aside a little money for some fishing tackle for William.

As the coachman's eldest son Jack had felt obliged to volunteer to fight in this war. He did not blame his father for this – it was just the way of things. He had heard of the soldier's longing for home and family and today he was experiencing it at first hand.

Chapter 27

Michael paused by the gate to catch his breath after the walk from the station then made his way up the path and knocked on the door of 'Solway View'. He had arranged to meet James here so that they could go to the St. Patrick's night dance together. It was unlikely that Pete Casey would be able to accompany them as he had somehow managed to persuade Miss Birks to go to the 'ball' with him and was picking her up from the women's hostel. It was Michael's first visit to his son's lodging. He had been asking James to introduce him to 'Our Lady', Mrs McBain, for some time, at first to satisfy himself so that he could genuinely reassure Annie that her son was being well cared for, but now after a couple of months without any mishaps on James' domestic front, simply out of curiosity.

The door was answered by the lady in person and Michael introduced himself.

"Ah so you are Mr Quinlan, young Jim's father," said Mrs McBain. "Do come in please."

Michael removed his hat and was ushered into the front parlour, an inner sanctum into which no guest and certainly none of the occupants of the loft were ever permitted to visit; it was the 'Holy of Holy's' according to Pete Casey. He was invited to sit and offered a cup of tea, this again being an unheard of privilege, which he gratefully accepted. They chatted for some minutes and Michael found Mrs McBain to be a much friendlier and indeed more caring person than he had been led to expect. She obviously knew more about James than the lad was aware of and Michael suspected that, although she would never have owned up to the fact, she was keeping a motherly eye on his son. They got around to discussing their home lives. Michael told her of his worries about his scattered family: Annie and the young ones at home, himself and James in Scotland and Jack in Mesopotamia. She sympathised, and hoped that the war would soon be over and they could all be together again. When he asked about her own family a hint of sadness crept across her face. 'The doctor', her husband, had died some years ago, she had a son whose job had taken him to Canada before the war and was now obliged to continue working there until it ended, she had a daughter who had been studying medicine in Glasgow but had enlisted as a nurse and was now serving in France. Like Michael she felt that she would see little of her family until this 'stupid war' was over.

As they were chatting, Pete Casey came down the stairs ready to go out, but on hearing the voices from the parlour and recognising Michael's, he turned and retraced his steps. James had just finished dressing for the dance when Pete came back to the loft.

"Hurry yourself Jim, 'Our Lady' has your father trapped in the parlour. I think she has a notion to take him over to the forge at Gretna Green and turn herself into your mother."

They came down stairs together and Pete knocked tentatively on the parlour door. Mrs McBain came out and looked at Pete standing there clean shaven and with his hair slicked down, wearing a brand new shirt and tie, freshly brushed suit and highly polished boots. "Who on earth is this vision of loveliness?" she said.

Michael had followed her out into the hallway. "Mr Casey has a date with a girl," he told her.

"Och the poor wee lassie," she said in an exaggerated Scottish accent. "Well if you two would-be Romeos are going to terrorise those poor factory girls you had better be off. Don't be late and don't make any noise coming in."

She turned to Michael and held out her hand. "It was very nice to meet you Mr Quinlan. Please call again any time and I'll tell you all about what your young scallywag of a son has been up to."

James blushed and bolted for the door.

The Central Hall at the burgeoning new Gretna Township was, in common with many of the other buildings at the site, serviceable but not yet completely fitted out. On entering the hall Michael and James – Pete had gone to meet Miss Birks – followed the crudely hand-painted signs on the bare walls directing them to where the St Patrick's night function was to be held. On the way they passed an open door marked 'cloakroom' where Michael deposited his heavy coachman's coat and bowler hat. James had not worn an outside coat. Father Conlon met them by the entrance to a large room with a small raised platform at one end for the band, and trestle tables and chairs arranged along both sides leaving the central floor area clear for dancing. Conlon collected their two shilling entrance fees, money ostensibly to be used for 'church funds' but which in reality was destined to enhance the coffers of the Irish Republican Brotherhood. A door to one side bore another sign directing dancers to a room where 'light refreshments' were available. About half of the tables were occupied when Michael and James entered, several by what appeared to be factory workers, the men sitting together on one side of the room while two or three tables crowded with giggling girls and young women sat opposite them. Michael suspected that the good Father Conlon had arranged things that way, although there were one or two obvious couples sitting together. Some tables were occupied by men who were clearly Irish navvies dressed in what passed for their Sunday best and all sporting shamrock in their lapels. They selected a table about half way into the room and sat down to watch the proceedings. Although in theory no alcohol was allowed a few bottles of stout were already in evidence and Michael guessed that something stronger was being secretly distributed under the tables.

Michael leaned across and said in a low voice, "I won't be stopping here till the end Jim, and if you want to keep your good looks you'll leave early too. This has all the makings of a Saturday night at Puck Fair and there'll be blood spilled before it's over."

James, who was of late beginning to see his father in a whole new light, was about to reply when he was interrupted by the grand entrance of Pete Casey and his lady.

Michael stood and said, "good evening to you young lady, I take it you must be the lovely Miss Birks I have been hearing about. I'm Michael Quinlan and this is my son James."

A smiling Miss Birks, looking a picture in a plain blue dress and with shoulder length brown hair, extended her hand. "Good evening to you Mr Quinlan. James and I have already met." (She stressed the 'James' who sank lower in his chair and hoped she would not mention where or when.) "And the name is Sarah."

"Glory be!" exclaimed Pete. "Haven't I been trying to get that out of her since the first time I laid eyes her."

"A lady will only divulge her name to someone she considers to be a proper gentleman, true Michael?" This delivered in a strong North Country accent.

"Very true Sarah, and by the looks of it your friends have spotted you."

They all looked over to where the factory girls were sitting and where there was much whispering, giggling and pointing. Sarah waved and they waved back. "If you will excuse us for a moment Michael I had better introduce Peter (stressed) to the girls or I'll never hear the end of it. You come too James I'm sure they would love to meet you as well."

James looked to his father for help but as none was forthcoming he was forced to tag along to meet the girls. The introductions were completed but the list of names rather passed him by. This was followed by an in depth inquisition. 'Peter' seemed to cope quite well with the loaded questions and more or less gave as good as he got, but James was totally out of his depth. He would have made a run for it had he not been rescued by Father Conlon calling for quiet.

The priest welcomed everyone to the first ever St Patrick's night dance in Gretna. He introduced the band and hoped that an enjoyable evening would be had by all. The 'band', a volunteer fiddler and accordionist hastily recruited after a plea from the pulpit, struck up a lively Irish jig. Everyone looked at everyone else and nobody made a move. This went on for a couple of tunes until eventually three of the factory girls got up and laughingly attempted their own highly unlikely version of a traditional Irish reel. The band held a whispered conference and agreed to try a waltz. To everyone's surprise, and the musician's relief, Pete asked Sarah to dance. She accepted and they took the floor soon to be joined by one of the couples. One of the factory workers plucked up the courage to ask one of the girls, others followed and the dance was under way.

James watched, fascinated as Pete guided Sarah expertly around the floor.

"Pete's a fair dancer," said Michael, "they make a grand couple."

"Did you and my mother do a lot of dancing when you were young Da?"

"That we did," Michael answered wistfully, "and if your mother was here now we'd teach these young ones a few tricks."

When Pete and Sarah came back James was anxious to know where his friend had learned to dance. "Sure and didn't I learn it at school from the Christian Brothers," was the explanation.

"What's a Christian Brother?" Sarah wanted to know. They laughed and Michael explained the joke to her.

"Never mind luv," said Sarah to James. "The next time they play a waltz I'll show you what to do."

Pete tried to mimic her accent but it didn't fit with his Irish turn of phrase "Luv is it, she never called me 'luv', did you me darlin' girl?" Sarah kicked him on the shin under the table.

James was quite enjoying watching the dancers. He had witnessed similar scenes at the village hall Sunday night dances at home but had never actually taken part. Pete was obviously practiced and was teaching Sarah the fundamentals of Irish traditional dancing and he hoped she would keep her promise to teach him a few steps. Several of the Irish navvies were also surprisingly at home on the dance floor, but for the most part they were merely taking part in some harmless horseplay with the factory girls. He recognised a few of the factory workers and was amused at the sight of a South African engineer he knew trying to dance an Irish jig with a girl from London.

Much to Father Conlon's relief it all seemed harmless fun, but he worried that he had not had a chance to carry out the main purpose of the evening, namely to gather information on how many of the navvies would be willing to join Daly in causing disruption to the factory in the name of Irish freedom. To this end he was disappointed with the turnout.

Michael was absent-mindedly tapping his feet in time with the music, but his thoughts were on other dance floors with Annie in his arms. Still he would have liked to dance, and he thought that Sarah would be willing to partner him if only to make fun of Pete, but he knew he would soon be out of breath and he did not want this to show.

The next dance was a waltz and Sarah literally dragged James onto the floor. He was awkward at first and unsure about where to place his hands, but she soon put him at his ease and he began to relax. With Sarah leading and counting time, 'one-two-three one-two-three' he began to get a feel for the rhythm and was soon mastering the basic steps; by the time the music stopped, much too soon for James' liking, she had extracted a promise from him that the next time they played a waltz he would ask one of the girls to dance.

An interval followed and they queued for refreshments, tea from a large urn for the men and a soft fruit drink for Sarah. While they sat with the drinks, Michael watched Father Conlon doing the rounds. He stopped and chatted briefly with the factory workers and stayed noticeably longer with the navvies and Michael was sure he heard the phrase 'fight for Irish freedom' mentioned. When he reached their table being introduced to Sarah seemed to throw him a little off balance but he quickly recovered. "Are you having a good time Miss Birks," he asked.

"Very good indeed," she answered. "I'm very glad I came."

The priest looked at Michael. "I was hoping to see a lot more of the Irish lads here."

"Oh you will Father," said Pete, "but they'll be in the pubs for a while yet. Building factories is hard thirsty work and they'll need to be well oiled up for the dancing."

"I was afraid of that, I'll have to keep an eye out for any that might have a drop too much taken," said a worried looking Conlon before moving on.

When he was out of earshot, Pete turned to Michael. "Did you hear what he was saying to the lads there about freedom for Ireland, I think he's a rebel at heart."

"I did," agreed Michael. "He started to say something along

the same lines at Mass this morning, but stopped himself."

"From the look of things at home Michael I'd say there'll be trouble there before long. There's plenty there who wouldn't mind taking advantage of the war. What was it the fella said? 'England's difficulty is Ireland's opportunity'."

Sarah was listening with interest. "At home in Yorkshire I kept hearing about trouble with the Irish, but since I came here I've found them to be nice friendly people. Apart from the one sitting here," she said giving Pete a dig with her elbow. "Are there really people who want to start a war over there as well as the one with the Germans?"

Michael explained that the great majority of Irish people would not want to take part in an armed rebellion, even though some of them would like to see the country have its own government separate from Britain. "But, like Pete here says there are some hotheads there as well who want to drive out the British by force."

"But where would they get the guns and things to fight against our army?" she asked.

James' mind was more on the factory girls and working up the courage to ask one of them to dance the next waltz with him than on what the others were saying. But he heard Sarah's remark and, being anxious to take part in the conversation, he blurted out in a loud voice: "Oh sure they're going to get a load of guns from the Germans. There's a fella called Casement over there now fixing it all up."

The silence that followed was deafening. Pete looked round quickly to see if anyone other than the four at the table had picked up the remark and found to his relief that everybody seemed to be too engrossed in their own conversations. James bit his tongue wishing the floor would open up. Michael sat rigid with a face like thunder and James saw that his father was, for the first time in months ready to lose his temper. But Michael managed to say in a reasonably level voice: "Where did you get that from James?"

"Sure didn't I hear about it around somewhere Da," he said.

Michael with effort still kept his voice down. "Where did you get that from James?"

James could see no way out and told them about the meeting in the back kitchen of Devlin's pub in Beaufort, about the Man from Dublin and what he had said about Roger Casement and the Germans.

Michael was about to speak but Pete laid a hand on his arm to stop him and then spoke himself in a graver tone than James had ever heard him use before. "Listen to me now Jim. You want to be very careful about talking like that in public places. If what you just said reached the wrong ears your life wouldn't be worth a bent farthing. There are people around that would do for you as quick as look at you and the rest of us as well if they thought we knew something we shouldn't. I don't think anyone heard you this time but for God's sake watch yourself. Do you hear me now?"

All James could say was: "All right Pete I will."

He looked at his father expecting to get another lecture but Michael, although obviously troubled, had been deeply impressed by what Pete had said and decided his best course was to reinforce the point. "Pete is right Jim you could easy get all of us into trouble."

James was suddenly faced with the realisation that up to now he had only been thinking of himself. But he was all of a sudden coming to terms with the fact that there were others involved, and the thought that he might have put them in danger hit him hard. The mood around the table had grown sombre and he knew that it was his fault. He felt he should say something but couldn't find the words. Mercifully the band struck up again and happily they played a waltz.

Pete stood and took Sarah's hand. "Come on luv," he said. Sarah stuck her tongue out at him but got up and joined him. Before they took the floor she urged James to go and ask one of the girls to dance before they were all on the floor.

James looked at his father expecting to be spoken to. But Michael had decided, partly to avoid spoiling the evening for Pete and Sarah and partly to let some of the heat out of the situation, not to say anything until later. He just nodded and James' relief overcame his apprehension about asking a girl to dance.

Her name was Kate. She seemed to be the youngest girl in the group and was certainly no older than James. She had come up from the West Country with an older sister drawn to work at the factory for the good wages. Once away from the high spirited influence of the rest of the girls she was every bit as shy as James. It took almost the entire duration of the dance for them to exchange names and say where they came from. They were just beginning to gain confidence and relaxed enough to enjoy the dance when the music ended. As he came back to his father a slightly happier James could not wait for another waltz to be played so that he could ask Kate to dance again.

Michael, sitting on his own, was thinking about how best to handle an extremely difficult situation. He noticed that the hall was gradually becoming more crowded. Groups of navvies were beginning to filter in and while they were in high spirits none seemed totally inebriated. Thus far all had passed the scrutiny of a clearly agitated Father Conlon and he had not turned any away. Pete brought Sarah back and excused himself to go to the toilet. When he returned he quietly told Michael that he had seen Liam Daly outside with another group of navvies all of whom seemed to be quite drunk. Michael pulled out his watch and announced that he had had enough for the night and it was time he started back to Dornock. He was on early shift tomorrow and at his age he needed his rest. Pete nodded and volunteered to fetch his coat and hat for him.

James was looking a little mystified so Michael explained: "Liam Daly is outside and has drink in him. If he comes in and sees me he might start trouble, so it'll be better all around if I'm not here. Will you walk down to the station with me Jim? It won't take long and you can come back and dance with that girl after."

He said good night to Sarah, who assured him that they would indeed meet again and they managed to leave the hall without incident.

Daly came in with Mick and a group of four or five navvies, all of whom were clearly under the influence. After some discussion Father Conlon allowed them into the dance on condition that they behaved themselves. Daly and Mick went into the cloakroom and the priest followed. He found the two waiting for him and, to his great relief, both were perfectly sober.

"Sure we haven't touched a drop Father," said Mick. "We took a stroll around the factory and we got what the boys in Dublin wanted." He handed Conlon some sheets of notes. "We met them eejits down the road. Sure they'll swear an oath on the Holy Bible that we were with them all night."

Conlon had in fact caught a few words of what James had let slip regarding Casement and the Germans, enough to at least recognise the significance. He was about to mention it to Daly but something stopped him. He caught a glimpse of the butt of the revolver in the inside pocket as Daly hung up his jarvey's cape, and he decided that for the time being it would be better to keep the information to himself.

Chapter 28

When they left the dance they walked for the first few minutes in silence. Michael was about to open the conversation when James spoke up: "I'm sorry Da, I should have kept my mouth shut or maybe told you about what happened in Devlin's before. I suppose what Pete said was right and that kind of talk could put everyone in danger."

"If the likes of Liam Daly heard you talking about things like guns coming from Germany they would shut you up for good, and if they didn't do that they'd make sure you carried the can for whatever devilment they have in mind." He let that sink in.

"Face the facts Jim, you're a factory worker for the Ministry of Munitions doing war work. If there was trouble here with the rebels and it came out that you knew something about it you'd be put in the jail whether you were part of it or not. The people in charge here can't afford to take chances and I'd lose my job too, then where would your mother and the young ones at home be."

"What can we do now Da, will we have to inform on them?"

Michael knew the significance of what James had just said. The word 'informer' had, over many years, been burned into the Irish consciousness. After centuries of struggle for freedom by various factions from the Kings of Ulster to the Fenians and up to the current Irish Republican Brotherhood the most contemptible figure to the Irish was the informer, despised by friend and foe alike. While it bothered him that James had not said anything before tonight he understood his son's reasons for not doing so. Even Michael, who had never in his life entertained a single thought about joining the nationalist cause in any of its guises, still felt an Irishman's fear of being branded an informer. But the real possibility of James and his friends, and indeed himself, being drawn into a potentially dangerous situation had the effect of making him feel better about passing on what James had told him.

The only way he could see of protecting his family and other innocents was to make sure that Daly and his fellow conspirators failed in whatever scheme they were planning.

"Leave it to me Jim," he said. "I know the very people to handle this. But remember what I said now, watch yourself and keep your mouth shut."

The lesson was not lost on James, "I will Da."

"Good man," said Michael. "Now go on back and dance with that nice looking girl. And for God's sake stay away from Liam Daly and his crowd."

When Michael got back to Dornock there were several people moving about in the hut. Some were changing shifts and some were coming in from a night out in Gretna or Carlisle. It was impossible to talk to Alistair McGregor in confidence so they went out into the night. He gave Alistair a full account of what he had heard about Roger Casement and the German arms. The only deviation from the whole truth was that James had volunteered the information rather than letting it slip out on the spur of the moment.

McGregor gave him a quizzical look but accepted the explanation. He sensed the importance of what they had learned and was impatient to pass it on. "I'll have to report this to the commander ASAP, but I suppose we can't do anything before morning, it's too late now. I'll contact him first thing. I'm sorry Michael but it looks as if the rumours of trouble in Ireland are true and I'm sure that doesn't give you any pleasure."

"No pleasure at all Alistair," said Michael sadly. "There'll be yet more Irish dead with nothing to show for it. May the Lord have mercy on their souls."

Michael knew that he was in for a disturbed night, the first for some time. He would spend it tossing and turning and the pain in his chest would return to bother him.

. . .

When James returned to the dance he was surprised to find Pete and Sarah waiting for him outside the hall and even more surprised to find the girl, Kate, with them.

"I think it's time to call it a night Jim," said Pete. "Liam Daly is in there with a lot to say for himself as usual. I'd say it won't be long before he starts on at one of the factory men and there is bound to be trouble. Some of them boys are a lot tougher than they look and there will be ructions. Sarah wants you to walk young Kate here back to the hostel."

Sarah was looking unusually flustered. "I think it's for the best James. Kate here has had enough anyway, unless of course you want to go back to the dance that is."

Wild horses would not have dragged James back inside as long as there was the possibility of being with Kate. "Sure I'll see her home. Is that all right with you Kate?"

Kate nodded and smiled shyly.

Sarah touched his arm; "Thanks James. I'd like Pete to stay here with me for a while in case any of the other girls needs help."

Pete laughed. "I tell you what I think; some of your lovely English roses have very dangerous thorns and if it comes to a fight it's not them that'll be needing help."

When James and Kate had left, Pete patted Sarah on the back. "Good girl yourself, your plan worked fine. If I told him to stay out of the dance or Daly would start on him he'd go in anyway to show that he's not afraid of anyone."

"Maybe," said Sarah. "But I think he learned a good lesson tonight."

James walked Kate the short distance back to the hostel and even managed to strike up a halting conversation. He told her a little about his home and family. When they said goodnight and he left the hostel he thought about going back to the dance but it had lost its appeal and so he headed back to Solway View instead. Soon after he got there 'St Patrick' Murphy came in and, unusually for him struck up a conversation. He asked if James had heard of the 'terrible goings on' at the dance. James told him what he knew. 'St Patrick' muttered something about the ungodliness of dances, said his prayers and went to bed.

He lay on his bed waiting for Pete, his mind half on the trouble he knew he had caused, and half on asking Pete how to go about asking Kate to go out with him. Sleep would not come easy.

. . .

Father Conlon sat in his room in the little annex at the rear of the church that passed for a presbytery. He was still stunned by the way events had turned out at the St. Patrick's dance that the police were at pains to point out he had organised. On arriving home following the fracas he had gone into the church to pray for guidance but none had been forthcoming. The police had interviewed everyone who was still standing, including himself, in an effort to establish exactly who had thrown the first insult, the first punch or the first bottle, but were none the wiser. One minute the dance was in full swing and the next there was chaos. The dancers seemed to divide into two warring factions, the navvies on one side and the factory workers on the other. There was much punching, kicking and wrestling, tables were overturned, cups smashed and clothing torn. Those unfortunates who found themselves on the floor were trampled underfoot. The factory girls screamed and stampeded out of the doors then sneaked back to watch the fun, totally ignoring Sarah's pleas to go back to the hostel. The police arrived in some strength, calmed things down, held their interviews, took names and addresses, issued a warning that this was not the end of the matter, and sent everybody home with the able-bodied helping the walking wounded.

The priest worried that there would be arrests and court appearances and that he would be called as a witness. He was deeply concerned about what he would say if called to give evidence under oath because he knew that Liam Daly and Mick had started the affray and it was obvious to him that they had done it coldly and deliberately, and not as a result of drink. The pair had then disappeared well before the police arrived. He had seen them slip away and noticed Daly checking on the gun in his cape pocket. The promptness with which the police had arrived and the number involved indicated to him that they had been tipped off and he again suspected Daly. Could he now swear on the bible that he knew nothing? His one consolation was that he had not told Daly about what he had picked up from young Quinlan regarding the German arms. He did not think it beyond the bounds of possibility that Daly would have used the revolver had he known. He was glad that he had held back, but he would have to report the incident to The Man from Dublin on his next visit.

. . .

Commander Wilson was just putting the telephone down as McGregor was shown into his office. The old sergeant stood to attention and saluted. Wilson was tempted to invite him to sit but thought, rightly, that the man would be more comfortable if military etiquette was observed.

"Stand easy sergeant." McGregor relaxed but before he could make his report Wilson continued. "Have you heard anything about trouble at a dance organised by the priest Conlon last night? I've just had the civilian police on to me about it."

"Only a bit of barrack room gossip sir."

"It's strange but the police seem to have been tipped off that there would be trouble. You don't think our man Quinlan was involved do you?"

"No sir, Michael left the dance early to bring me some news that I think you should hear." He went on to relay the message from Michael regarding the German arms.

The commander sat up. "Good Lord, I'd better get this off to London immediately." He thought for a moment. "You say this came via Quinlan's son, is it possible he might be involved in some way?"

"Och no sir," said McGregor, "he's just a young recruit caught out in no-man's-land and not knowing which way to turn. His father will straighten him out sir."

"Very well sergeant. Quinlan has done well not to cover anything up regarding the boy but I shall have to report this in full. Please let him know that."

"I think he understands that sir. If I might say something sir, Michael is very worried about the laddie's safety if Daly and his gang got hold of this information. Is there any way we can help him out there sir?"

"I'll certainly give it some thought sergeant," said Wilson, "but in the meantime I must get this off to the people in London. Thank you sergeant, that will be all for now." McGregor saluted and left.

. . .

"Now that is interesting," said The Man from Whitehall over the telephone. "We did of course know about the bold Sir Roger being in Germany. Apparently he has been trying to recruit men from among Irish prisoners-of-war, but without any success I'm happy to say. But asking the Germans to supply them with weapons, now that is where the Hun might be more than happy to oblige. From what you say it looks to me as if the rebels have been using this as a recruitment ploy, and not being too security conscious about it, which in turn means that whatever they are planning must be happening quite soon."

"What can be done about it?" asked Wilson.

"There's only one way to get an arms shipment into Ireland and that is by sea, so this looks like a job for the Royal Navy wouldn't you say commander?"

Wilson could not make up his mind whether his superior was making fun of him so he changed the subject. "Can we do anything about some protection for Quinlan's son? I fear that if anything were to happen to him it would hit Quinlan hard and we might lose his cooperation."

"You could be right, Commander." There was silence for a moment. "Get in touch with 'Patrick' through your intermediary and ask him to contact me. We'll see what can be done, but under no circumstances must we tip our hand and alert the other side."

Wilson felt a tinge of resentment, he felt that he was being sidelined once again and major decisions were being made without his input. But all he could do was to carry out the order.

"There is one other thing," said Wilson. He related what had happened at the dance the previous evening and what the civilian police had told him. "It sounds to me as if the thing was started deliberately and the police were informed beforehand. I wondered if I might not take advantage of the situation to have a chat with this Father Conlon personally – making an effort to work with local religious leaders etc., that sort of thing. I'd like to hear for myself what he has to say."

"Now that is a good idea. You are learning Commander. He might just be their weak link so let's apply a little pressure. But again I stress be careful not to arouse his suspicions."

Chapter 29

Nitro-cotton, or 'gun-cotton' as it became known, was produced by charring cotton waste with a mixture of nitric and sulphuric acids. Munitions workers filled large stoneware pans with the acids, then added the raw cotton waste and left it to soak. When ready the nitro-cotton was first washed in boiling water and then in cold, with powdered chalk added, to remove any traces of excess acid. It was dried in warm air using a centrifuge. The finished material was transported to the next processes in rubber bags.

This extremely hazardous process, with an ever-present danger of acid splashes and fumes, was carried out by the female workers, the 'Gretna Girls' as they became known – girls whose ages ranged from as young as sixteen year old Kate to women in their fifties and even sixties. They wore khaki uniforms trimmed with red and comprising pyjama style trousers, a long-sleeved belted tunic and a mob cap. Because the water on the floors, not to mention the mud and slush of the site itself, many of the girls took to wearing rubber wellington boots. The greatest danger of accidents stemmed from foreign bodies being dropped into the mixtures, which became more and more volatile as more ingredients were added. Strict safety precautions were introduced to prevent this and other risks. Rules were rigorously enforced. Any of the girls caught carrying or wearing metal objects, even buttons on their underwear, had money taken from her wages as punishment.

Enforcing these safety procedures was the responsibility of the Ministry of Munitions Women's Police Service who carried out random but frequent checks. The WPS was a national police service and had their own inspector on site and the ever-increasing number of 'Gretna Girls' demanded an ever-increasing number of policewomen. This in turn meant an ever-increasing workload for Commander Wilson. He needed help, and was on the point of contacting his superior at Whitehall when he decided that it was high time he exercised his own authority. He promoted Brown to be his deputy with the rank of inspector and with responsibility for day-to-day policing matters, leaving himself free to concentrate on security issues. And after some thought he promoted Michael Quinlan to take Brown's place. Wilson firmly believed that Michael had all the necessary qualities to do a competent job, if he hadn't he would not have entertained the idea, but if pressed he would have to concede that there was a second reason for choosing the former coachman. The new post would give Michael added authority and greater freedom of action in carrying out his undercover role of helping to counter the scheme being hatched by Daly and Conlon. And it would be possible for him to report in person and so speed up the process. The commander may not still have fully accepted the concept of 'cloak and dagger' methods, but he was quickly learning how to employ them.

Michael was extremely happy with his new appointment; he felt it afforded him greater opportunities for protecting James.

Once Wilson had explained his new duties to Michael, he briefed the men who would have to work under the new senior policeman and was gratified not to find any signs of hidden resentment at the appointment of the apparently well liked and respected Irishman. The only awkward moment for Michael was when Wilson told him that he should make any urgent reports by telephone and gave him the appropriate numbers. Michael had never in his life been faced with the necessity of using the instrument and had to request a crash course.

Alistair McGregor heard the news on the thriving factory grapevine and came to the stores to congratulate his friend. They were chatting in the stores office when they were interrupted by the old two piece telephone attached to the wall. Michael had a moment's panic but managed to put the earpiece to his ear and say a hesitant 'hello' into the mouthpiece. It was Wilson calling to explain his decision to interview the priest, Father Conlon, and to ask him to get someone to find McGregor and send the sergeant to him. Alistair, who had been finding Michael's efforts on the telephone highly amusing, was mortified when his new boss told

Wilson that the sergeant was in fact in the office and he could talk to him in person. Before he could do anything about it the sergeant found the telephone in his hands and it was his turn to panic.

Chapter 30

The old soldier in the army greatcoat with the sergeant's chevrons and wearing a battered tam-o'-shanter was becoming a familiar figure limping around Gretna. Two navvies lounging on a street corner came to attention and saluted as he approached.

"The top of the morning to you general." Alistair ignored them and stumped past.

"That's the old bugger from the huts at Dornock, Quinlan's pal," said Liam Daly. "He spends a hell of a lot of time mooching around here these days. I'll lay odds that he's doing something for that bloody coachman on the Q. T. Come on we'll see what he's up to, we have time before we have to meet The Man."

"Did you hear that Quinlan got promoted?" Mick knew very well that Daly would have heard but wanted to gauge his reaction.

"I did, and I'll tell you this, the bigger they are the farther they fall and that bastard is going to fall a hell of a long way."

Before he could say any more Mick grabbed his arm and pulled him back around the corner. "Will you look at that? The old fella is going into the church. What is he after there? Maybe he's seen the light and wants Sean to convert him."

Alistair went into the church, but conversion was the last thing on his mind. He removed his tammy and called out softly: "Hello. Is there anybody about?"

There was no immediate reply so he inched further up the aisle as quietly as his wooden leg would allow and called again.

"Can I help you?" The priest, wearing his long dark cassock, came out of the sacristy door to the right of the altar.

"Ay I hope so padre, if you are (he looked at the official looking envelope in his hand) The Reverend S Conlon the RC chaplain?"

Conlon looked curiously at the letter, "I'm Father Conlon."

Alistair pulled himself to attention. "Och well. I'm sergeant

McGregor and I have a letter for you from Commander Wilson."

A hint of concern joined the curiosity on Conlon's face as he took the envelope. "And who might this Commander Wilson be?" He was perfectly well aware who Wilson was and the lie did not sit easily on his conscience. It seemed as if telling lies had become an all too frequent necessity of late and the thought disturbed him.

"Commander Wilson, padre? He's in charge of security up at HM Factory," explained Alistair who knew an untruth when he heard it.

"Do you know what this is about?"

"Not exactly padre. But I'd guess that it has something to do with the punch-up at the dance the other night."

"But that has nothing to do with this man Wilson. The local police are dealing with the incident." Conlon was getting nervous.

Alistair felt that he had gone as far with worrying the priest as Wilson wanted him to. "Och well I wouldn't know about that. I'm only the regimental runner. I just deliver the orders." He came to attention again. "If that'll be all padre I'll be on my way. I have other business to conduct here in Gretna."

Conlon, still gazing at the envelope, nodded and the sergeant left.

When he emerged from the church the two navvies who he knew to be Daly and Mick, and whom he realised had been following him, had disappeared. As he walked down the street towards the station he met another man in dark clerical garb who seemed to be heading for the church carrying a small suitcase. He waited until this second priest had gone some distance then turned to follow him.

Father Conlon was still standing in his church reading Wilson's letter when the two navvies entered. "What did that bloody old soldier pal of Quinlan's want here?" demanded Daly shortly.

"He brought a letter from that commander Wilson at the factory." The reply conveyed the priest's nervousness.

Daly made to snatch the letter but Conlon managed to prevent him doing so. "I haven't read it myself yet, and keep your voice down in the church."

They stood glaring at each other when a voice from the still open doorway called out the traditional Irish saying on entering a room: "God bless all here."

They turned and were surprised to find a second priest standing in the aisle. Daly was about to ask him to state his business, but looked again and burst out laughing. "Jesus Mary and Joseph, aren't you the grandest looking priest I ever laid eyes on."

Much to Father Conlon's displeasure The Man from Dublin gave them a mock blessing before asking, "What's all the argument about?"

"Father Sean here just got a love letter from the sailor boy at the factory, Commander Wilson," said Mick.

"What does he want?"

"I haven't had a chance to find out yet," said Conlon crossly.

"Well we can't stay here shouting about it," said The Man from Dublin. "I told you to lay on somewhere private for us Sean. That buffet at the station is getting too chancy. We'll sit down with a cup of tea and find out what the head security man wants."

Father Conlon was glad to get them out of the church as he found both their attitude and language upsetting, and the sight of The Man from Dublin dressed as a priest deeply disturbing. He led the way out through the sacristy and was saddened but not surprised to find that he was the only one to genuflect and make the Sign of the Cross as they passed in front of the altar. He conducted them to the priest's private quarters behind the church. As they filed out McGregor left his vantage point and set off to report to Commander Wilson.

When they entered the priest's room where he had arranged chairs for them. Daly threw his cape into a corner and there was a distinct thud as the revolver in the pocket hit the floor. This proved to be the last straw as far as Father Conlon was concerned and he turned on the former jarvey.

"Don't ever let me catch you bringing that thing into my church again." He was visibly trying to hold his temper. "And while we're at it you can watch your language in the house of God."

Before Daly had a chance to come back at him he turned on

The Man from Dublin. "What's the idea of pretending to be a priest of God, it's blasphemous!"

"Easy now Sean, desperate times call for desperate measures and sure what better disguise could I have for a meeting in a church?" He pointed to the case he had placed on the floor. "Things are beginning to happen at home and I couldn't take a chance on anybody wanting to know what's in there, but nobody ever stops and questions a priest."

Conlon was far from pacified. "What have you brought over this time, more guns, I suppose."

"No guns Sean, but something a lot more dangerous. You'll have heard the saying 'the pen is mightier than the sword', well I'll show you how that works in a minute when everyone calms down."

He could still sense Daly's anger and turned to face him with his back to the priest. "Sean's right though Liam you shouldn't be taking guns into the church."

Daly caught the broad wink that accompanied the statement and relaxed.

"All right, now Sean give us a look at that letter."

The priest handed it over and The Man read it. "What happened at the dance?"

"These two here started a fight and I'm sure they did it deliberately. They tipped off the police as well and left me to sort it all out with them. Now the security man at the factory wants me to go and see him about it."

The Man turned to the two culprits. "It looks like the plan worked lads if this fella Wilson is worried enough to want to talk to Sean. If you get another chance to drive a wedge between the factory workers and the Irish navvies you should take it."

Conlon was astounded. "Do you mean to say that this was all set up and nobody told me? Who do you think I am? Some eejit you can kick around anyway you like? Well I won't stand for any more of it."

The Man waited for a minute then looking directly at Conlon he said slowly in a level voice, "Look Sean, you were happy enough to join us when all you had to do was preach rebellion

181

from the safety of the pulpit at home. But this is the real thing, so get it straight, you're in it now and you're in all the way because there's only one way out and you know very well what that is. If I think you're not up to it I won't take any chances at all with you. Priest or no priest I'll see you dead before I'll put The Cause in danger. So you'll stand for what I say you'll stand for."

As soon as he had clearly explained the reality of the situation to Conlon, The Man turned on Liam Daly. He made it plain to the hot headed rebel that he was to stop carrying the revolver around with him. 'If you get caught with that gun on you the game will be up for all of us. And like I just told your man Sean here you'll be made to pay for it. So for Christ's sake use your head Liam. The way things are going around here I'm thinking I'll have come over more often."

There was silence for several minutes as he let the message sink in. Mick, who was the only one to escape censure, was the first to break it. "Sure they'll be good lads from now on, and we'll all be the better off if we hold our tempers."

"All right," said The Man, "first things first. What about this invitation from the security man, Wilson?"

Ironically Conlon and Daly were for once in agreement, albeit for different reasons. Daly was all for a simple solution i.e. tearing up the letter and telling Wilson what he could do with his invitation, "I'll tell him myself if it comes to it." Conlon's reasoning was more complex; he worried that getting involved with the head of the factory security force could only serve to aggravate what was rapidly becoming an extremely complicated situation. At least that was how it seemed to him and he felt that they should be under no illusions about it. This would not be a single meeting but the first of many if Wilson meant what he said about cooperation with the local churches. He didn't mention the fact but he was extremely nervous about a meeting, which would almost certainly require him to commit further sins by telling even more lies.

The Man from Dublin listened but was adamant that the invitation would be accepted. This Commander Wilson must not be given the slightest reason to suspect that Father Conlon was anything other than what he appeared to be, a Catholic priest whose only concern was for his flock. Plans were too far advanced at home to risk anything going wrong at this end. Conlon would accept the invitation, offer all the assistance he possibly could and promise to cooperate fully in whatever the security man had in mind.

"Now," said The Man, "it's time to talk about more important business." He picked up his case, placed it flat on the table and opened it. Much to Father Conlon's consternation he removed a cassock similar to the one he was wearing himself. Underneath the cassock was an assortment of clothing, which could only have been the property of a clergyman. He felt inside and took out a book which Conlon immediately recognised as a breviary, a catholic priest's prayer book from which, among things, he read his obligatory daily office. From inside the back cover of the breviary he withdrew a single folded sheet of paper. He opened it and passed it round. The animosity still evident between members of the group was diminished and they read the contents.

"That," said The Man, standing up and assuming the schoolmasterly stance he unconsciously adopted when preaching Irish Nationalism, "is the gist of what will be presented to the Irish people, the British government and, it must be said, the world in general in the near future. The final draft of 'The Declaration of the Irish Republic' is at this minute being prepared for publication by our own printers. It will signal the start of the rebellion that will finally set Ireland free."

He explained what the revolutionary leaders in Dublin had decided they wanted done at Gretna in support of the uprising at home. The leaflets were to be distributed as quickly and as widely as possible immediately the proclamation was read by Padraig Pearse and the uprising began. The rare use of Pearse's name was designed to drive home the importance placed on the action by the leader himself.

Reactions to the change of plan varied.

"Ah for Christ's sake!" Daly jumped from his seat and banged his fist on the table. "What would we be wanting with bits of paper? Guns are the only things that'll get this job done."

The Man carefully explained again how the main object of the exercise was to cause maximum embarrassment to the British but Daly was still not convinced. "Give me a machine gun and I'll embarrass the bastards."

Father Conlon, whose religious feelings were still quite hurt by The Man's shameless impersonation of a Catholic priest, which to him bordered on the sacrilegious, was almost comforted by the thought that the leaflet campaign might replace the need for bloodshed, at least as far as his 'parish' was concerned. But this heartening assumption was shattered when Mick, who had thus far sat quietly reflecting on what he had heard, began to question The Man.

"The boys at home know what they're doing all right. If this notion works it'll give the Brits a grand headache here on the mainland to go with the one they get at in Ireland. But does this mean that the chances me and Liam took nosing around the factory at night were all for nothing?"

"Not at all Mick, you'll still get your chance for action, there's nothing like a good kick in the backside to go with a headache."

"And tell me now? How are we going to do that? Are we going to plant bombs in the arses of their trousers?"

"No you're going to use some spent acid and water."

"Christ Almighty!" interjected Daly, "we're going to piss on them."

"Only in a manner of speaking Liam," said The Man. "Those brainy boys at Dublin's famous Trinity College have made the job easy for you. Listen now and I'll tell you how it's done."

The solution was a simple one and even Daly could grasp the principle. If spent acids were to inadvertently find their way into a quantity of nitroglycerine enormously high temperatures would be generated and large quantities of dangerously toxic nitrogen peroxide fumes given off. Unless immediate remedial action was taken to cool the mixture down the nitroglycerine would explode with devastating effect. The only way to prevent an explosion was to add, and to keep on adding, large quantities of cold water to the mixture until the temperature was reduced. This in itself was an extremely perilous undertaking. The factory designers would obviously have known of this problem and would have put systems in place to deal with it. All that was required was for Mick and Daly to work around the safety measures.

"How?" said Mick.

"The only tricky bit is getting the acid into the nitroglycerine – you have to watch how you handle the stuff. The 'brains' are sure that there will be plenty of spent acid lying around the factory. You don't need much and any old acid will do, and you can put it into any of those big vats that have nitro in them. Then all you have to do is turn off the water supply and run like hell. Even if they catch on quick and some smart munitions worker turns the water on again it will be too late and up she goes."

Mick thought hard for a while and then said, "I think it can be done. It won't be hard to find some acid lying around in that place and hide it there until it's wanted for the job. If the water is as important as you say it is the controls will be well marked and easy to get at, and there will be a notice to show even a complete eejit how to turn it on and off. I'll tell you what we'll do; I'll be able to do the acid bit on my own if Liam can start a ruction in another part of the factory to cause a diversion."

This was more to Daly's liking and he interrupted Mick: "Now you're talking. I'll cause a diversion all right."

"Good," said The Man. "That will keep the factory police, and with any luck the local coppers too, busy while we are handing out the Proclamation. We'll break the news to the navvies at Mass. Sean will preach a sermon on the righteousness of The Cause and I'll say a few words at the end. We'll hand out the leaflets as they leave the church, the altar boys can give us a hand. I'll bring them over a few days before the off and I'll stay here until the day."

He looked directly at Conlon. "You're going to have a visiting priest for a few days whether you like it or not. I'll leave you to make the arrangements. All right Sean?"

Conlon was not 'all right'. "So all this will happen on a Sunday will it?"

"That's right Sean, the first Sunday after the rising at home," The Man lied.

"Well you're not going to use the altar boys, I won't allow

you to get children mixed up in this." Conlon was adamant.

Before The Man could retort, Mick spoke up. "Sure there'll be no need to use the kids, there are sure to be a few men at Mass only too ready to give you a hand after they hear what Sean has to say and you tell them that the rising has started at home. I'd say you'll be able to give them handfuls of the things to spread around far and wide for you."

The Man from Dublin could see the logic in this and nodded. "All right, we'll finalise that the next time I come over. In the meantime put your mind to what you have to do in the factory Mick. Now there is something else we have to think about and it's this."

He paused to make sure he had their attention. "As soon as things are finished here I want to go straight back to Dublin to join the fight there. If you want to come with me that would be grand because they'll need all the help they can get."

Both Mick and Daly said that they definitely wanted to go and join in the uprising.

"Good lads," said The Man. "So I'll leave it up to you to make some arrangements to get us out of here before we get caught and spend the whole rebellion in gaol. You can come with us if you like Sean. Your masters up in Armagh won't be too happy but it's up to you. If you decide to stay here you can tell the Brits we forced you to help us at gunpoint, and that'll suit us fine because it will give them one more thing to remember us by. Think about it Father Conlon."

Father Conlon was silent. He was beginning to realise that it was just one more in a long list of things he had to think, and more importantly pray, about.

"How long have we?" said Mick, "How soon will they want us to be ready?"

The Man considered this before replying. Daly and Mick knew that the rising was planned for Easter, but he remained cautious about confirming this in front of Conlon. He could see that the priest was becoming more and more concerned about his role in the affair and he worried that there were definite signs of conflict between the man's nationalist leanings and inbred religious beliefs. The thought of human bloodshed as opposed to the sacred bloodshed in the Passion of Christ at Easter might be enough to tip the balance and the priest could easily become a liability.

"No more than a month," was the only information he was prepared to impart.

He stood up and repacked his case. "Well I have a train to catch. Have a look around to make sure there's nobody out there that shouldn't be Liam. You go with him Sean and come back to tell me when the coast is clear."

When they left The Man turned to Mick. "Keep a close watch on those two Mick. Sean is wavering and Liam is too eager to use that gun I gave him. Between the pair of them they could make a complete bags of this. And, keep this under your hat, the day is Easter Sunday. Casement will land on Good Friday and the guns will be there soon after."

. . .

McGregor went directly from the church to the administrative centre with all the speed he could muster. He demanded to be taken in to see Commander Wilson immediately, but was forced to wait impatiently while a pedantic new security man, clearly suspicious of Alistair's tramp-like appearance, questioned him closely. Luckily Brown came in, recognised him and conducted him to Wilson's office.

"And you say there was some disagreement between them sergeant," said the Commander after the sergeant had made his very clear and detailed report.

"Yes sir, they were definitely arguing in the church before the second clergyman arrived and it went on after he went in. I couldn't catch exactly what was being said – the hearing is not what it used to be sir – but the padre Conlon was no' very happy. I couldn't swear to this sir, but I think the reason might be that the new man was no' a real padre at all. They went into the rooms at the back of the church and shut the door so I decided it would best to come straight here and report to you sir."

"Well done sergeant, you took exactly the correct course of action." At this McGregor momentarily came to attention. "And you are sure that you have never seen this second clergyman with the case, if in fact he is one, around the area before."

"Dead sure sir, but I'd say that he was on his way from the railway station."

"As he was carrying a suitcase perhaps he intends to be around for a while." Wilson was thinking aloud.

"If he is it won't be for long sir," said Alistair, "that case was no' big enough to carry enough kit for a long stay."

"Very well McGregor, I'll take it from here for now. I want you to find Quinlan and talk to him about what you've found out. He may even know this man from your description, but in any case tell him to keep a sharp look out for him, especially around the church. And once again I must say well done sergeant."

"Thank you sir," the sergeant saluted and left.

Immediately after McGregor left, Wilson telephoned the office in Whitehall and asked to speak to the Director. While he was waiting for his superior to come on the line he set the wheels in motion to find 'Patrick', but found the operative difficult to locate.

He felt it would be dangerous to send McGregor back to Gretna to keep watch on the meeting as he would almost certainly be recognised, and the same thing would happen if he sent Michael Quinlan. So, in the absence of 'Patrick' he resolved to deal with the situation himself. He decided to trust McGregor's instinct that Conlon's visitor would not be staying long in Gretna, and that he had been making his way from the station when first spotted. He called for a railway timetable and tried to make an estimate of what time the bogus priest might leave Gretna. When he thought the time was right he walked down to the station and went into the waiting room from where he could watch all that was happening on the platforms. He had not been there long when, obviously having timed his arrival with some care, a priest carrying a small suitcase entered the station just in time to board a train for Carlisle.

Wilson briefly considered following but, heedful of his superior's constant demand for caution, decided not to. Instead he went to his office and sent off an accurate description of the Man from Dublin to Whitehall.

Chapter 31

Commander Wilson was gratified, if a little surprised, that Father Conlon had accepted his invitation. Before his meeting with the rebel priest he reviewed the events of the last few days and all in all he had reason to feel satisfied with the way things were turning out. Indeed it might be said that he was feeling quite pleased with himself. Even The Man from Whitehall had expressed his satisfaction.

For his part, Father Conlon spent much of his time before going to see Commander Wilson deep in thought. He prayed for guidance, but deep down he knew that he had brought most of his problems on himself. He still passionately supported The Cause of Irish Nationalism, mainly because he abhorred the notion of Catholic Ireland being subject to Protestant Britain. But he was learning that while theory was one thing practical reality was quite another and he was finding the lesson extremely unpalatable. As the Man from Dublin had intimated, it was easy to preach rebellion from the safety of the pulpit in a land where the local priest always enjoyed considerable respect and often wielded not a little power within his parish. But without having planned it he suddenly found himself firmly entrenched in the front line and, due to the nature of the covert movement he had chosen to join, there could be no going back. He had been told in no uncertain terms that once in he would not be allowed out again where he might pose a potential danger to The Cause. It caused him considerable disquiet to learn that he was completely expendable, and it was time to review his position.

He had for some time suspected that he was not being kept fully informed by the others about what was happening at Gretna. Now he was certain of it. The fight at the St. Patrick's dance had been prearranged behind his back. Then there was the incident where young Quinlan had let slip something about Roger

Casement and some German arms, he certainly had not been privy to any information concerning that. The obvious conclusion was that he was not fully trusted and was merely being used as a pawn. That fact alone made him glad that he had not mentioned to any of the others what he had heard the lad say. He was convinced that had he done so he would have been responsible for the boy's death. It was becoming obvious that Liam Daly would not hesitate to use that revolver. In this instance the priest had overruled the rebel. He had spoken, preached and written at length about Irish heroes of the past who had died a martyr's death for the sake of their country, and on occasion he had asked himself if he would be prepared to follow in their footsteps. At the time it had been easy to believe that he would, and he remained convinced that this answer was still valid. But being found in a remote bog or deserted ditch with a bullet in his head was definitely not his idea of a martyr's death. The trouble was that he had never thought about exactly what he did have in mind. The alternative, dying on a battlefield while attempting to take other men's lives, was equally abhorrent to him.

The Man from Dublin had provided one possible solution when he asked what the priest intended to do after the rising began, and the action at Gretna was successfully completed. He had not been openly threatened by The Man but he now knew that he would not be permitted to walk away scot free. The idea that the others would corroborate a claim that he had been forced at gunpoint to join them simply did not ring true, and in any case such a story would not be believed. The thought of his expendability came back to haunt him.

After much thought and prayer the only solution which presented itself was to see the affair through to the bitter end. He would then surrender himself to the authorities, and hopefully he would have the opportunity to expound his support for the nationalist cause in court. But he was mindful that he would have to tread extremely carefully if he were to live long enough to achieve this.

. . .

"Ah Father Conlon, do come in, I am Commander Wilson, head of security at His Majesty's Factory, Gretna." Wilson extended a welcoming hand, which was rather limply accepted. "Do please sit, I'm sorry about the bare nature of the office but until the main factory buildings are completed my personal comfort has a low priority rating. I'm extremely grateful to you for taking the time to come here. I've been meaning to contact you, and other local community leaders, for some time but pressure of work etc. I've heard of your work in the Catholic Church, and I'm glad to finally have the opportunity to meet you in person."

He paused to let Conlon wonder whether he meant work at the church in Gretna or his involvement with the nationalist cause in Ireland. Wilson had been well briefed by The Man from Whitehall.

"I regret the fact that it has taken that unfortunate incident at the dance the other night to hurry things along." He noticed that Conlon was about to say something but didn't give the priest the opportunity. "Yes I know that strictly speaking this is a matter for the civilian police and I imagine that you have spoken with them, so perhaps I had better explain my interest."

"I would like to hear that," said Conlon.

Wilson continued. "Well, I am responsible for security here, which on the face of it means preventing any attempts at sabotage, the obvious suspects being the Germans. But this establishment is so vitally important to the war effort that I have been instructed to deal with anything that might interrupt or delay operations here, and it seems to me that trouble between the factory workers and the builders could well cause such delays. Don't you agree?"

Conlon nodded.

"As I said any legal action is up to the civilian authorities, but if there are troublemakers around, be they factory workers or builders, then I need to know. I don't suppose you have any idea of which side actually started the fight?"

"None at all," lied Father Conlon. But Wilson sensed his discomfort.

"Shame," said Wilson. He thought for a moment. "Look Father Conlon, I know you are not obliged to, but I would appreciate it if you would let me know of any other events you have planned. I certainly don't wish to make it difficult for people to organise social events, on the contrary, I believe they are badly needed, but being pre-warned will help to nip any trouble in the bud."

"I'll be happy to do that Mr. Wilson," said Conlon. The use of 'Mr' was not lost on the Commander.

"Good," said Wilson, "and if I can help in any way with what you are doing at the church please do not hesitate to ask." He took out his watch. "I'm sorry to rush you Father, but I really must dash. Thank you again for coming."

He stood and extended his hand. The priest had no option but to follow suit.

For Conlon the brief meeting had posed more questions than it had answered. Why had he been invited to go to the factory for what had turned out to be the most superficial of reasons. It could only mean that Wilson had wanted to meet him in person. He wondered why, and the thought worried him.

In this, Commander Wilson had achieved his purpose.

Chapter 32

Sir Roger Casement stood with the small group on the quayside gazing at the lines of German submarines as the rain swept in off the North Sea. With him were two fellow nationalists, Bailey and Monteith, and a German naval officer. He did not like these underwater killers. Although he had elected to become a soldier for a cause he held dear, the concept of the U-boat with its inability to distinguish between combatants and innocent victims represented an aspect of modern warfare he found repulsive. The few hours he had already spent aboard one had added a physical dislike to his moral objections. But the German Military High Command had insisted that his best, if not only, chance of returning to Ireland to join in the planned uprising was to accept their offer of transporting him home by submarine. Today they would make a second attempt to achieve that objective.

Twenty four hours previously they had boarded the cramped, oily, smelly U-20 at the Wilhemshaven base. They had not been at sea for more than an hour when he was approached by members of the crew who, with obvious pride, told him that theirs was the boat which had sunk the liner *Lusitania,* and his revulsion at the use of submarines was confirmed. He accepted the fact that he had chosen to become fully committed to the cause of Irish Nationalism and that this would involve some loss of life, but the thought of innocent women and children being slaughtered without mercy went against every moral fibre in his body. In the event, however, the boat developed engine trouble and was forced to return to the base. Here he would be transferred to another boat due to go on patrol in the North Atlantic.

Although he knew that he was wasting his breath he turned to the German Naval officer standing beside him and said, "I really should be travelling with the arms shipment. Those rifles are my responsibility and I would much prefer to remain with them."

Captain Heydal who was, for the second time, waiting to see him off shook his head. "Impossible" was all he had to say.

Officially the German was there to represent Count Bethmann-Hollweg and Count Rudolph Nadonly, the members of the High Command with whom Casement had negotiated the arms shipment. But the Irishman suspected that Haydal was also under orders to make certain he and his companions finally left Germany for good. He also had an uneasy feeling that the reason the Germans had put forward for not allowing him to accompany the arms shipment were not entirely valid. The Russian rifles had been loaded aboard the German cargo vessel *Libau*, which had been disguised as a Norwegian fishing boat and renamed *Aud Norge*. The crew under the command of Captain Karl Spindler were all German sailors posing as Norwegian fishermen and had sailed from the Baltic port of Lubeck three days previously. The Germans argued that if the ship were to be stopped and boarded by the Royal Navy, and a well known Irish nationalist was found to be on board, they would not be able to keep up the pretence of being neutral Norwegians. In fact their fate would be sealed and they could be shot as spies. Casement did not agree, he felt that if the ship was boarded the arms would be found and under those circumstances no cover story would stand up. But there was nothing he could do about it and eventually the *Aud Norge* had sailed without him.

Casement was in fact becoming increasingly frustrated by the German attitude towards him and his mission. True, they had supplied the arms and had put considerable effort into fitting out the bogus fishing vessel as well as providing her volunteer crew, but he still suspected that they were following their own agenda and he was being used as a pawn in one of their many propaganda games. He was so concerned that he had asked an Irish-American friend, John McGory, to travel to Ireland via Denmark to warn the nationalist leaders of his fears. Had he known that the *Aud Norge* had been fitted with demolition charges and would be scuttled at the first sign of trouble his fears would have been confirmed. The Germans for their part, while they were willing to support a rising by Irish rebels as a way of hindering the British war effort, had no intention of being drawn into an Irish adventure themselves.

For now, Casement had no choice but to go along with the German arrangements and so he boarded the U-19.

News that the *Aud Norge* had sailed, and of Casements departure, would be radioed to the German embassy in Washington where the ambassador, Count Johann Heinrich von Bernsdorff, would pass it on the leader of *Clan na Gael*, John Devoy, for transmission back to Dublin.

Chapter 33

Michael was sitting in 'his office' watching the comings and goings in his new domain. It had not taken long for him to get to grips with what was involved in the post of the senior Ministry Police officer responsible for one of the factory's main storage facilities. He had not expected to find being in charge to be any less strenuous than being an ordinary policeman and this proved to be the case. In fact he found that he had more to do, much of it paperwork which was something totally new to him, but with the help of Inspector Brown and the cooperation of his colleagues he was soon coping well. As the work of completing the factory progressed and further production processes came into operation so the activity around the stores increased and with it the need for extra vigilance by the security staff. As a result of his increased responsibility, Michael found that he was much better informed not only about the factory processes, although much of the technical jargon was beyond his comprehension, but also about the progress being made towards full production. So he knew that the first batch of cordite would soon be produced and sent on its way to other munitions factories to be finally prepared for use at the battlefront. From what they read in their newspapers the whole country was by now aware that, with the war well into its second full year, the need for munitions had reached crisis point.

In spite of the extra workload, however, there were compensations for the new senior security man. One very welcome advantage was that, although he was on call twenty-four hours a day, he no longer had to work shifts. Even though he made a point of visiting the stores in the late evening, and went to work early in the morning, he was enjoying regular sleep and meals, and it served to bring about a marked improvement in his general health. The pains in his chest became less severe and visited him less often, and he found that he was not quite as prone to suffer from shortness of breath. McGregor, who now considered them to be of equal rank, remarked that he was looking 'braw'.

The only cloud on his horizon was the persistent worry that James might still be in danger because of what he had said at the dance. Things seemed to have quietened down and little more was coming to light about the suspected rebel plot. Daly and Mick had not been seen for some days and it was noticeable that he and Pete Casey had not been approached by Father Conlon after Mass the previous Sunday morning. But the uneasy feeling would not go away. He hoped and prayed that James had learned a sharp lesson at the St Patrick's dance and would be more careful in future about what he said and where he said it. But to make things more difficult, James was now working at the Mossband site at Longtown, almost nine miles away over the English border. Even with his greater freedom of movement it was impossible for Michael to watch out for any potential danger to his son over there, but he did have an ally in Pete Casey. Although still working on the new township site at Eastriggs, Pete promised to help look out for James when he was off shift. He consoled Michael with the thought that even if anything came of James' outburst at the dance, and this seemed to be increasingly unlikely, the danger of anything happening to him at work was extremely remote.

Pete, however, was now faced with a further complication involving Michael's son, which it was largely of his own making, and which he was reluctant to discuss with the lad's father. To say that James had a girlfriend would be an exaggeration but he was certainly seeing a lot of the young factory girl, Kate. Ever since the dance and the walk back to the hostel with the girl, James had pestered Pete to get him another meeting with Kate.

"Why don't you do what we used to do at home in County Cork?" said Pete.

"What was that?"

"Ask her for a date yourself, or is that too much of a job for a thick Kerryman?"

"Ah sure I don't like to, I'm not any good with women, I wouldn't know what to say to her."

"Tell her you're mad for her, tell her she's the sweetest

colleen you've ever laid your black Irish eyes on, tell her that if she won't walk up the aisle with you next Sunday morning to be married by Father Conlon you'll drown yourself in the Solway Firth. Tell her anything you like but for God's sake leave me alone."

But in the end Pete gave in, or more accurately, Sarah gave in for him. She arranged for the four of them to go to the cinema in Gretna. They sat and watched the flickering silent images on the screen and when they came out Pete said to Kate, "Sure didn't you get more conversation out of Rudolf Valentino to-night than you'll ever get out of your man here, but good luck to you anyway."

The ice, however, had at last been broken.

Below the new township at Gretna was a piece of land along the Solway shore which became rather grandly known as 'The Beach'. There actually was an area of sand uncovered twice daily by the receding tide and behind this was a jumble of rocks. Along the shoreline a gravel path had been laid with park benches evenly spaced every twenty or so yards for visitors to rest and admire the view across the Firth. Now in the early spring sunshine it was becoming a popular spot for off-shift factory workers to sit or to promenade along the path.

It was Saturday afternoon when James and Kate walked to the far end of the path and sat on the last bench. Due to their shift times it was the first opportunity they had to meet since going to the cinema. James had been forced to tell his father that he would not be accompanying him into Carlisle this week and had to confess that he was going out with Kate instead. Michael tried to act as if he was taking the matter seriously, but couldn't prevent himself from smiling. He had suspected that James would not be satisfied with just one dance with the girl from the hostel, and he had just received confirmation from Pete Casey. The news that his son was 'going' with a girl actually came as a relief to him and he agreed with Pete that even if the rebels were planning to harm James they would not make a move while he was with the girl. So he had given James his blessing, and assured him that he was well able to manage going to the post office by himself, but rather spoiled his son's relief by saying he couldn't wait to pass on the good news to his mother.

The waters of the Firth were beginning to recede exposing the wet sand. Seagulls and other wading birds were beginning to gather to feed on morsels washed up by the incoming tide. The couple sat in silence looking south across the water to where the Cumbrian Mountains were just visible against the backdrop of the light evening sky. James was deep in thought.

"A penny for them," said Kate.

"I was just thinking that if my brother Bill was here he could put a name to every one of those birds, and a lot of other birds and animals too."

"Didn't he want to come here then with you and your father?"

"Oh he wanted to come all right," said James, "but Da wouldn't let him. With Jack in the army in Mesopotamia someone had to stop at home to look after my mother and the young ones."

He had already told her about his home and family and a little about the village of Beaufort. She was a good listener and he found it was a comfort to talk to her about the people and things he was starting to miss now that the novelty of life at Gretna had begun to wear thin.

"Have you never thought about joining up yourself James?" asked Kate quietly.

"Sure of course I have," he replied. "I would have gone with Jack but my father wanted me to come here to help him make some money. He's afraid that he'll never be able to get a job as a coachman again because he says the days of the horse are over. So he wants us to put some money in the bank for my mother in case he's out of work when we go home after the war."

He explained how Beaufort House had been closed and his father laid off work due to the war.

"But I'll tell you Kate, I very nearly did join up in Carlisle a couple of months ago. I would have too but my Da was in poor health and I couldn't leave him. If I did that I'd never be able to face my mother again."

He told her about the girls he met in Carlisle who gave him the white feather. A cloud passed across Kate's face and all she said was, "Oh."

In the silence that followed, James worried that Kate might be thinking badly of him for not being in uniform. The mention of the feathers had obviously upset her so he changed the subject.

"Tell me this Kate, why did yourself and your sister come all the way up to Gretna to work? Sure there must be a lot of war factories around Bristol that are crying out for girls like you."

It was a few minutes before Kate answered. She laid a hand on his arm and said, "It's a sad story James, and I don't want to burden you with it. Besides it would spoil our afternoon out."

James considered this, something he had said had obviously brought back a memory she would rather remained hidden. So he spoke gently to her. "They have a saying at home that we all have a heavy cross to bear, but it gets a lot lighter if someone gives you a hand to carry it. I'd like to help you to carry your cross Kate."

Eventually Kate told him: Several months ago her sister, Rose, and some friends started to hand out white feathers to the local men who hadn't yet volunteered. They said it was their patriotic duty to shame young men into going to war, and to begin with they believed it, but as time went on it became more of a game to them. Then after a few months news started to come through from the front, and War Office telegrams began to appear informing families that a father, son or brother had been killed in action. One was a young man who lived just a few doors down the street and whom Rose had been 'walking out' with. Although the boy had a job that would have excused him military service, Rose had been adamant that if he loved her he would volunteer, she was ashamed, she argued, to be seen with someone out of uniform who would look so handsome in one. When the telegram came with news of his death, Rose blamed herself and, in their grief, the boy's family also held her responsible. The affair caused a rift between the two families who had been friends for years, and in the end Rose decided that the only thing to do was to leave home. She came to Gretna and, rather like James and his father, Kate had come with her.

"Oh, those horrid telegrams, why do they have to give people the news that way?" Kate burst into tears and clung to James, and in spite of the circumstances, for the first time in his life he experienced the pleasure of holding a girl in his arms.

The moment passed and Kate dried her eyes. "I'm sorry James I shouldn't burden you with my troubles."

"Ah sure 'tis no trouble at all Kate," he said lightly. Then he became more serious.: "I hope to God that one of them telegrams never comes to my mother about Jack. I don't know what she'd do without Da being there."

. . .

James and Kate were not the only ones thinking about the effect on families when news of a death on the battlefield reached home. Thousands of miles to the east on the banks of the Tigris Jack Quinlan and members of his gun crew had just returned to their posts after having been detailed to help with burying the dead from yet another fruitless attempt to relieve the besieged troops in Kut-al-Amara. One man had recently received a letter from home which included news that a very good friend had been killed in France. Jack and his fellow soldiers knew that news of casualties on the Western Front reached home quickly and telegrams were sent to families almost immediately to avoid people finding out from the casualty lists in the newspapers before being officially informed. But what of the men they had just helped to commit to the hard stony ground of Mesopotamia? How long would it be before their families received the terrible news?

The Tigris corps had moved to the left bank of the river and for several days the artillery had, as far as supplies of ammunition would allow, bombarded the Turkish positions around the battle scarred Hannah Define and Fallhiyeh. When the infantry were sent in on April 5th and 6th they were repelled with appalling losses. Next day the artillery was in action again and on the 8th yet another frontal assault by the infantry was ordered and again it failed. As usual the attacks were poorly coordinated. Troops who actually managed to fight their way into the enemy trenches were not properly supported and were soon driven out again by the Turks.

The net result was yet again thousands of casualties.

Eventually the telegrams would reach the families at home. Many of them would simply say 'missing in action presumed dead'. Hundreds of the men who fell in Mesopotamia have no known graves.

Chapter 34

As the *Aud Norge* battled its way through rough weather out into the North Sea, two figures were battling their way through wind and rain along the old Solway Viaduct.

"Christ Mick," said Liam Daly, "is this the only way you could think of for us to get away after the ructions at the factory? The Man said to find an escape route home, not to get blown into the bloody sea or get a train up our arses."

The fine spring weather had broken and been replaced by strong winds and rain. They had already made one attempt to walk along the viaduct from the Scottish side but had gone only a short way when a heavy goods train appeared out of the misty rain coming from England, and they had to scramble back the way they had come. The viaduct had been closed to passenger traffic and was now used exclusively by goods trains bringing raw materials to the Gretna factory. They would soon be making the return journey loaded with Gretna's finished product, cordite. Mick knew that he was taking a chance on meeting a train on the viaduct because he had not been able to find a timetable. There must obviously have been one to avoid hold-ups and accidents but it had not been published as it would have been for passenger trains. He noted the time and direction of the train and added it to the list he was compiling in a small notebook. As the train approached the viaduct it slowed to a crawl and gingerly made its way across the estuary. Even when travelling at a snail's pace the weight of the locomotive and heavily laden wagons caused the structure to vibrate alarmingly. It had been designed to cross the tidal estuary at the top of the firth at a time when trains were much lighter and slower, and by the outbreak of the First World War it had already been in use for some sixty years. The rails ran on an iron carriageway supported by pylons evenly spaced every twenty yards or so along its length and, from a distance, it resembled a structure assembled from matchsticks.

Once all of the wagons were actually on the viaduct, Mick rose up from where they were hiding in the bushes and looked along the track. "Sure it's wide enough for us to walk along either side of a train, the big danger is being shook off the thing because there is nothing to hold on to. But we can do it all right."

Daly was not convinced. On their first attempt the wind had caught his jarvey's cape and he could feel the Webley revolver banging against his thigh. "I hope you're right there Mick because I was nearly blown off by the wind."

"You'll have to take that cape off or you'll have the choice of being drowned by the rain or drowned when you hit the water down below there."

The train passed and they started out again along the track. They had not gone far when Daly saw the wisdom of Mick's words and shrugged out of the heavy cape. He stuck the revolver in his trouser belt and folded the cape over his shoulder. The structure was still vibrating slightly and it shuddered as the train picked up speed again on its way to Gretna. They crossed to the English side without further incident although by this time Daly was wet through and thinking he was right about there being an easier escape route.

"All right, so we can get across that bloody bridge, but what do we do then? If we walk all the way to Carlisle the peelers will be up off their fat backsides by the time we get there and they'll be waiting for us.

"You're right there Liam, you're not as big an eejit as I thought," said Mick. "So we'll have to leave this railway behind us as soon as we can." Much to Daly's surprise he produced a detailed map of the area from an inside pocket and began to study it. "Now we follow the rails for a while and, according to this, we come to a *boreen* that goes under the track."

"Where did you get that thing from?" asked Daly.

"Sure didn't I send Father Conlon to get it for me from the Town Hall in Carlisle, I told him to say he wanted it to find his way around his parish is case he had to visit the sick."

Daly was impressed. "Jesus Mick, aren't you the great one for planning things. What would we do without you? But tell me this; will Father Sean be coming with us on the day? To my way of thinking he'd only slow us down."

"He would too," said Mick. "We'll tell him he can come if he wants to, but I'd like to leave him behind and use him as a sort of decoy. We'll see what The Man thinks about it."

Daly thought about it for a minute then voiced his solution to the problem. "I'll tell you this, if either one of them two slows me down they won't make it all the way across that bridge, they'll be going for a swim if you see what I mean."

Mick said nothing, but he made a mental note to watch Daly very carefully and look out for his own skin if things went wrong.

They walked on for several hundred yards to where the track ran onto an embankment and a little further on they came to where the *boreen*, no more than a farm track, ran under the railway through a small tunnel. They scrambled down the slope and clambered over the fence at the bottom onto the muddy lane. Mick set off northward towards an area of woodland and Daly followed.

"Where will this take us?" Daly wanted to know.

"Longtown," said Mick.

"Longtown? Why would we be wanting to go anywhere near there for Christ's sake, I thought the idea was to get away from the bloody factory."

"You're right there Liam but sure isn't that the last place the Brits will be looking for us?"

Daly thought about it but was still not quite sure. "And what do we do then? Walk all the way to Liverpool for a boat, or are we supposed to swim home?"

By now they had reached the patch of woodland. Mick left Daly to keep a look out while he went to look around the wood. When he returned he grinned at Daly and said, "It couldn't be better, there's an old cowshed in there that hasn't been used for years." He held up his hand to prevent Daly interrupting and went on. "This is what we'll do; we'll lift a motor car in Carlisle or somewhere and hide it here. Then we'll wait until dark and drive to Stranrear for the boat to Larne. If the boys at home are doing the business the Port of Dublin will be closed and the only thing going in or out will be British warships, so we'll be coming down from Belfast instead."

"My life on you Mick," said Daly. "Sure I never doubted you for a minute."

. . .

Over the years spent living in the shadows he had developed a sixth sense. He couldn't say exactly where, he couldn't say exactly when and he couldn't say exactly by whom, but the last time he visited Gretna his instinct had told The Man from Dublin that he had been watched. He was, therefore extremely reluctant to go back there before the uprising, which was now imminent, especially as he was carrying the printed leaflets in his suitcase. So he decided to take a chance and arrange a last meeting with Mick and Daly in the Carlisle station buffet. Father Conlon had not been invited as The Man felt that two priests sitting in the buffet with a couple of navvies was likely to arouse comment. He raised an eyebrow when no objections were forthcoming but put it down to the fact that Conlon was still unhappy at the thought of his being disguised as a priest. Had he known that the real reason for there being no objection he might have treated the matter more seriously. The truth was that Conlon had decided that they would only tell him what they wanted him to know whether he went to the meeting or not.

The Man was not prepared to take unnecessary risks and he ordered Daly to remain outside and loiter around the station keeping his eyes open. This time there were objections, but Daly calmed down when The Man gave him the case full of leaflets and told him to guard it with his life. As Daly walked along the platform The Man was disturbed to see that one side of the jarvey's cape hung lower than the other under the weight of the revolver in the pocket.

When they were seated at the secluded table at the end of the long room, Mick passed The Man the newspaper he was carrying. The Man opened the paper and looked at the map fixed inside with the escape route marked in red.

He nodded with satisfaction. "That's good Mick, I think it will work, but there is one big problem. I see that Liam is still carrying the revolver around with him. I'm afraid that it was a mistake to let him have it at all."

"He won't let it out of his sight," said Mick, "and if I tried to take it off him he might turn it on me."

"So it's as bad as that is it? Is there any danger of him using it before we're ready?"

"He'll use it sometime there's nothing surer. I think we can hold him off until the ructions start, but as soon as the balloon goes up he'll start shooting, and I'd say he'll start with that old coachman. The thing is that Quinlan is now a factory policeman and if Liam kills a copper the whole place will be up in arms and we could all get caught. But I'll tell you this; I won't be taken alive, if I have to give my life for The Cause I will, but I'd rather die in Ireland."

"That makes two of us," said The Man who thought things over for a while. "Listen here Mick, if Liam starts shooting as soon as those leaflets are in circulation the coppers will have to concentrate on him and it will be easy for us to get clear, especially if they find this map on his body."

He was confident that Mick would go along with this and was not disappointed. "That's fine with me. If Liam keeps them busy enough we could just catch a boat train for Stranraer. But we'll have to keep him quiet until the time is right."

"Do you think he could be trusted to mind those leaflets for the next week or so?"

Mick considered this. "That's the funny part of it, I think he could. The truth is I think they'd be safer with him than they would be with Father Conlon."

"I agree," said The Man. "This is what we'll do..." He explained and left Mick in the buffet while he went to talk to Daly.

"Listen Liam," said The Man as they stood pretending to look at the train timetable. "It'll be your job to look after what's in that case. I don't like the idea of leaving them at the church with Sean Conlon, and Mick has to organise things at the factory as well as stealing a car. Don't let them out of your sight and don't go anywhere near Gretna. Keep your head down here in Carlisle. Do you understand how important it is to keep these things safe until we want to use them?"

"Sure of course I do," said Daly. "It's great to see that things are moving at long bloody last."

"Good," said The Man. "The rising is set for Easter Sunday. I'll be coming to Gretna early on Good Friday, so bring the case to me over there that morning. Until then it's your responsibility ok."

"Don't worry I'll be there. But what about causing a diversion at the factory?"

"We'll have plenty of time to talk about that on Good Friday," said The Man. "And keep this map with you as well, if Mick get's caught in the factory we don't want them to find this on him."

When Daly turned round to reassure him, The Man from Dublin had gone.

. . .

The 'Gretna Girls' who would be carrying out the final stages in the manufacture of cordite had completed their training and were ready to begin the dangerous paste mixing process. Although the factory itself had not as yet been completely finished, all of the essential equipment they would need had been installed and tested. In spite of the hazards involved in the process, Kate and her friends were proud to be engaged in such essential war work, and could hardly wait to start work in earnest. Most of them had family members or knew someone serving in the armed forces and even those who did not were eager to do their bit for 'Tommy'.

James had been deeply affected when Kate told him that she would be thinking of his brother in Mesopotamia while she was at work, and he knew his father would be equally pleased to hear this. In a way it was almost as if she would be praying for Jack.

Cordite paste was produced by mixing the nitro-cotton with nitroglycerine in large shallow lead-lined mixing bowls of about five feet in diameter. Solvents in the form of ethanol and ether were added. The mixing could not be done by machine, to do that would be much too risky, so it had to be carried out entirely by hand. The girls lived under the constant threat of explosion as well as the many other health hazards connected with handling dangerous chemicals.

Once it was mixed the paste was passed through leather sieves into clean rubber bags and transported on the special trains to a cordite press house. Here it was forced through dies to produce long strings of explosive material. It was from these strings, or cords, that the term 'cordite' was coined. The cords were cut into lengths and dried in stoves to evaporate the ether and other surplus chemicals. Batches of finished cordite were sent by rail to the Woolwich Arsenal for testing and from there to the shell filling factories. The filled shells were transported to the docks for shipment to the troops at the front.

Chapter 35

Wireless signals between Germany and her foreign embassies were intercepted by the Royal Navy and deciphered in Room 40 at the Admiralty. Commander Wilson, still a member of British Naval Intelligence in spite of his wartime posting at Gretna, knew about the Navy's decoding operations and understood the seriousness of the situation when The Man from Whitehall telephoned to pass on the latest reports from '40'. Recent intercepts indicated that the arms shipment had sailed from Lubeck. They did not know exactly which ship the arms were on but it would certainly be sailing under a neutral flag, and it was thought that the most likely place to land the arms would be some remote spot in the south-west of Ireland. The guns could obviously not be unloaded at a busy port and it was unlikely that the Germans would risk sending them through the busy shipping lanes of the English Channel or the Irish Sea. The political situation in the north of Ireland would make it difficult for the rebels to hide such a large number of weapons there, so that left the west coast, and the deserted bays and hills of the south-west would be ideal for the purpose. The Intelligence Service had also received reports of a submarine leaving the base at Wilhelmshaven, ostensibly on a routine patrol but with three mysterious passengers on board.

"There is nothing to suggest that the two events are connected," said The Man from Whitehall. "But I'd lay odds on one of those mysterious passengers being Casement himself."

"Does this mean that you expect a nationalist uprising in Ireland to be imminent?" asked Wilson.

"I'm afraid that we have to draw that conclusion Commander, and my guess would be that it will take place over the Easter weekend. A great many of our masters in government do not agree with my reading of the situation, they still believe that nothing is going to happen in Ireland until after the war, which in my view is being dangerously short sighted. They could of course be right but I'm not prepared to take any risks, so I want you to be on your toes up there."

"I suppose," said Wilson more in hope than expectation, "that you don't want the civilian authorities to pick up those rebels we already know about."

"No," said The Man from Whitehall. "If we do that and nothing happens over in the Emerald Isle we will be accused of aggravating the problem, so it is essential that we catch them in the act." Before Wilson could interrupt he went on. "But we do have to be properly prepared for all eventualities which means you will need some help."

Wilson took a deep breath before speaking. "The factory has just begun to produce cordite and, according to the technical people, there are dozens of places where an act of sabotage could be carried out. As we can't possibly cover every eventuality we will have to adopt a different approach and I've pressed the factory management to try and prioritise the most obvious danger areas for me. I'm getting to know my men here pretty well and I'm certain that several can be trusted to keep their mouths shut if I brief them fully on all aspects of the situation. My intention is to form a special group, which will be split into small teams and placed in the most vulnerable areas. If they know exactly what they are up against and have descriptions of the suspects we have already identified, it will make it easier for us to adequately cover the factory area. The civilian police would have difficulty finding their way around inside here and might prove to be more of a hindrance than a help. That, however, still leaves us with the problem of my men having no authority off Ministry property, and since the affray at the dance, Conlon and co. will know that."

"I'll leave you to do what you think best in the factory proper Commander but, you are right, the civilian police will have to be involved. You had better contact the senior man locally and bring him on board."

"I'm afraid it is not quite as simple as that," said Wilson. "The factory crosses the Scotland – England border and each country has its own separate laws and police forces. We could easily run into a difficulty with jurisdiction."

"Damn!" said The Man from Whitehall, "I should have thought of that. Look, you had better get on with what you need to do in the factory and I'll go and have a word at the Home Office. We need to have some liaison arrangement in place, not just for the present emergency but for the duration of the war. I'll give this priority and get back to you."

With that he rang off.

Wilson felt that he could now safely assume to have been given carte blanche to deal with all security matters within the confines of the factory and, glad to be acting on his own initiative, he set about planning his campaign. He drew up a list of the men he thought would be most suitable, most of them already in senior positions, and after some thought he added the name of the Women's Police Inspector. These would form what he called his special 'task force' to deal with emergencies. But before he contacted anyone else on his list he set about finding Alistair McGregor, and when the old sergeant came to his office he explained fully the latest position. He held nothing back as he had come to have complete trust in the old soldier.

"Now sergeant, I want you to concentrate your efforts on Gretna, paying particular attention to the railway station and Father Conlon's church, you can leave the factory to the rest of us. But please be careful not to arouse the slightest suspicion. For the reasons I have just outlined, and you are to keep those to yourself, we simply cannot afford to tip these people off. Do you think you can manage that?"

"I'm sure I can sir," said McGregor. "I'm getting well known around town now, in fact people are beginning to stop me for a wee blether. I often go to the Institute for a cup of tea and I can easily spend more time there."

"All right, sergeant I'll leave that up to you." He would have liked to tell McGregor about the existence of 'Patrick' and his associate but, as they were not under his direct control, he felt that this would be stretching his authority too far.

"But before you go sergeant there is one rather more delicate matter I should like to have your opinion on. I'm concerned about whether I should enroll your friend Quinlan in this new task force I am putting together."

He held up his hand as he could see that the sergeant was about to say something. "Oh I trust the chap completely, but this thing is liable to have repercussions beyond this factory and even beyond this country. If the Irish Nationalists are, as we suspect, planning some mischief here to coincide with a rebellion over there then I could be placing Quinlan in a very awkward position indeed. It does not matter whether the rebellion in Ireland is successful or not, there will certainly be recriminations afterwards, there always are. If the rebels were to find out that Quinlan had a direct hand in thwarting their plans here then it could be difficult if not dangerous for both him and his family when he goes home after the war. These people tend to have long memories."

"I see your point sir," said McGregor, "but I wouldn't worry about Michael. To tell you the truth I've talked to him about this myself. The way he sees it is that capturing these rebels as you call them sir is the best way to keep them from getting at his son after the lad opened his mouth at the dance about those German weapons. Nothing has happened yet but, in my opinion sir, they could be waiting for the balloon to go up before they do anything. To be honest sir I think he would rather be in the know than be left out of it."

"Well thank you for that sergeant," said a relieved Commander Wilson. "I will see that he is fully briefed and included in the task force."

Chapter 36

U-19 was a Mittel-U class boat built at Danzig. It had a displacement of 650 tons on the surface and 830 tons when submerged. Powered by a 1,700 horsepower diesel motor on the surface it could reach a top speed of 15.4 knots. Underwater, power was supplied by a battery-driven 1,200 horsepower electric motor which gave it a top speed of 9.5 knots. U-19 had a range of 7,000 miles on the surface. It could remain submerged for a distance of 80 miles at its maximum diving depth of 164 feet so the length of time it could spend under water before having to surface to recharge the batteries was approximately 8 hours. These were of course all theoretical figures which assumed operating in ideal conditions, which were rarely if ever found in either the North Sea or the North Atlantic. Armaments consisted of a 105mm deck mounted gun, and the boat carried six torpedoes fired from twin tubes, two in the bow and two in the stern.

The 35 man crew endured extremely cramped living and working conditions for long periods and so they resented having to provide space for Casement and his two companions, none of whom were fellow submariners or even sailors of any kind. The three Irishmen were obviously unwelcome intruders into this very private underwater world where extra bodies would mean a greater drain on their precious oxygen supply should they have to remain submerged for any length of time. The Captain, whose name Casement had not been given, was the only one on board who made an effort to be friendly towards the three uncomfortable and uneasy passengers. In the tiny curtained off cubicle which passed for the Captain's private quarters he explained to Casement, in excellent English, why he was not sorry to have him on board for at least part of the patrol. He had, for once in the war, been given clear orders – transport Casement and his companions to Ireland and land them safely on a deserted beach in County Kerry.

For the first time in the long history of naval warfare, submarines were being widely deployed as an offensive weapon. At the beginning of the war neither side had any clear ideas on how best to deploy them. For the most part the German Military High Command reacted to changing overall strategic situations and political necessities rather than develop clear operational or tactical procedures. Propaganda formed a major part of the German war effort and they were always conscious of world opinion regarding the use of U-boats. The life of a U-boat Captain was already difficult enough: dealing with the everyday running of these early boats with their mechanical limitations, changing weather and sea conditions and simply keeping themselves and their crews alive required a great deal of skill and effort. According to U-19's young Captain, constantly changing political thinking leading to vague and sometimes totally inappropriate orders, served to complicate their lives even further.

At the outbreak of war the Germans decided that U-boats would only be used against warships, and in this they met with some success. But as the stalemate of trench warfare set in on the Western Front, and it became obvious that there would be no early end to the war, German Military Command issued orders for both allied and neutral merchant vessels to be attacked in the waters surrounding the UK. At this stage U-boat attacks on merchantmen were carried out on the surface, crews were allowed to disembark and the ships sunk by gunfire. Then in May 1915 the U-20 sank *The Lusitania* with torpedoes, and a great many neutral American civilians lost their lives. In August the passenger liner *Arabic* was attacked and several more American non-combatants died. Bowing to American pressure all U-boat activity in the English Channel was suspended, and the boats were withdrawn from this area. Then in March 1916 the Germans loosened the restrictions and captains were given permission to resume attacks on British merchant ships in the Channel, providing they did not appear to be carrying passengers. Soon afterwards U-29 sank the liner *Sussex* and the orders were changed again. Captains were ordered not to sink without first giving the target a clear warning.

According to the Captain of the U-19 it was easy to issue

orders from the comfort of Naval Headquarters but extremely difficult to implement them in action. It was not always easy in foul weather to distinguish between friend and foe let alone determining a target's nationality and trying to ascertain whether it was carrying passengers. If a U-boat Captain dithered he could easily lose the chance of sinking an enemy ship, and if he returned from a patrol without a kill he would be at best criticised and at worst court-martialled.

Casement listened politely but was not impressed. He thought that the account of a U-boat Captain's lot he had just listened to had been carefully rehearsed. He had noticed the 'kill' symbols on the submarine's conning tower as he boarded, and watching the competent way the Captain handled his boat and the obvious rapport he had with his crew, Casement had no doubt that this young man would not 'dither' – he would go for the kill and worry about the consequences afterwards. Once again he had the uneasy feeling that he was being used as a pawn by the Germans. He wondered if, as a well known Irishman with many friends and contacts across the Atlantic, the Germans were hoping he would present a sympathetic account of the U-boat war to the Americans. If this was so they would be disappointed, Casement's basic moral objection to the concept of submarine warfare would never allow him to make an apology for it.

He asked the Captain what he thought about German involvement in the planned nationalist uprising in Ireland but it was obvious that the submariner knew nothing beyond his orders to land the three passengers secretly on a beach at Banna Strand. It disturbed Casement to find that his host also knew nothing about the arms shipment. As he understood the situation he was supposed to arrive in Ireland two days before the arms were landed and he had expected the submarine to have had some contact with the bogus trawler. It was obvious that the Germans were not coordinating the operation and he could only hope that his colleagues in Dublin had made proper arrangements to receive both himself and the arms shipment.

The anxiety coupled with the movement of the boat on the surface and the cramped conditions served to make Casement quite ill and he spent the remainder of the voyage in extreme discomfort.

. . .

Further radio intercepts by the Royal Navy confirming the existence of the German arms shipment were passed to the Under-Secretary for Ireland, Sir Matthew Nathan, but without revealing the source. He was, therefore, doubtful of the accuracy of the information and failed to act immediately with the result that the British authorities in Dublin Castle were not informed.

Not far from 'The Castle' the rebel leaders, Pearse and Connolly, had also received the news via *Clan-na-Gael* in America that the arms were on their way. The arrangements with the Germans were that Casement would come ashore on April 19th, Good Friday, and travel directly to Dublin. The arms would be landed two days later on Easter Sunday, and distributed to units across the country. The uprising would have already begun by then, but it was felt that at that point the authorities would be too occupied with trying to suppress it to have time to interfere with the landing. There was nothing in the signals from Washington to suggest the need for a change of plan.

They sent for the Man from Dublin who was briefed and ordered to return to Gretna.

Chapter 37

Gathered in the police station in Carlisle were The Man from Whitehall, Commander Wilson, 'Patrick' and the senior police officers from both the Gretna and Carlisle stations. Both of the policemen were officers with many years service and would have been retired by now had they not been retained because of the war. They had been delegated by their respective Chief Constables under orders from the Home Office with instructions to cooperate fully with the security services at the Gretna factory. The fact that they knew each other and had cooperated in the past was in the eyes of the Man from Whitehall a distinct advantage. He completed the introductions and briefed the policemen on the entire situation, stressing the importance of the Gretna factory to the war effort. He gave them descriptions of the suspected rebel saboteurs who had so far been identified and when he came to the priest who had visited Father Conlon he had information which was new to both Wilson and 'Patrick'.

"We have not been able to find a name for the man you described Commander, but we believe him to have been very active in recruiting members for the nationalist factions all over Ireland. This means that he is almost certainly not the Roman Catholic priest he appeared to be, so don't be drawn into thinking that he actually is a Man of God. The next time he visits Gretna, and I'm convinced that he will be back, he may be wearing a different disguise."

Wilson made a note to remind McGregor and the other members of his new 'task force' of this point.

The Man from Whitehall continued: "With less than a week to go until Easter we don't have much time to prepare, but prepare we must. It is essential that as soon as things begin to move everyone is kept informed, so some form of communication system must be set in place. I suggest that all of you report to Commander Wilson on a daily basis. In fact several times daily would not be overdoing things in my view. You may have nothing to report yourself but someone else may be on to something that you need to know about. Do our friends from the police have any objections to the operation being coordinated by Commander Wilson?"

Neither policeman raised any objection. The instructions they had been given by their respective Chief Constables had left them little choice in the matter.

The officer from Gretna said, "Would I be right in thinking that any crimes committed by the suspects are most likely to take place at night?"

"That depends," said The Man from Whitehall. "I would expect an uprising in Ireland to begin in the early morning and if they are planning for action here to take place simultaneously then that would seem to be the obvious time. But you are right inspector, we don't know for certain and we must be on our toes. Can you have your telephone manned twenty-four hours a day Commander?"

Wilson thought he could see a solution to a problem which was still giving him some concern. "I propose utilising a second telephone which will be manned by one of my people through the night and I will check in on a regular basis myself like everyone else. The man I have in mind is called Michael Quinlan and as he was the one who first brought all of this to light by recognising the suspect Daly, he should be ideal for the job."

"Good," said The Man from Whitehall. "And on the same subject can we assume that police assistance will be available overnight if required."

Both police inspectors nodded in agreement. Then one of them brought up a subject everybody had in mind:."I've got clearance from my Chief to issue firearms should I deem it to be necessary. If these suspects are who you believe them to be they will almost certainly be armed, so I do not intend to take any chances and at the first sign of trouble I will give the order for firearms to be issued."

His colleague nodded in agreement and The Man from Whitehall turned to Wilson. "What about you Commander?"

"We do have a small supply of handguns available. My men have not been specifically trained to use them, but there are several ex-soldiers and policemen among them who have had some experience. However, I must stress that the factory has just begun producing cordite and, paradoxically, guns don't really have any place in a munitions factory. There are a lot of innocent people, especially the factory girls, around who are already in considerable danger without being placed in the line of fire. It would only take a spark, or a stray bullet, or a flying chip to get into a vat containing nitroglycerine or onto a table loaded with cordite paste and the saboteur's work would be done for them. It really would be better if any shooting took place well away from the materials we are dealing with."

"Yes I see your point," said The Man from Whitehall. "I'm afraid that rather nips the idea of catching them in the act inside the factory in the bud."

The policeman from Carlisle spoke up: "If these people are arrested do they have to be handed over to the security services or will they be charged by us and taken to trial in the usual way?"

"They would eventually have to stand trial in the usual way, but under the wartime emergency powers they would first be handed over to us. And a lot would depend on how their colleagues in Ireland are dealt with once the rebellion has been crushed. Do you have something in mind Inspector?"

"Well," said the Inspector. "As I understand the situation we have to prevent these people doing something which would disrupt the operation of the munitions factory, while at the same time you want us to catch them red handed committing the crime of sabotage. We could simply arrest this man Daly and his chum and hold them for a short while, say in connection with the affray at the dance the other week, but even if we could prove anything against them they would probably get off with a fine. If on the other hand we hold them on suspicion of sabotage without any real evidence they will get off and we are in danger of handing the Irish nationalists a propaganda victory. An alternative is of course to arrange for Daly and this 'Mick' to simply disappear but we don't know how many others may be around or who they are. And we would be on dangerous ground if we were to interfere with the priest. On the other hand if we do nothing we are in danger of allowing them to commit an act of sabotage which in turn will also give them a propaganda tool. All of which of course assumes that a rebellion will begin in Ireland over the Easter weekend."

"That sums it up nicely," said The Man from Whitehall. He looked at the other policeman. "What about you Inspector? What's your reading of the situation?"

"I believe that we are dealing with some very devious people," said the inspector from the Gretna station. "I agree that the incident at the dance was deliberately staged, probably to cause trouble between the factory workers and the Irish navvies. Any trouble of this sort will happen outside the factory so the sooner this affair is settled the better I will feel. I intend to keep a close watch in and around Gretna, and be prepared to react immediately at the first sign of trouble. You say you already have a man looking out for the suspects in Gretna Commander."

"Yes," replied Wilson, "an old soldier, I'm using him because he is unlikely to arouse suspicion."

"I've seen him around," the inspector remarked. "I'll detail one of my chaps in plain clothes to watch the railway station. That way we should be able to note all comings and goings and if the priest moves he can be followed. If you let your man know they can work together."

"Good," said The Man from Whitehall. "I believe that is all we can hope to achieve for the moment, please set things in motion as soon as you get back. So unless anyone has anything else to say we'll leave it there for now."

"There's just one thing," the Carlisle policeman looked directly at 'Patrick'. "I'm sure that I've seen you around Carlisle with the navvies, but I'm not sure of what exactly your role is in all this." (Good point, thought Wilson.)

"'Patrick' works directly for me," said The Man from Whitehall. Turning to his agent he went on: "I don't want you to come out into the open unless you have to but it is essential that you work with these gentlemen. So get to know the other watchers and concentrate your efforts on Gretna, leave the factory to the

Commander. Your employers will not see much of you for a few days but I'm sure that you can come up with a plausible story if questioned."

He turned to the two policemen. "Should you need any assistance and I am not available you can assume that 'Patrick' has full authority to act for me."

As the meeting broke up, Wilson noted that The Man from Whitehall had not fully answered the policeman's question. Nor had he mentioned the fact that 'Patrick' had an accomplice.

. . .

In Mesopotamia the artillery of the Tigris Corps used what ammunition they could gather to bombard the Turkish trenches of the Sannaiyat line for two days on 20th and 21st of April. The infantry attacked on 22nd along a narrow strip of firm ground through the swamps. They took the first and second enemy trenches but suffered such heavy losses that only a few got through to the third line. A Turkish counter-attack was repulsed with great difficulty but a second attack proved to be too strong and the few remaining British troops holding the captured trenches were forced to withdraw. By mid-morning the remnants of the attacking force were back at their starting point.

On this occasion by mutual consent members of both the Red Cross and Red Crescent went out to tend to the wounded.

Jack Quinlan gazed at the empty ammunition boxes and realised that there could be no more attacks until fresh supplies arrived. There was barely enough left to put up a fight if the Turks mounted an attack.

Chapter 38

It was early morning on Holy Thursday April 20th. Michael was sitting in his cubicle in the hut at Dornock having just returned from eating breakfast with Alistair McGregor. He had been up all night manning the telephone as part of the special security arrangements. Alistair McGregor, who had completed his janitor's duties before breakfast, went off to resume his look-out in Gretna. Michael felt dog tired from a long night spent taking and passing messages, none of which contained any definite information. Things were very quiet on the Gretna front, ominously quiet according to Commander Wilson. Nothing had been seen of either Daly or Mick for several days and Father Conlon had not left his church or received any suspicious visitors. Although feeling some discomfort in his chest, Michael sat on his bed to reread his latest letter from Annie.

After assuring him that she and the younger children were well, the letter concentrated on her concern for her three eldest sons. She enclosed a letter from her soldier son in Mesopotamia and as he read it Michael was struck by the contrast between how Jack described the war to his mother and what he had written in the letter to himself and James. In his letter to his mother he went to great lengths to reassure her that he was stationed well away from the fighting and was not in any real danger. This was in stark contrast to the real situation he had described to his father and brother. Michael was glad that he and James had decided not to forward their letter to Annie, but he knew his wife well enough to be able to tell that she was not convinced by Jack's account. She mentioned that several telegrams had been delivered in the Killarney area bearing the terrible news of young men being killed in action. None had as yet come to Beaufort, but Michael knew she dreaded the thought of receiving one to say that Jack had fallen. The only way Michael could think of to ease her worry was to write and say that nearly all the soldiers being killed were engaged in the fighting on the Western Front and that there was very little fighting in Mesopotamia. But he feared that this would not settle her mind.

On a lighter note, he had to smile at her reaction to his news that James was 'courting'. She was full of questions about Kate: How old was she? Was she a local girl? Did she come from a good family? Did he think she was 'suitable'? She saved the inevitable Irish mother's question until the end; was she a good Catholic? Michael thought about telling her that the romance was somewhat stalled at the moment because of opposing shift patterns. With the factory now producing cordite as fast as it possibly could Kate was working long hours on shifts, which rarely coincided with James', although they still met whenever they could. But to tell Annie that would only cause her to worry about the possibility of James having his heart broken, so he would just write back and tell her that everything was fine with her second son.

Then there was the question of what to do about William. With the coming of spring he was hard at work on the farm where he was employed and in his spare time doing an excellent job of getting the cottage garden into shape. On top of that he had to look after the pony and drive her and the youngsters to Mass on Sundays and into Killarney on Saturdays. But what worried Annie was that he had still found time to take two fine spring salmon from the river Laune. Although they had eaten one, and William had sold the other to the Great Southern hotel in Killarney, Annie was uncomfortable with the thought of the salmon having been illegally caught. To make matters worse she did not know where her son had got the necessary fishing tackle from. He said he had borrowed it from a friend but she feared that he had taken it from the tackle room at Beaufort House. Michael guessed that this was true, but what struck him about the incident was how much the world, and the way he viewed it, had changed. Before the war it would have been unthinkable for the coachman's son to have helped himself to fishing tackle from the 'House', and even if he had escaped the attention of the gamekeeper, the pre-war Michael would never have stood for William poaching salmon. Now he was much more inclined to treat the matter leniently. He remembered what Jack had said in his letter and so he would write and suggest to Annie that she use some of the money she had saved from what he and James had sent home to buy some tackle of his own for William. To further alleviate her worries he would tell her that with the 'House' closed for the war he did not think that His Lordship would mind William taking a few salmon. While Annie would wonder at this change in her husband's attitude, she would accept his decision and at least one of her worries would be eased.

He put off replying to Annie, writing to her would give him something to do during the long hours waiting for the telephone to ring tonight, and Alistair would post it for him when he went into Gretna tomorrow. Then he remembered that tomorrow would be Good Friday and the post office might be closed, but he intended to go to Carlisle on Saturday if he could get away, and would post it himself. The Easter Weekend would mean little at Gretna this year, the requirement for cordite would override any thoughts of celebration either sacred or secular. But Michael determined that he would make an effort to visit the church occasionally and hoped that James might do the same. Had he been at home the whole family would have gone to confession for Easter, but this year it might have to wait until he could get into Carlisle. His conscious bothered him about this, but confessing to Father Conlon was something he would prefer not to do. While he had little regard for the man he still had great respect for the priest, but under the circumstances could not make a full and honest confession to him. He fretted for a while but in the end tiredness overcame him and he dropped into a fitful sleep.

. . .

While Michael Quinlan slept at Gretna, aboard the *Aud Norge* still flying the Norwegian flag, Captain Karl Spindler was wide awake. The Captain was becoming increasingly uneasy. He was nearing his destination and entering the sea area known to the British as the Western Approaches, and he feared that the sight of a Norwegian trawler in these waters would arouse suspicion. So far the voyage had been uneventful. They had seen a great many merchant ships and a few British warships but had largely been ignored. The one anxious moment occurred when the Royal Navy destroyer *HMS Bluebell* had approached, but it did not challenge them. Spindler's orders were to deliver the arms to the Irish rebels who would meet him on a deserted beach in Tralee Bay. Once the arms were unloaded he was to make his way home as best he could. At the first sign of trouble the crew were to don their German naval uniforms, hoist the German ensign and scuttle the ship. His orders did not contain specific dates or times and he assumed that the Irish would be ready to receive the weapons as soon as he arrived at the rendezvous. He had heard nothing from his superiors since leaving Lubeck so he assumed his orders remained unchanged. To Spindler it seemed that The Military Command were going to a great deal of trouble to deliver some outdated Russian rifles to a rebel faction in a small corner of the British Empire. He would follow his orders to the best of his ability, but the safety of his crew would come first. So he took a deep breath, doubled his lookouts, ordered the crew to have their naval uniforms close to hand, and turned in towards the coast of County Kerry.

Completely unknown to the Germans aboard the *Aud Norge,* just a few hours ahead of them was the U-19, with the by now quite ill Casement on board. The U-boat was preparing to submerge before entering Tralee Bay on the last leg of its voyage.

In Dublin the rather cumbersome communications system between Berlin and the Irish Republican Brotherhood, via Washington and *Clan-na-Gael*, had produced nothing to indicate any changes to the agreed timetable. Casement would arrive in County Kerry early tomorrow morning and be conducted directly to Dublin. Two days later the German arms would be unloaded and distributed to rebel units across the country.

Before setting out on his journey to Gretna, The Man from Dublin was briefed by Pearse and Connolly. He was given the good news that Eoin McNeill had been persuaded by the imminent arrival of the German arms shipment to alter his position and throw the full weight of his Irish Volunteers behind the uprising. Pearse then turned to the question of what they wanted The Man to do once the Proclamation of the Republic had been circulated among the Irish navvies at Gretna and he had made his escape. At first The Man protested about being given what he saw as a lesser role in the uprising. But having been reminded of the real purpose of the rebellion he realised that, in the context of the long-term fight for an Irish Republic, he had been presented with an extremely important opportunity.

Chapter 39

Because of the necessities of war the trains ran a normal service on April 21st 1916, Good Friday. In the Gretna area it was essential that the workers had transport to the great munitions factory where the production of cordite went on unabated over the Easter period, uninterrupted by celebrations either sacred or secular. The Man from Dublin had travelled overnight to Liverpool and arrived in Carlisle in time to catch an early workers train to Gretna. He still wore the dark suit and Roman collar of a priest knowing that he would stand out in the company of the workers going to the factory and would be remembered later when his mission there was finished and the hunt for him began. With luck the authorities would waste time looking for a clergyman while he made his escape wearing the military uniform he had brought with him. None of his associates knew the details of his escape plans, each had been given a different version. But clever as his ruse was it backfired, for as he got off the train he was spotted by the plain clothes policeman covering the station who had been told to expect a priest.

The policeman watched as The Man stopped and spoke to a navvy. Under the pretext of asking for directions he muttered to Mick, "How are things going here?"

"So far so good," was the reply, "I'm all set to do the business in the factory and Liam will be here any time now with the papers."

"How are Liam and Sean holding up?" asked The Man.

"Father Conlon spends most of his time on his knees praying for guidance, but I think he will be ok. Sure there's nothing he can do now but go along with us. But I saw Liam yesterday and I'd say he's getting primed for action. If we don't watch him he might blow up and do something stupid before we're ready. Settling things with that old coachman is about all he can think about.

Anyway he still thinks we're all going out together over the viaduct so that should hold him together for another couple of days and after that we'll be all right. But all the same we'll have to watch him."

"Is that so? Well I'll have to keep a close eye on him. They're all set at home for Sunday morning. When it's all over here catch the first train out that you can and I'll see you either here or in Stranraer. Then it's Dublin and the rebellion for us. Up The Republic." The Man made a show of thanking the navvy for his help and set off up the road.

The policeman followed until he noticed that the old soldier had also seen the man in the priest's clothing and was following him. They exchanged glances and the policeman went to report in.

Commander Wilson received the news and made sure that all those involved were informed and on their toes. He was, however, somewhat worried about Michael Quinlan. He could not help noticing that for some days the former coachman had shown distinct signs of being unwell. Whether he was suffering with some physical ailment or from anxiety brought on by the gravity of the current situation, or simply tiredness from working the night shift, he could not tell, but in any case he was loath to interrupt Michael's sleep. But he had to face the fact that Michael was the best suited of all the people at his disposal for what he wanted done. At some stage he might need someone to go inside the church and Michael was the obvious choice, so he would let him sleep for a few hours and then he would have him woken up.

Liam Daly paced impatiently up and down the platform at Carlisle as he waited for the Gretna train. After nearly a week cooped up in his lodgings, going out only for food, and forcing himself to stay away from his favourite pubs, he was nearing the point where it would not take much to drive him into an uncontrollable temper. Not being a reader and having nobody to talk to, he had played solitaire until he could no longer tolerate the game and threw the cards on the floor. After that he spent most of his time cleaning, unloading and reloading, and generally playing with the Webley revolver until he could hardly wait to use it in anger. He had tried to open the case he had been given the responsibility of guarding but found it locked and he cursed The Man from Dublin for not letting him have a key. He did not know where Mick was or what he was up to and this too helped to fuel his temper. Mick had paid him his only visit the previous day to reassure him that everything was going according to plan. He assured Daly that he had stolen and hidden a car for their escape back to Dublin to join in the rebellion, but the rebel's state of mind was such that he wondered if Mick had actually come to check up on him.

His train arrived and he boarded with the case. Being on the move again and the thought of going back to Gretna served to calm his nerves. As he left the train and made his way to the church he was easily spotted by the vigilant watchers, in spite of the mild April weather he still wore the heavy jarvey's cape.

Wilson rang Whitehall to report that the suspects had all arrived in Gretna. Three of them, Conlon, Daly and the mysterious priest were in the church. The man known as 'Mick' was at present on the loose but was somewhere in the area and would soon be located.

When Daly reached the church he went directly to the priest's private apartment and was warmly greeted by The Man from Dublin. "Good man yourself Liam." The Man slapped him on the back, "I see you've brought the goods with you. Did you have any bother?"

The rebel had by now regained some of his former composure. "Not a bit," he said. "But I saw that bloody old soldier hanging around out there in the street. He's always around and I'm beginning to have second thoughts about that old bugger."

The Man saw this as an opportunity of giving Daly something positive to think about. "I noticed him too. There might not be anything in it but to be on the safe side I think we should make sure and take him out of the game if you see what I mean. I'm sure that you can handle that for us after dark tonight, but make sure you do it quietly. No guns yet Liam, but after the rising starts you can do all the shooting you want."

"I'm your man," said Daly. "And where is himself, the parish priest today?"

"Sean is in the church getting ready for the Stations of the Cross this afternoon, but I think he's spending a lot of the time on his knees."

"I don't trust him one bit," said Daly, "he'd inform on us at the drop of a hat."

"You could be right there," said The Man. "But we need him until after Mass on Sunday morning, after that I couldn't care less what happens to him."

"Sure won't I make him a part of my diversion to give Mick a clear run, him and that high and mighty coachman."

The former jarvey sat and took off his cape. The Man looked on with some concern as Daly took the revolver from the pocket and almost lovingly caressed it. He was about to say something on the subject but let it pass.

. . .

Michael was roused by one of Wilson's men at midday and told to go to the Commander's office in civilian clothes. As he entered the office, Wilson was just finishing off a telephone conversation. Michael caught the last few words: "…so things are really beginning to heat up. Yes, under the circumstances I agree with what you advise regarding the priest."

The Commander replaced the receiver and looked up. "Ah Quinlan," he said, "thank you for coming so promptly. Please sit down. I'm sorry to have got you out of bed so early, but things are actually beginning to move."

He explained what had transpired during the morning. "Now, I should like to have someone take a look inside the church. I doubt if Daly and our friend posing as a priest will actually be in the church proper, but I must be sure of that. I certainly don't want either ourselves or the police barging into a House of God for no valid reason. Do you think you could find a good excuse to take a look inside?"

"Sure that's no bother at all Sir," said Michael. "I was going there anyway for the Stations of The Cross. We always have that at three o'clock on a Good Friday. I'll go over there early and hang around for a while after."

The promise of an early conclusion to the affair caused Michael to lose much of his inbred reluctance to being involved in something that might be construed as violating the sanctity of the church. He was still very much concerned for James' safety, and the news of Daly's arrival back in Gretna served to heighten his anxiety. So he was resolved to do whatever was necessary to see the threat to his son removed.

"Good," said Wilson. "But I must say that you don't look at all well, Quinlan. Are you sure you can manage."

"Oh I'm all right Sir. As soon as this is all over I'll be my old self again in no time at all."

"Very well," said Wilson. "But please be careful. I don't think that they would start anything inside the church proper and especially during a service, but at the first sign of anything being even slightly amiss I want you out of there, and not only for your own good. Any kind of trouble in the church could ruin everything. I will make sure that the police and our own people know you will be inside the church for the afternoon service and if the worst comes to the worst you can call on them for help."

"Yes Sir, I'll be careful all right. My son James will be there and I'll be making sure that nothing happens to him."

Chapter 40

Father Conlon came in from the church. He looked at Daly and the revolver with obvious distain and received an arrogant sneer in return. He said nothing but went into his kitchen and prepared some tea and cheese sandwiches for lunch. Being a Friday, and a Good Friday at that, he was not prepared to provide his 'guests' with meat no matter how many snide remarks it drew from Daly.

Following many hours spent in prayer, the priest had made up his mind that he wanted no more to do with The Man from Dublin and Daly. These men were nothing like the brave Irish patriots fighting to free Catholic Ireland he had imagined when he first decided to support the call for a republic rather than the concept of home rule, which seemed to be perpetually discussed but with never a single sign of progress. He firmly believed that people like Pearse, Connolly and Casement and many others were good men fighting for a just cause, and he could accept the fact that drastic measures were sometimes necessary. But he could no longer accept the disregard for human life, the deviousness, and the total disrespect for The Church exhibited by The Man from Dublin and his accomplices. The fact that this was the Holy Season of Easter did not seem to bother them in the least. He had resolved to wash his hands of them.

But he realised that he would have to wait until after the fast approaching Good Friday service. One look at Liam Daly and the way he was handling the revolver left him in no doubt that the slightest provocation would drive the man to use the weapon. The priest could not risk any trouble with the church full of innocent worshippers.

They ate in silence until The Man from Dublin said, "You're very quiet there Sean, is everything all right? You have nothing to do until after Mass on Sunday morning when we hand out the Proclamation and I say a few words about it. Until then just carry on as normal. I'll be here to look out for you, and if anyone asks tell them I'm a friend staying for the Easter."

"What about him?" asked the priest, pointing at Daly.

"Ah well, Liam will be around, he has a bit of business to do tonight but he'll be back tomorrow morning."

Daly pointed the revolver menacingly and said, "Don't be worrying about me Father. I'll do my job, you just make sure you do your bit."

Much to The Man's surprise and Daly's disappointment the priest failed to show the slightest sign of fear. He got up without a word and went back through the sacristy to the church. At the front of the building, he opened the main doors and looked out. The familiar figure of Michael Quinlan was walking up the street towards him and he felt a moments panic. The service was not due to begin for another half an hour and if Daly in his present mood were to spot Michael here on his own, his hatred for the coachman was more than likely to boil over and God alone knew what would happen. The priest felt he had to prevent Michael going anywhere near the church until it was full of worshippers and he would be relatively safe. He went out, closed the doors behind him, and walked down the street to meet Michael.

"Good day to you Michael," said the priest. "If you're here for the Stations of the Cross you're a bit early, we won't be ready for a short while yet."

Michael took out his watch. "You're right Father, sure it's only half two yet. It's this shift working, it makes a man lose track of time altogether. Anyway I'm here now so I might as well go in and say a few Hail Marys while I'm waiting."

"No don't do that Michael, I've locked up the church while I came out for a bit of air before the Stations. Take a walk with me for a short way, there's something I want to ask you, and I'm sure Our Lady won't mind a bit."

Much as he wanted to see inside the building, Michael felt he had no option but to agree, and the priest led him away from the church.

"What was it you wanted to know Father?"

"Well Michael," said the priest "It's like this, you work for that man Wilson up at the factory. I only met him the once after that terrible do at the dance. So tell me what sort of a man is he?"

"In what way do you mean Father?"

"Well I have a bit of a problem and I think he might be the man to help me out. Is he a reasonable kind of a fella who is ready to listen and keep it to himself if I tell him something in confidence, or is he one of those stiff military men who go by the book all the time?"

"No," said Michael. "He's not a bit like that. The Commander is a real gentleman and I'm sure he'll listen to anything you have to say to him Father."

Father Conlon sighed with apparent relief. "I'll take your word for it Michael and have a chat with him."

"Do you want me to fix it up for you Father, I'll be seeing him later on today when I go to work?"

"No, no thanks Michael," said the priest, "I have his telephone number. I'll give him a call."

They turned and walked back towards the church where a small crowd had gathered waiting for the doors to be opened. Michael spotted James and went over to talk to him while the priest hurried to open the church.

James was concerned by his father's haggard appearance. "Are you all right Da? You look a bit under the weather."

"I'm just a bit tired Jim," Michael assured him. "I'm giving a hand on the night shift this week and I'm not used to it. Where's Pete Casey? I thought he'd be here."

"I don't know," said James. "I haven't seen a lot of him all week. He comes in late at night and leaves early in the morning. I suppose he's busy working like the rest of us. Even the fella Pete calls 'St Patrick' is coming and going all the time these days."

Michael laughed. "Pete is busy with the lovely Sarah is what I think. And how's that young Kate? I have a letter here from your mother asking after her."

James was once again surprised by the changes the last few months had brought about in his father, but he still found himself blushing. "She'll be off work soon and she's coming over to meet me here after the Stations so you'll see her yourself."

Michael couldn't help smiling as they went in to join the congregation. Once they were inside the church, Alistair McGregor left the place from where he had been watching and moved up to the open church door to mingle with a few latecomers who, in their peculiar Irish way, preferred to listen to the service from the porch or just outside.

The Stations of the Cross were completed without incident and Michael noted how much more assured Father Conlon seemed to be than he had been of late. That, and what the priest had said about talking to Wilson, would be worth passing on to the Commander. The congregation began to file out of the church but Michael lingered and James, still concerned about his father's health, stayed with him. They were the last two left in the church when they were approached by Father Conlon.

"I'm sorry lads you can't stay here. I have to lock up now."

Before they could reply the clear sound of a telephone ringing could be heard through the open sacristy door. As a concerned looking Father Conlon turned to go and answer it they heard someone pick it up and speak. There was silence for a few minutes before an animated conversation could be heard. The by now extremely agitated priest ushered Michael and James towards the door and turned back up the aisle. He had gone only a few steps when there was an angry shout and Liam Daly burst into the church from the sacristy with his jarvey's cape flowing and brandishing his revolver.

Daly grabbed the priest by the throat. "It was you Conlon, you informed on him" he roared. "You're the only one around here who knew about him, so it must have been you for sure."

The priest stood his ground and looked directly in the gunman's face. "Take that gun out of my church Daly," he said firmly. "And who exactly is it that I am supposed to have informed on?"

Daly caught the movement at the back of the church as Michael and James collected their senses and started to leave the pew to make for the door. He pushed the priest aside and ran up the aisle to block their path, and turned his gun on them.

"So maybe it wasn't Conlon at all," he yelled. "It was you,

you bloody coachman turned copper. You informed on him. Well here is where I settle things with you for good."

Conlon regained his composure and got hold of Daly's arm. "Informed on who Liam? And for the last time take that gun away from here."

Daly shook him off. "Casement," he shouted. "Roger Casement, he landed at Banna Strand this morning and was taken by the Brits as soon as his feet touched Ireland. The only way they would know about him was if some informing bastard told them."

By now Daly was obviously beyond reason. He pointed the revolver at Michael who was still seated in the pew finding it difficult to breathe. "And I think it was you, and even if it wasn't it's all over for you here and now."

"It wasn't Da at all it was me Liam." James shouted from where he stood in the aisle. "I told them about Casement and the German guns."

Daly waved the revolver between Michael and James. Father Conlon got between the gun and James and in an effort to further confuse the gunman said, "That's right Liam. James told everyone the night of the St Patrick's dance. I knew all the time but I said nothing because I was afraid of what you might do. But you are not going to hurt anybody in my church. You'll have to kill me first."

Daly said nothing. He hit Conlon on the side of the head with his gun and as the priest slumped to the floor he took deliberate aim at James.

Before he could squeeze the trigger the door crashed open and a figure hurtled through into the church. As he got between Daly and James the gun went off.

The shot echoed and re-echoed around the church and Alistair McGregor fell to the floor with a bullet in his chest.

Chapter 41

The Man from Dublin was angry, very angry. He was angry at the news that Casement had been captured; he was angry about the little amount of detail he had been given over the telephone regarding the circumstances of the capture; he was extremely angry with Daly for his reaction to the news and he was angry with himself for having told Daly the news in the first place. He should have known better, he should have paid more attention to Daly's unbalanced mood and realised that hearing about a setback to the plans for an uprising would be just the thing to send him over the edge. Even after years of conditioning himself to maintain his self-control it required a supreme effort of will by The Man to marshal his thoughts and examine the situation calmly and logically. But once he had regained his composure he was able to think it through quickly and clearly.

On the telephone he had been assured by Pearse that the uprising would still take place. But Casement's capture, which might well lead to the loss of the German arms, would necessitate some adjustments to the timetable. Pearse had left it up to him to decide on the best course of action to take at Gretna, but the nationalist leader had been adamant that the new mission he had been entrusted with at their last meeting was to take precedence over everything else. In view of this The Man decided he had to get away from Gretna as soon as he could. He quickly ripped off his Roman collar, jacket and trousers. It took less than a minute to take the army uniform from his case, pull on the trousers, button the tunic up to his throat and put on the cap. He put the priest's clothes back in the case and took out his own revolver, smaller than the one he had given Daly but no less deadly. He opened the other case and tipped the Proclamation leaflets out to make a pile on Father Conlon's living room floor. These could not be left here at any cost, if the authorities discovered them they would be alerted to the imminence of the uprising. He struck a match and set fire to the bottom of the pile. A fire would not only destroy the evidence but also create a diversion. A crowd was gathering outside the church where several of the congregation had lingered to chat after the service and were now wondering what was going on inside. He was about to go around the side and mingle with them when the sound of the shot from the church stopped him in his tracks. He would have to do something about Daly. He turned and ran into the church intent on shooting the jarvey, and Conlon too if he happened to be there.

As he entered he took in the scene at a glance: The body on the floor, James helping his father out of the pew and Conlon, with blood on his face, grappling with Daly in the aisle. The priest was shouting as he struggled for the revolver.

"I will not allow you to kill anyone else Daly."

None of the crowd outside had as yet dared to step inside the church but in the distance the sound of a police whistle could be heard. The Man from Dublin was about to shoot Daly and Conlon when he realised that he could turn the situation to his advantage.

He pulled the bleeding and weakened priest off Daly and threw him to the floor. "Come on Liam" he shouted urgently, "we have to get away from here."

Daly looked at him. He was confused by the army uniform but recognised the wearer. "I'm going nowhere until after I settle up with this pair."

"No Liam," shouted The Man. "We'll take them with us as hostages, nobody can lay a hand on us while we have them alive. We'll take them over the viaduct to where Mick left the car. You can do what you like with them then."

He did not give Daly a chance to argue. Grabbing James, he stuck his gun in the lad's face and said, "Come on you help get the old man moving, the two of you are coming with us."

He pushed them towards the sacristy door. Daly was caught up in the mood of urgency and followed without question.

They exited the church into a cloud of smoke pouring out of the priest's quarters which hid them from the growing crowd. As they rounded the back of the building The Man suddenly stopped.

"Christ Liam," he said, "we've left Conlon alive to inform on us. You go on with these two, I'll go back and take care of him and catch you up. Go on Liam run!"

Daly, his mind now intent on escape, did as ordered. The Man turned back but instead of going into the church he dived into the smoke filled doorway of the priest's rooms. He ruffled his uniform, held the soldier's cap over his nose and staggered out again to where a uniformed policeman was holding back the crowd. The policeman caught him as he faked a collapse.

"I... I came to see the priest and saw the smoke." He coughed and cleared his throat. "I thought that he might be inside but I couldn't get all the way in. The whole place is on fire."

"You're lucky to get out alive," said the policeman. He turned to the crowd, "I can't leave here but can someone take this brave chap down to the Institute and get him a cup of tea?"

"It's all right," said The Man. "I can manage to get there under my own steam. I could do with that cup of tea and maybe something stronger if they have it." As if suddenly remembering something he added: "By the way I saw three men going around the back and I'm sure one of them had a gun."

"Bloody hell! I'll have to pass that on." The policeman blew his whistle to summon help. "All right you go to the Institute but wait for us there. The inspector will want a statement from you. What's your name by the way?"

"Smith, Private John Smith of the Royal Irish. I'll wait for you at the Institute."

The Man from Dublin did not go to the Institute. He took a circular route to the railway station, caught the first train out which, by good fortune happened to be going to Carlisle. He had a perfunctory wash and brush up in the gentlemen's toilet and a cup of tea and a sandwich in the buffet. Within less than an hour after leaving Gretna he was aboard the boat train to Liverpool. Before arrival at the port he changed back into his clerical garb and by the next morning he was back in Dublin.

· · ·

"Hurry up you lazy old bastard." Daly gave Michael a kick on the behind as he struggled along the railway line helped by James. "Tell him to move his arse or I'll shoot him here. I only need the one hostage."

They were stumbling along the railway towards the Old Solway Viaduct as fast as Michael's breathless condition would allow. So far they had not seen any sign of either pursuit or the Man from Dublin.

"I bet the daft bugger has been taken," said Daly. "Well I'm not hanging around waiting for the likes of him. If he doesn't hurry up he's on his own."

A late afternoon sea mist was rolling in off the Irish Sea and settled around the Solway Firth. As they were about to step onto the viaduct they had to jump aside as a goods train passed going towards Carlisle. They were roughly halfway across the bridge when Michael collapsed.

"For God's sake Liam," shouted James. "He can't go any farther. Why don't you just leave him here and take me. If you leave him alone I'll help you to get away."

Daly stopped, listened and peered into the mist. There was still no sign of pursuit.

"To hell with the pair of you," he shouted. "I don't need either one of you any more so I'll be on my way alone."

He pointed his gun at Michael. "Say your prayers coachman, this is where I settle up with you once and for all."

Michael closed his eyes and prayed. James cried out, "No Liam."

The shot rang out and the body tumbled over the side of the viaduct.

Chapter 42

Several hours before the incident at the church in Gretna, in the early hours of that Good Friday morning, the submerged U-19 nosed its way carefully into Tralee bay. The Captain took his time inspecting his surroundings, both land and sea, through his periscope before bringing his boat to the surface. He climbed to the unlit conning tower and carried out a second thorough 360 degree search through his powerful binoculars. Satisfied that there was no immediate danger he went below and left the conning tower to his first lieutenant and the lookouts.

Roger Casement was by now quite ill. He had not eaten for days and the combination of seasickness, claustrophobia and anxiety had left him in a state of total weakness. With his companions, Bailey and Monteith, he sat white-faced in the submarine's tiny wardroom. The Captain reported that they had arrived off Banna Strand, and while there was no sign of the Royal Navy or indeed any other shipping, he had not detected any activity ashore. And he had certainly not seen the signal light he had been told to expect.

They discussed the situation for a few minutes and the Irishmen decided that as it was still very early and the local volunteers who were to meet them would be on the scene before long. The U-boat captain did not agree, he wanted to put the trio ashore immediately and be on his way. He was not prepared to put his boat and his crew at risk sitting on the surface in enemy waters for a second longer than he had to. Monteith and Bailey argued that they would need some form of transport for Casement who was obviously unfit to travel. Under normal circumstances the captain would have simply dumped his three unwanted passengers on the beach and left the scene with all possible speed. But he had to consider the orders he had been given to try and convince Casement to adopt a more sympathetic view of submarine warfare.

Although he suspected that he had failed in his attempt to accomplish that particular aim, he realised that abandoning the Irishman would certainly put an end to whatever chance of success remained. So he accepted a compromise.

Monteith and Bailey were put ashore and went to search for the local sympathisers and seek their help. As soon as they made contact they would signal the submarine. When nothing was heard from them by the time the eastern sky began to lighten the German Captain had no choice. He launched the dingy for the second time and two of his sailors rowed Casement ashore. As soon as his men returned he submerged and left to get on with what he saw as the real war.

On his own, Casement managed to make his way to an ancient stone ring near Ardfert called McKenna's Fort. He had only been there for a couple of hours before he was discovered and arrested by members of the Royal Irish Constabulary.

The authorities made no attempt to suppress news of the arrest. On the contrary, they sought to publicise it and the news had reached Dublin by midday. Pearse and Connolly conferred and decided to arrange a meeting with as many members of the Military Council as could be contacted quickly. It was while they waited for the members to assemble that Pearse telephoned his agent at Gretna.

Much of the hastily arranged meeting was taken up in a heated discussion about exactly what had happened to Casement. What seemed obvious was that the authorities knew in advance when and where he would land, which could only mean that someone had informed on him. Various theories were put forward as to who the traitor might be. Virtually every individual and organisation involved in the rising was blamed.

Pearse sat in silence. He was conscious of how few people, including most of those present, knew the exact details of Casement's return to Ireland. He agreed that the authorities must have been pre-warned but at this stage a witch hunt for informers would result in attention being diverted from the main issue, the rising, and he was determined to avoid that.

In his opinion there were two other possible sources the

authorities could have gleaned the information from. Firstly, the Germans who he had come to realise considered their involvement in Irish affairs as being of minor importance, and as such their security measures attached to the enterprise were probably not as stringent they might have been. Secondly, and in Pearse's opinion the more likely cause, was the cumbersome communication system requiring messages to be relayed back and forth across the Atlantic. He did not of course know of the existence of Room 40 but he realised that British Naval Intelligence must be putting a great deal of effort into intercepting and interpreting all German wireless traffic. And they would also be interested in transmissions from America destined for recipients other than their own administrative offices in Dublin.

If his theory was correct, he told his colleagues, and the British had picked up information about Casement from wireless transmissions, it was very likely that they also knew about the arms shipment. Both Pearse and Connolly were confident that, as the arms were not due to arrive until early on Sunday morning, there was time to divert them to a different location. The rebel leaders agreed and orders were immediately issued to revise the plans for receiving and unloading the *Aud Norge*. Several delegates raised the possibility of mounting a rescue attempt as Casement was being taken to Dublin Castle, but before any definite plans could be made, news reached them that the British authorities had sent their prisoner directly to London.

The Nationalist leaders at this meeting were to a man deeply committed to The Cause and, in spite of the setback, unanimously agreed that the uprising should go ahead as planned. A meeting of the full Military Council would be held and the proclamation announcing the establishment of the Irish Republic would be issued from the steps of the General Post Office on Easter Sunday morning immediately before the action began.

Had they known the situation regarding the *Aud Norge* at that precise moment, they may not have exhibited such confidence.

The bogus Norwegian trawler with her cargo of captured Russian rifles was already off the entrance to Tralee Bay. Captain Spindler had dropped anchor among the Magharee Islands off

Rough Point to wait for nightfall before entering the bay and being contacted by the rebels.

But at 6.20 pm, just as he was preparing to weigh anchor, the *Aud Norge* was apprehended by *HMS Bluebell* and ordered to proceed under escort to Queenstown in Cork Harbour.

Chapter 43

"Da, Da it's all right."

Michael could hear James' urgent voice as if in the distance. He opened his eyes, blinked and turned round to where James was staring in puzzled amazement. It took him several seconds to register the fact that the man standing in the mist holding the still smoking revolver was Pete Casey.

"Where's Liam Daly?" was all Michael could manage to say.

"Pete shot him Da," said the incredulous James, "and he fell off the side into the water."

"He's not in the water yet." Pete stuck the gun in his belt and went past them to where the collar of the jarvey's cape could be seen snagged on a protruding iron bolthead and was swaying gently with Daly's body still attached. He bent to loosen the cape and James, thinking that he meant to drag the jarvey back onto the viaduct, went to lend a hand. Before James could reach him Pete had un-snagged the cape and coldly and deliberately let the body drop down into the fast-flowing outgoing tide. There was a splash and as they looked down into the murk the body could just be made out face down with the cape spread out over it rushing out to sea like a dark stain on the water.

"Jesus Pete, I thought you were going to pull him up. Maybe he wasn't killed dead," said James.

"He's dead now all right," said Pete. "It's better all around this way Jim. We'll all be better off if he just disappears, no one will be asking any questions."

James automatically crossed himself. He was about to ask what was really going on when Pete looked round in alarm. "Mind out there Michael or you'll fall in after him."

Michael was getting groggily to his feet and swaying dangerously close to the edge. James caught and steadied him while Pete took a small flask from his pocket and held it to

Michael's lips. "Take a swig out of this Michael," he said, "it'll bring the roses back to your cheeks."

Michael coughed as the unaccustomed heat of the brandy burned his throat, but it seemed to revive him.

"Come on," said Pete, "the sooner we get off this bloody viaduct the better. If the fog gets any worse we won't see the edge and there's a chance of getting knocked off by a train."

The mist thinned out as they left the viaduct and moved away from the Firth. As they approached Gretna supporting Michael between them James could not contain himself any longer. "How did you come to be on the viaduct Pete, and where did you get the gun from?"

"All in good time Jim," said Pete. "Sure I'll tell you the whole story later on. But first things first lads, you have to tell me what happened in the church back there."

Although slowly recovering, Michael was still out of breath so James relayed to Pete everything that had happened. He stopped when he reached the point where Alistair McGregor had been shot and looked at his father.

"He saved our lives Da," he said quietly. "Alistair saved our lives."

"He did too Jim," said Michael, "and so did Pete here God bless him. But I have to go and see how Alistair is. Sure I don't know whether he's alive or dead."

"Leave that to me Michael," said Pete. "Jim you take your father over to 'Our Lady's'. Mrs McBain was married to a doctor and she'll know what to do for him. Wait for me there until I find out how the land lies. And for God's sake keep your mouths shut the pair of you. There are people running around here with guns thinking you're informers. You've had two close calls today and if the wrong people find you it could be a case of third time lucky."

"He's right there Jim," said Michael. "We'll say nothing to anyone until we hear from you Pete. And you'll be sure to let me know about Alistair."

"I will Michael," said Pete. "Before I go Jim is there anything else you can tell me about the church?"

"There is just the one thing," said James. "The fella that was dressed as a soldier, I saw him before. He was the one who came down from Dublin to talk about a rising to drive the British out of Ireland. In Devlin's kitchen back in Beaufort it was, where I heard about Roger Casement and the German guns. Liam Daly was there too."

"All right," said Pete. "Now go on and take your father over to the lovely Mrs McBain." With that he was gone.

James helped his father up the path and rang the bell. Mrs McBain came to the door, took one look at Michael and ushered them into her front parlour.

"My, but you don't look at all well, what ever happened to you Mr Quinlan?" she said as she directed Michael to a chair by the fire.

"He was feeling bad on the way home from the church," said James. "Pete Casey thought it would be a good idea to bring him here for a bit of a rest. I hope you don't mind Mrs McBain, Pete will be here in a while and then we'll take Da back to Durnock."

"Take him back to those wooden huts? You'll do no such thing young man, at least not until he is looking and feeling better than he does now." She called the maid to make some tea and bring some scones. Once Michael had drunk some tea and eaten a scone he began to feel better.

"I'm sorry to trouble you Mrs McBain," he said. "I don't know what came over me, but sure I'll be all right before long."

"Oh don't worry about that, it's no trouble at all," she assured him. "You just rest here for a wee while and we'll see how you get on. Now I have to go and see about dinner for my guests, you will join us of course Mr Quinlan if you feel up to it."

Michael began to protest, but Mrs McBain was adamant. James was unsure if he was invited to eat with the guests or in the kitchen with the navvies as he usually did.

When she left Michael said, "I hate to be causing this woman so much trouble and not being able to tell her the whole story Jim."

"We'll have to wait until Pete comes back before we can do anything at all Da," said James. "God knows what he was doing on the viaduct or where he got a hold of that gun. But we'd be dead if it wasn't for him."

"We would too Jim," said Michael. "I think there's a lot more to Pete Casey than meets the eye. But the first thing we should do is say a prayer of thanks for him being there."

"Yes and one for Alistair McGregor too," said James.

. . .

Father Conlon, suffering from delayed concussion caused by the blow to his head from Daly's pistol, had been taken to hospital in Carlisle where he was in a private room under police guard. As he was being initially treated in the church he was heard desperately but incoherently trying to say something: "Mick" … "the factory" … "water in nitroglycering"' were the only words the police could decipher, but when Commander Wilson was told he quickly realised their significance. He immediately arranged a thorough search of the factory by all the forces at his disposal, with a warning to be careful if Mick was spotted as he was almost certainly armed.

Having done all he could at the factory, Wilson had returned and was now in what remained of the priest's living quarters, together with 'Patrick' and the Gretna police inspector, sifting through the ashes.

'Patrick' kicked some ash aside and bent down to pick something up. "Well now will you look at what we have here." He held all that remained of a sheet of paper, it had been completely destroyed by the fire except for the top couple of inches. The words on the charred paper were just about legible:

POBLACHT NA H EIREANN

THE PROVISIONAL GOVERNMENT
OF THE
IRISH REPUBLIC
TO THE PEOPLE OF IRELAND.

"Good Lord," said Wilson. "What on earth would something like that be doing here?"

"I don't know," said 'Patrick', "but it looks as if there were quite a number of them. I'd say that this was why the fire was started – to destroy all trace of them. I expect Father Conlon should be able to tell us if and when he comes round, but for now we had better report this to London and let them sort it out."

"I'll get straight on to Whitehall," said Wilson. "He'll know the right people to contact."

"Use the phone in the station Commander," said the policeman, "it's closer than your office."

Wilson spoke to The Man from Whitehall for several minutes then handed the telephone to 'Patrick'. When they had rung off they approached the police inspector. "He will pass the information to the right people but in the meantime he wants all this kept very quiet," said Wilson.

The inspector nodded. He had seen enough of The Man from Whitehall's methods to have expected this, but he was not quite as prepared for what 'Patrick' had to say: "As far as the priest, Father Conlon, is concerned there should be no immediate legal action taken against him. The powers that be are concerned that if a rebellion in Ireland is imminent arresting him would only inflame the situation here. For the present, at least until we have a clearer picture of what is happening in Ireland, we are to treat him as an innocent victim rather than one of the perpetrators and let him carry on as normal, assuming of course that he recovers. This will be cleared with your Chief Constable so you won't have to take responsibility inspector."

The real reason, the policeman suspected, was that they were hoping that the priest would be contacted by any other rebels there happened to be in Gretna.

As they left the police station Wilson said, "I'll have to get back to see how things are at the factory. But I should like to call in on Quinlan on the way, to see how he is and to make sure he understands about the priest. Under the circumstances do you want to come with me?"

"I think I will," said 'Patrick'

Mrs McBain came to the door. "Good evening madam," said Wilson. "I am Commander Wilson, head of security at HM Factory." He turned to 'Patrick'. "And this is…"

"Och I know that rogue well enough," she said, "that's Peter Casey, one of my lodgers."

Wilson gave 'Patrick' an old-fashioned look. "Quite so madam, Peter Casey," he said. "I believe that one of my men, Michael Quinlan, was brought here earlier feeling unwell, I wonder if we might look in on him for a moment?"

"Oh do come in please," said the lady of the house, "poor Mr.Quinlan is not at all well, although now that he has rested and had something to eat he is feeling better."

Michael stood up as they entered the parlour, but Wilson motioned him to sit down. "I'm terribly sorry that you and your son have been subjected to all this Quinlan," he said. "How are you feeling now?"

"A lot better thanks to Mrs McBain here," said Michael. "Give me a few minutes and I'll be ready to come over to the factory with you and make my report."

But Mrs McBain wasn't having any of that. She examined Michael's face and listened to his breathing. "I wasn't married to a doctor for thirty years without picking up some medical knowledge," she said. "I don't think he should go anywhere to-night, least of all to one of those draughty huts. He must stay here, I have a spare guest room and he can use that. Then we'll see how he is in the morning and decide whether or not he should see a doctor."

Before Michael could protest James spoke up. "That would be grand thanks Mrs McBain. It would be a load off my mind if he didn't have to do any more running around today."

"Yes," said Wilson, "it's extremely kind of you Mrs McBain. I'll see that you are recompensed for the room."

"We can talk about that later Commander. I suppose there are some medical facilities up at the factory?"

"Yes madam. There is always a nurse on duty and a doctor on call from Carlisle hospital."

"Well I suggest you take him there in the morning if necessary. Excuse me now gentlemen while I go and see about the room."

When they were alone, Wilson spoke to both Quinlans: "From what Pat… I mean Peter here tells me you two have had some very narrow escapes. But I would strongly suggest that you say nothing about what has happened for the time being. The man Mick and this fellow dressed as a soldier are still at large and extremely dangerous, and we don't know how many others may be on the lookout for you. So please be careful, there have been enough deaths for one day."

"Have you any news about Alistair McGregor?" Michael asked quietly.

Wilson hesitated, but Pete answered. "I'm sorry Michael, he's gone," he said. "He was dead before he hit the floor."

Michael crossed himself while James fought hard to hold back a tear. "May the Lord have mercy on his soul," said Michael. "He saved Jim's life."

"Amen," said Pete. "It's small consolation I know but he died like a soldier – it's how he would have wanted to go."

There was silence until Wilson spoke. "They have taken his body to the county mortuary in Dumfries. Do you know if he had any family that we could contact? He died under my command and I should like to at least write to them."

"He had a son in The Royal Scots doing his basic training," said Michael. "His other son was killed in a train crash not far from here."

"Well that's something to go on," said Wilson. "I'll get the police on to tracing him. One other thing Quinlan – Michael – Father Conlon is in hospital in Carlisle with severe concussion. For the moment we are treating him as a victim of Daly's so when he comes out of hospital he will be carrying on as normal. He must not know that we are on to him, is that clear?"

"Yes sir," said Michael. James looked puzzled.

"Good," said Wilson. "Now is there anything else you need. If not I have to get back to the factory so I'll have to leave you in the safe hands of Mrs McBain and Peter here."

Pete saw him to the door. "Do you think there is any danger of Mick or any of his friends coming here tonight?" asked Wilson.

"If they do I'll be ready for them," came the reply.

The Commander had left when Mrs McBain returned with a bottle of malt whiskey and some glasses. "I thought we all deserved a wee dram," she said. "I don't suppose I'll ever know what's really going on here but *slainte* to you anyway."

The Irishmen recognised the Gaelic toast to good health, *slainte* they replied.

Pete and James helped Michael up to bed and then went up to their own sleeping quarters. They were alone in the loft. Being a Friday night the Clancy brothers were out on the town as usual. 'St Patrick' was out, presumably at work.

James was getting over the shock of almost being killed twice in one day and his curiosity was getting the better of him. "What's going on Pete? Is Da mixed up in something I don't know about? He seemed to be well in with that Commander Wilson. And what were you doing on the viaduct with a gun?"

"I'll have to leave your father to tell you his side of it himself Jim," said Pete. "But we're all getting over a hard day so I'm for my bed. I'll tell you everything in the morning."

There was a noise from below. Pete started and reached for his revolver and watched the trapdoor opening. Then he relaxed as 'St Patrick' came into the loft went to his corner, knelt and said his prayers, and went to bed without a word.

Downstairs, Michael also said his prayers. He prayed for the soul of his friend Alistair and his religious faith moved him to include one for Liam Daly. When he had finished he fell exhausted into the first comfortable bed he had slept in for months.

James couldn't sleep, especially when he noticed that Pete spent the night by the open trapdoor with his revolver at the ready.

Chapter 44

As Michael slept, and James lay awake watching Pete, both were as yet unaware that they owed their lives, in part at least, to Sarah and Kate.

Kate had left the Women's Hostel and was walking to the church to meet James when she ran into Sarah who, for reasons she did not explain, decided to accompany her. As they neared the church they saw the crowd gathered outside and their light-hearted chatter was interrupted by the shouting from within. At the sound of Daly's gun going off Kate froze but Sarah shook her into action.

"Quick Kate!" she yelled in the girl's ear. "Run down to the institute and fetch Pete. I know he is in there. Go on Kate, run!"

When she was sure that Kate had grasped what was required of her and had set off down the street, Sarah looked around and made a quick inspection of the local shops. Most were closed but the Post Office was open. Inside there was a small queue at the counter. She roughly pushed the waiting customers aside, waved her Ministry of Munitions Women's Police Service warrant card in the postmaster's face and demanded to use the telephone.

Outside again she almost collided with Pete Casey, "I've telephoned Commander Wilson," she said.

They ran to the church together. Pete looked at the crowd thronging around the main doors. "Come on round the back." He set off and Sarah followed. The clanging of a bell signalled the approach of the Fire Brigade.

Smoke was still pouring out of the priest's quarters as they ran round the back of the church. Pete spotted the Gretna police inspector talking to a uniformed constable and they went over. "What's happening Inspector?"

"All we know at the moment is that one man has been shot in the church and the priest has been injured. I'd lay odds that this fire has been started deliberately as a diversion. Apparently a soldier tried to look inside but failed to get in. He told the constable that he'd seen three men making off and that one of them had a gun. I'm organising a pursuit."

Pete thought for a moment. "No don't do that," he said. "I have an idea of who they might be. I think the man with the gun is Liam Daly and he's holding the other two as hostages. If we send a large party after them he's liable to turn his gun on them. It's best if I go after them alone."

"Do you think the men he's holding are Michael Quinlan and James, there is no sign of them here," said Sarah.

"I'm afraid I do," said Pete. "You stay here with the inspector until Commander Wilson arrives and I'll go after Daly. He's always talking about going over the viaduct and I'll bet that's where he's making for."

"All right," said the policeman. "But in the meantime I'm putting out a general call for them."

Sarah and the inspector went into the church. A uniformed sergeant was preventing a protesting navvy from entering. He turned and looked suspiciously at Sarah. "It's all right sergeant," said the inspector, "she's with the Ministry Police. Who was that and what was he doing in here?"

"I know him," said Sarah. "He's the one they call 'St Patrick', according to Pete he's spends a lot of time praying, he's probably harmless."

"Fine if you say so," said the inspector. "Now what's the story here sergeant?"

Commander Wilson came in just as the sergeant was making his report. "Well sir the old soldier is dead and the priest is in a bad way from a bang on the head. I've sent for an ambulance which should be here any minute. He keeps trying to tell us something but it doesn't make any sense. Something about the factory and someone called Mick, then he mentioned 'water' and 'nitro' something or other."

Sarah drew a sharp breath and Wilson turned quickly. "Good Lord they are planning to sabotage the factory. Come on Miss Birks, we have to get back there."

Outside they met a worried Kate. "What's going on Sarah?

Where's James, I was supposed to meet him here."

Sarah thought quickly: "There is an emergency at the factory Kate," she said. "James is all right, he's with Pete and they will be back later. In the meantime you can help, so come with us." She looked at Wilson who nodded.

Wilson organised the search while Sarah and Kate went around warning the Gretna Girls to be extra careful as there was a rumour of an acid leak.

Later that evening, Wilson was able to tell Sarah about the rescue on the viaduct. She went to find Kate and told her that James was looking after his father who had been taken ill, but that she would be able to see him tomorrow.

. . .

While all the action was taking place in and around Gretna, Mick had spent the day quietly in Carlisle. He had planned to remain in the city until the time came for him to implement his part in the uprising by causing disruption in the factory on Easter Sunday morning. But as the day wore on he was conscious of a growing feeling of unease.

He strongly suspected that The Man from Dublin was not being honest with him regarding his plans for leaving Gretna, but this did not really bother him. He had, after all been a party to deceiving Liam Daly about their escape so he wasn't complaining. Having been an active member of the Irish Republican Brotherhood since boyhood he well knew how things were done when working on highly secret missions. In any case he had made contingency plans of his own. What he was convinced of though was that The Man from Dublin would not leave him in the lurch, unless it was absolutely necessary in the context of the overall strategy being implemented by the Military Council in Dublin. He had worked with The Man before and he knew that he was, like himself, totally committed to The Cause. But he was worried about Daly. If anything went wrong there was no doubt that it would be because of him. It did not really matter to Mick if things went wrong in Gretna, his concern was for his own part in the operation, which he would carry out irrespective of whether other aspects of the plan succeeded or not. But he thought it best to make sure of his ground and he decided to go back to Gretna later that evening.

He waited until he knew the station would be crowded with navvies and factory workers coming off and going on shift, intending to mingle with them on the train. But as he stood on the platform he began picking up snippets of conversations between the workers who seemed to be discussing something that had happened at Gretna. He approached a couple of the Gretna Girls and asked what was going on. They told him that something had triggered off an emergency at the factory, they had been told to be extra careful because there was a danger of an acid leak and the factory police were carrying out an extensive search. On top of that there had been trouble at the Catholic church in Gretna, they did not know exactly what but they had heard that it involved shooting and a fire.

"I knew it," he thought to himself. "That bloody Daly couldn't wait." The details of what had happened at Gretna were of little consequence; the important point was that *something* had happened and he had to consider what effect it might have on his part of the operation.

He caught a train to Dornock and walked back to Eastriggs where hundreds of men were still building a complete new town. He wandered over to join a group of navvies taking a break.

"I hear there was a fire at the church in Gretna, and people got hurt, does anyone know if Father Conlon is ok?"

"The last I heard was that they took him to the hospital in Carlisle," said one. "He's better off than that old soldier who hangs around. I hear that he was killed. God rest him."

"How did it happen?" asked Mick.

"Pat here says he was shot, but sure you can't believe a word this eejit says."

"I'm telling you he was shot," came an indignant voice. "Some fella broke into the church and shot him. When Father Conlon tried to stop him he got a belt on the head. It was like the Western Front up there. The gunman set fire to the church and made a run for it, and the coppers are still after him."

They continued to argue but Mick had heard enough and slipped away. On the way back to Gretna he mulled over his position. It was obvious the game was up as far as the scheme to distribute leaflets in conjunction with the uprising at home was concerned. But there was no reason to think that the uprising would not go ahead as planned, and his best chance of playing a meaningful part might be by causing disruption here at Gretna. One snag concerned him; Father Conlon. Now that things had started to go wrong the priest was not to be trusted, someone had said or done something to cause the alert at the factory and Conlon was the only possibility. And if the authorities knew about an attempt to disrupt production at the factory they would know about him, and even now be searching for him. The longer he stayed in the area the slimmer would be his chances of success, so if he was to act at all he must act quickly.

Back in Carlisle mingling with the workers getting off the train he went to the left luggage office and retrieved the leather case he had left there. He went to the toilet and changed into the new smart suit, shirt, tie and shoes. He checked the revolver, replaced it and the navvy's clothes in the case and left the station acting like a prosperous businessman. He avoided the pubs and cafes frequented by the navvies and went to one of the city's most exclusive hotels. After a casual meal in the dining room he left and caught the last train back to Dornock. Nobody paid any attention to the well dressed traveller. Leaving the station he carefully inspected his surroundings, and satisfied that he was not being watched he slipped behind some darkened buildings, changed clothes once more and secreted his case.

By now it was past midnight. The factory was ablaze with light, but this did not deter him. He had made good use of the shadows cast by the lights on his previous nocturnal visits. Some of the builders were still working on the Eastriggs site. He picked up a scaffolding plank and carried it on his shoulder holding it with both hands so that most of his face was obscured and walked unchallenged into the factory proper. The alert was obviously over and there did not seem to be any obvious extra security measures in place.

Inside, he found one of the specially designed trolleys used for moving materials around the factory. He left the plank and pushed the trolley to the spot near No 2 Nitrator where he had hidden the container of spent acid. With the acid in the trolley he entered a building where nitroglycerine was being washed in pre-wash tanks, and stood by the tank nearest the door as if taking a breather. There were five men working in the house but they took little notice of the labourer pushing a trolley. Had things gone to plan he would now have waited until Daly began his diversion and then introduced the acid into several tanks of nitroglycerine. But there was no Daly and no diversion, and there was no chance of interfering with the water supply as planned.

He removed the stopper from the neck of the container, took a deep breath, heaved it into the nearest tank of nitro, and ran from the building. Outside he collided with a man approaching the building and knocked him to the ground winded.

There was a shout of alarm as one of the nitroglycerine workers witnessed what had happened. The men began to frantically add water to reduce the temperature, but it had already reached danger point and was still rising. The five men realised that they were not succeeding and abandoned the house just as the man outside, who happened to be their foreman, was getting to his feet. In spite of their warnings he went around and entered the building by the back door. Through the fumes he could see that there was still room in the tank. He stayed in the house and continued adding water until the temperature was reduced.

By now the alarm had been raised and everyone in the vicinity alerted to the danger. With everyone's attention directed to the building with fumes pouring out of it, Mick had no difficulty in slipping away to receive his bag and change into the business suit. He waited long enough to realise that the expected explosion was not going to happen, and disappointed, walked to Annan. From there he caught an early train to Dumfries, from where he caught the boat train for Stranraer. By Saturday evening he had reached Larne and was on his way to Dublin intent on taking part in the uprising on Sunday morning.

．　．　．

In the early hours of Easter Saturday morning, while Mick was making his escape, Captain Spindler and the crew of the *Aud Norge* were being taken prisoner. Spindler had chosen his spot well. As they approached the sunken reefs around Daunt's Rock he ordered his men to change into their uniforms and hoist the German naval ensign. When they were over the reef they took to the boats and the captain scuttled the ship. The consignment of arms sank to the bottom with it.

The Germans were picked up by their escort, *HMS Bluebell*, and held as prisoners of war.

Chapter 45

The Man from Whitehall was extremely busy when Commander Wilson called to report on the attempted sabotage. The arrest of Roger Casement, the capture and subsequent scuttling of the *Aud Norge* and the discovery of the Proclamation of the Irish Republic at Gretna left him little time to deal with matters at the factory.

The intelligence service at Dublin Castle had suspected for some time that a rising was being planned, but the leading representatives of the London Government in Ireland had persuaded themselves that there was no immediate cause for worry. Only the Lord Lieutenant of Ireland, Lord Wimborne, seemed to have realised the gravity of the situation and demanded that warrants be issued for the arrest of all the known nationalist leaders. But the Assistant Secretary, Sir Matthew Nathan, decided that there was no need for immediate action. One reason behind this fateful decision was that spies inside the Irish Volunteers had informed him that Eoin McNeill had changed his mind yet again because of the loss of the German weapons and had decided not to take part in the uprising. The problems were compounded by the fact of the Easter weekend. The senior government official in Dublin, Augustine Birrell, was in London and so took no part in the decision making in Ireland.

All of which left the security services in London, already severely stretched by the war, to deal with the escalating crisis. In spite of his volume of work, The Man from Whitehall considered what Wilson told him and expressed the opinion that the danger at HM Factory Gretna had now passed. He was convinced that an uprising was imminent and he rightly concluded that, with the failure of their plans at Gretna, the surviving rebels would have fled to Dublin to take part.

. . .

Michael was feeling much better after a good night's sleep when Commander Wilson called at Solway View on Easter Saturday morning. He was in the dining room eating breakfast with James and Pete Casey aka 'Patrick'. Both had been promoted from the kitchen for just this one occasion. Even Mrs McBain had expressed satisfaction with Michael's improved condition and had flatly turned down any suggestion of being paid for the room. The commander was offered a cup of tea which he gratefully accepted – he had been called out when Mick had caused the disturbance in the early hours and had not rested since.

In reply to the Commander's anxious enquiry about his health Michael answered: "Sure I'm fine again now sir. Give me an hour to go over to Dornock for the uniform and I'll be back to work in no time at all."

Physically Michael seemed fine but Wilson suspected that emotionally he must still be suffering from the ordeal of yesterday. He told Michael that with the death of Liam Daly and the fire at the church, the emergency was over for the time being and he could take the weekend off.

Pete Casey raised his eyebrows at the mention of the emergency being over but said nothing, he had begun to develop a high regard for Commander Wilson's judgement. But he raised them slightly higher when a message came from the factory asking James to report for work immediately irrespective of what shift he was on. There had been an 'accident' during the night which had damaged some equipment and, as James had helped during the installation, the engineers thought that it would save time on the repairs to have a labourer who already knew what was required.

James hesitated and looked at his father. "Go on Jim, sure I'll be fine and you'll be better off at work. It'll take your mind off of yesterday," said Michael.

Pete nodded. "He's right Jim. And I'll get a message to her so that she knows where you are." Michael grinned and it was Wilson's turn to raise his eyebrows.

When James had gone, Wilson explained what had happened yesterday in Ireland with the arrest of Casement and the sinking of the ship carrying the German guns. He went on to tell them about the sabotage attempt at the factory during the night. The rebel known as Mick had been recognised as the saboteur, he had not been apprehended and it was thought that he had fled back to Ireland. Wilson did not mention The Man from Whitehall in front of Michael, but Pete knew that the commander would have reported in and that his assessment of the situation had been accepted. Now in possession of all the available information, Pete, in his role as 'Patrick' agreed that the 'emergency' was indeed over for the time being at least.

He spoke to Michael. "I'd say that he's right. With Daly dead and Father Conlon in hospital there is nothing more for any of 'the boys' to do here."

He did not mention the discovery of the 'proclamation' leaflets which remained top secret, but went on: "With a rising set to take place any day now they will all have gone home to join it for sure. You can rest easy Michael, Jim will be safe enough while he stays around here, but I'll warn him against going too far afield for a while yet."

Michael breathed a sigh of relief and Pete left for the factory with Wilson. They went to discuss progress with Sarah who, in her capacity as a Ministry Women's Police Inspector, was helping with the investigation into the 'accident'.

James could not as yet manage to think clearly about the events of Good Friday. The death of Alistair McGregor had been more of a shock than the events on the viaduct where he had been too concerned about his father to take in everything that was happening. And not having slept very well while watching Pete keep guard all night had left him drained. He knew that he should be giving thanks for Alistair's sacrifice and for Pete's timely intervention, both of which events had certainly saved his life, but the overriding emotion he felt as he went about his work was relief that his father had survived and was looking better.

Michael stayed for a while and chatted with Mrs McBain. He thanked her again for her hospitality, mentioning lightly that she must have some Irish in her to be so welcoming. On the way back to Dornock he could still hear her warnings to 'take it easy now' ringing in his ears.

He hesitated before entering Alistair's 'billet' but went in and gazed sadly at the neatly made bunk and the old soldier's 'kit' precisely folded in the best military fashion. He touched nothing but knelt and prayed for his friend.

Returning to his own cubicle he sat and thought of home. He looked at his watch and it occurred to him that at about this time, Annie would be taking the family to church to make their confessions in preparation for going to Holy Communion on Easter Sunday morning. It saddened him to realise that this would be the first time in over twenty years that he and Annie had not made their Easter confessions together. Then he remembered something which would go at least some way towards rectifying this, he had thought before about going to confession himself in Carlisle and he resolved that today he would do just that. While he was there he could also find out what the Mass times were for Easter Sunday. With Father Conlon in hospital, Pete and James might want to attend Mass in Carlisle as well.

He was ready to leave when James looked in for a short while during his lunch break. When Michael explained what he intended to do, James reluctantly withdrew his objections and walked with his father to the station.

Chapter 46

James saw his father off from Dornock on the 1.45 to Carlisle that Easter Saturday afternoon, April 22nd 1916.

The train was not overcrowded as the departure did not coincide with a shift change at the Gretna factory, but people were taking advantage of the fine and sunny weekend weather to travel for pleasure, so neither was it empty. Michael found a seat in a compartment with just three other passengers. One of the passengers was John Campbell of Carlisle, a joiner at the factory who later described the bare facts of what happened next:

> "At 1.47 on Saturday afternoon the gentleman entered the compartment of the train I was travelling in to Carlisle. About 5 minutes after the train started the man fell forward on to the knees of one of the passengers opposite to him. He was lifted up and artificial respiration tried without effect. The body was taken to Carlisle and the matter reported to the Station Officials and a doctor was called."

The Station Master ordered the buffet to be cleared and Michael was taken inside and laid on the floor. The doctor, Charles Crawford Aitken, arrived soon afterwards from his practice in Carlisle but it was too late. Michael Quinlan was dead.

The body was taken to the police mortuary and an investigation begun to find the identity of the deceased, and a search organised to find his home and family. With the demands of wartime, and the fact that the death had occurred on a weekend the investigation would not normally have been afforded a high priority. But later in the afternoon as the police inspector sifted idly through Michael's meagre personal effects he found the Ministry of Munitions badge, and a letter addressed to Michael Quinlan. The name rang a bell and he suddenly remembered that this was the man who had manned the telephone at the factory during the search for the Irish rebels. He rang Commander Wilson and asked him to send someone to make a preliminary unofficial identification to confirm his suspicions.

Wilson came personally, confirmed the worst and went back to Gretna with the shocking news.

In the event it was Sarah who eventually found James sitting with Kate on a bench at The Beach and gently broke the news of his father's death.

Chapter 47

With Father Conlon still in hospital a supply priest came from Carlisle to say Mass at Gretna on Easter Sunday morning. James attended but rather went through the motions, concentrating neither on the priest nor the service. The joy of The Resurrection passed him by. It was not that he had lost his faith, his beliefs remained unshaken, but his mind was now on other things. The events of Good Friday had been effectively driven from his mind by the news of his father's death, but not even that sad fact took precedence in his thoughts. His father was dead and, although he believed that it would happen at some ordained time in the future, for him there would be no immediate resurrection. For the moment James' overriding concern was how, and indeed what, he was going to tell his mother.

Thoughts of his mother brought memories of Easters past. He knew that at that moment she would be doing everything she could to ensure the feast was celebrated in the way the family had always done. William would harness the pony and drive the family to early Mass. He suspected that on this particular Sunday his mother would give a special reminder to William and the children to pray for their father and brothers. He knew that he and his father would be in her prayers and that she would make special mention of Jack who, in spite of his reassurances, she secretly feared was in mortal danger. They would have gone without breakfast in order to comply with the fasting requirements for Holy Communion, but after coming home from the church, breakfast would be a joyous affair. His mother would boil eggs and add a little cochineal to the water, which would turn the shells bright red without harming the insides. The children would laugh with delight at the sight of the magic eggs, which could be eaten only on Easter Sunday. James held back a tear as he contemplated the shock it would cause if news of Michael's death were to reach home today.

The obvious method of informing his mother was by telegram, and he knew that he would eventually have to face the painful duty of sending one. He realised that as soon as she received the wire she would immediately think that Jack had been killed in action, and learning that it was in fact her husband who had died would only serve to increase the pain. James remembered Kate's reaction to telegrams bringing dreadful news and he decided that he could not subject his mother to that ordeal today. It would wait until tomorrow.

He desperately wanted to go home and tell her in person but for the moment that was not possible. Tomorrow morning he was required to go to Carlisle to make a formal identification of the body prior to a post-mortem being performed. Even though it would be a bank holiday the country was still at war, and such formalities had to be carried out at the first opportunity. On Tuesday there was to be an inquest, which he would also have to attend. Then he would have to think about arrangements for a funeral. People were being kind and offering to help, especially Sarah, who offered to find out about the cost and bureaucracy involved in taking his father's body home for burial. For his mother's sake he thought this was what he would have to try and do. But all he could do today was go to Dornock and try to think of what he should do about his father's meagre belongings.

After Mass he had a brief word with Pete and then had to face the rest of the day alone. Everyone was busy, the war did not pause just because of one death and so neither could the work of the great munitions factory.

. . .

In Dublin that Sunday morning the full Military Council met to consider their options in the light of what had happened to Casement and the German arms. To further complicate the situation, Eoin McNeill had arranged for an advertisement in an Irish Sunday newspaper ordering a halt to all Irish Volunteer activity. This again left the republican forces much depleted. But along with the IRB, The Citizen Army and the Volunteers,

Cumann na mBann, ('The League of Women') formed in 1914 as an auxiliary corps to complement the Volunteers, were integrated into 'The Army of the Irish Republic'. Under the leadership of Countess Markievicz, the former Constance Gore-Booth and now the wife of a Polish nobleman, these women would play an important part in the rising.

The meeting agreed that the rising be postponed for twenty-four hours. It would now begin on Easter Monday, April 23rd 1916.

Chapter 48

At 11.00am on Easter Monday members of the Irish Republican Brotherhood, the Irish Citizen Army, the Irish Volunteers and the women of *Cumann na mBann* set out from Liberty Hall to occupy strategic buildings in the centre of Dublin. In spite of Eoin McNeill's order banning the Volunteers from taking part, sufficient numbers of that organisation did in fact muster and by midday all their objectives had been taken with little or no resistance. The insurgents set up headquarters in the General Post Office in Sackville Street (*now O'Connell St.*), Dublin's main thoroughfare, and declared the formation of the Irish Republic. Padraig Pearse, James Connolly and several other members of the provisional government based themselves in the building and the new green, white and gold flag of the republic was unfurled. Other buildings and places occupied included: the Four Courts, Jacob's Biscuit Factory, Boland's Bakery, and St. Stephens Green. Having taken their objectives the rebels set about organising defences and barricading themselves in. An assault was mounted on Dublin Castle, the seat of government in Ireland, the guards were overcome and a police sentry was killed, but for some unknown reason The Castle was not occupied.

There was no immediate response from the British military authorities as there were only an estimated 400 troops in Dublin at the time. The Commander-in-Chief, General Lovick Friend, was in England and the Dublin Garrison Commander could not be located. While reinforcements were being organised the first British troops to see action were a detachment of cavalry who charged up Sackville St. and were repulsed by the rebels. British troops did have some success when they managed to oust a small rebel force from a building known as The South Dublin Union. The British then began to occupy buildings around the rebel strongholds from where they could fire on the insurgents.

Unaware of what was happening in Ireland, James went into Carlisle and made the formal identification of his father's body. He decided to await the results of the post-mortem before sending a telegram home as he felt some definite information on the cause of death might help to lessen the pain, if not the shock. So he returned to Gretna and waited at the Institute where he had arranged to meet Kate when she came off shift.

Pete Casey and Sarah Birks had dropped the pretence of being a navvy and a factory worker, and of being a courting couple, although they obviously remained good friends. Sarah was now acting openly as an inspector in the Ministry of Munitions Women's Police with an office in the administration building. Pete's exact role was still somewhat obscure, but he spent much of his time liaising with The Man from Whitehall and Commander Wilson. He was also keeping a close eye on the improving condition of Father Conlon. James pondered his father's remark that 'there was more to Pete Casey than meets the eye' but although Pete's role had obviously changed his manner had not. He was still content to live in the attic at Solway View and, more importantly to James, he remained a friend. James had too much on his mind to enquire any deeper into who or what Pete really was. For the moment he was content to accept the situation at face value. But it was a concerned looking Pete who came looking for him at the Institute.

"What's up Pete?" asked James.

"It's started Jim, the bloody rising has started at home. I don't know the whole story but I hear Dublin has been attacked. There'll be ructions now for sure."

Although he had once considered joining it, a rebellion in Ireland was the last thing on James' mind. "Well I suppose it was always on the cards Pete. But I'm thinking more about what's happening here with my father dead and trying to take him home as well as telling my mother the news."

"God knows I'm sorry to be the one to say this Jim," said

Pete. "But I don't think there's any chance at all of taking Michael home now. If my thinking is right the whole country will be cut off and there will be no way in or out for the living let alone the dead until the fighting is over."

It took a moment for this to sink in. "How long will that be Pete? Will there be any chance soon of taking him home?"

"I'm sorry to say it but I can't see it happening Jim," said Pete. "As soon as the army gets reinforcements into Dublin the fighting itself will be all over in no time at all, a few days at the most. But the repercussions of this will last for years."

"So you don't think the rebels can win," said James.

"Oh they'll win in the end all right, but not now. The British army will crush the uprising and then the British Government will do the very thing the rebels want. They'll come down hard on the survivors with trials and hangings and firing squads and turn them into martyrs. And all that will do is to unite the whole of Ireland. Today there is hardly any support for the rebels but to-morrow everyone will be cheering the martyrs. Any Irishman even suspected of being a British sympathiser will have to look out for himself."

"So when will I be able to go home myself Pete? I'll have to see my mother and tell her about Da."

"The truth of it is I don't know Jim." Pete gazed sorrowfully into the distance. "You and me are in the same boat together. I've been working for the British security service and I came here to look for German spies not Irish ones. But the way things have panned out I don't think I'll ever be able to go back to Ireland again. You told Daly in the church that you had informed on Casement and someone else might have heard you like they did at the dance. Oh I know well that you didn't inform on anyone, you only said it to save your father, God rest his soul, but that won't mean a thing when the real troubles start at home."

James was crestfallen. "Are you telling me that we can never go home at all?"

"Oh sure you might get away with it yourself Jim, nobody else was actually in the church at the time except Father Conlon. I think he has had enough of the likes of Liam Daly and he won't say anything. But that fella dressed as a soldier, not long ago he was impersonating a priest as well, is a horse of a different colour. Now there is a very slippery customer and I wouldn't put it past him to remember you. For Christ's sake Jim watch out for him if you do go back."

"What about yourself Pete?"

"I'm afraid that I can never go back. I suppose I'm a bit like the priest. I'm disillusioned with the people I've been associating with. Except for Commander Wilson and Sarah Birks I wouldn't give you a penny for any of them. I'm for America – it's the only road open for me."

"What will you do there?" asked James.

"I think I'll spend most of my time trying to persuade Miss Birks to come and join me," answered Pete. "Anyway, in the meantime I'll keep my ear to the ground and try to let you know if the coast is clear across the water. But the way things are now you should be thinking about sending a telegram to your mother."

James said: "I was going to do it today but I was waiting until after the post mortem, anyway the post office is shut for the bank holiday."

"Ah sure can't you send wires by telephone these days," said Pete. "Come on I'll give you a hand."

While they were composing the telegram on a scrap of paper, Sarah came in. When she saw what they were doing she took it from them. "I'll send it for you from my office Jim," she said. "Your father was a factory employee and it's the least the Ministry can do for him."

When she returned she too wore a worried frown. "I've sent it off all right Jim," she said. "But the rebels have taken over the General Post Office in Dublin and the people here can't guarantee when it will get through. I have to go back to the factory now. What's happening in Ireland is bound to be common knowledge before long and Commander Wilson is worried about the effect on the Irish workers here."

When they returned to Solway View and went to the loft after dinner they found the McCarthy boys out as usual. 'St Patrick' Murphy went to his corner not to read as he usually did but to

273

write. Pete and James paid him scant attention. Next morning he posted his letter to an address in London and just a few days later German Intelligence learned of the failed Irish Nationalist plot to sabotage operations at the British munitions factory in Gretna.

Chapter 49

With the arrival of British reinforcements in the early hours of Tuesday morning the fighting in Dublin increased in intensity. But the British commander, Brigadier-General Lowe, still had only 1,200 troops in the city. He believed that the rebel headquarters were located in Liberty Hall and initially concentrated on isolating the insurgents there, and on securing the approaches to Dublin Castle. Later in the day rebel positions at St. Stephens Green were made untenable when British snipers and machine guns were able to get into the Shelbourne Hotel which overlooked their hastily dug trenches. Further British reinforcements were being sent from England and field artillery was on its way from their base at Athlone.

The women of *Cumann na mBann* organised and ran first aid posts, prepared and delivered meals, gathered intelligence, acted as scouts, carried despatches and transferred arms. Some rebel leaders however, Eamon deValera at Boland's Bakery and Eamon Ceannt at the South Dublin Union, would not permit them to occupy posts inside their strongholds. But at St. Stephen's Green, Countess Markievitz acted as second in command to Michael Mallin and took part in the actual fighting.

. . .

While the fighting continued in Ireland the 'Inquest on the body of the late Michael Quinlan' was being held at the City Police Office, West Walls, City of Carlisle. The Coroner was Thomas Slack Strong.

James testified that he had identified the body as being that of his father, who was employed at HM Factory Gretna. The last time he had seen his father alive was on Saturday 22nd at about 1.30pm. when he boarded a train at Dornock. His father had been going to

Carlisle on business. James was not asked the nature of his father's business and so did not elaborate. He stated that his father had complained of pains in his chest and that he sometimes suffered shortness of breath.

Doctor Charles Crawford Aitkin was sworn in and testified:

"On Saturday last about 2.15 in the afternoon I was called to the Citadel Station to attend to the deceased. When I arrived he was dead. On the instructions of the Coroner and in conjunction with Dr. Edwards on the 23 inst I made a post-mortem examination of the body of the deceased at the Police Mortuary. On external examination we found no marks of violence. On internal examination we found fatty degeneration of the heart and over distension of the right side of the heart sufficient in our opinion to account for sudden death from cardiac syncope."

The inquest found that: "Michael Quinlan died of natural causes namely Cardiac Syncope."

The coroner released the body for burial and, after commiserating with James, asked if he had made funeral arrangements. James said that due to Easter he had not, but had been hoping to take his father's body back to Ireland for burial. The coroner adjourned the proceedings and held a short conference with the police inspector and doctor. When they finished he dismissed the jury and brought the official proceedings to a close.

When the jury had left he called James into a side room with the policeman and the doctor. With some kindness the inspector told him that it would not be possible to take his father home at present. Martial Law had been declared in Ireland effectively cutting the country off to all but official traffic. This also meant that family members would be unable to travel to England for a funeral. The coroner suggested that under the circumstances responsibility for the funeral could be taken on by the local authority here in Carlisle. He offered to contact the chairman of the Board of Guardians who would be responsible for the arrangements.

It was up to James and he took his time in considering the suggestion. He was not at all certain of what exactly was involved and he worried about what his mother would think. He asked several questions mainly concerning the religious aspects of such a funeral. It transpired that if the authorities took responsibility his father would be buried in the 'dissenters' or Non-Church of England section of Carlisle cemetery. Should he wish he could arrange for a Roman Catholic priest to conduct the burial service. The alternative was to arrange a funeral himself. It would involve considerable time and expense and, with family members unable to attend, would not necessarily result in a more formal or worshipful committal. In any case a traditional Irish funeral would not be possible.

All three gentlemen advised James that what the coroner proposed was by far the best solution and he was eventually persuaded. It was not perfect and he would have a lot of explaining to do to his mother. But it was his decision and he would live with it.

. . .

While the inquest on one body was taking place in Carlisle a different type of inquest on thousands of bodies was being held in Mesopotamia. After the latest failure to break through to Kut-al-Amara a last attempt to supply the garrison was made via the river Tigris. The artillery supplemented by machine guns made every effort to cover the river steamer *Julmar* as she attempted to deliver food and supplies to the besieged troops. But to no avail, she was shelled and captured by the Turks while still several miles from her objective.

It was the end of the road for the besieged garrison. At first they tried and failed to negotiate an honourable armistice with the Turks. There was nothing left but unconditional surrender triggering off one of the greatest disasters ever to befall the British army.

Jack Quinlan could scarcely have felt worse had he known of his father's death – that news would not reach him for some weeks yet. The failure to relieve Kut was deeply felt by the artillerymen. The infantry had suffered terribly in their attempts to break through and might have succeeded had they had better support. Jack and the other gunners could often do no more than stand and watch the infantry die. Shortages of high explosive shells for the 18 pounders, coupled with incompetent tactical direction and lack of coordination, were the real culprits, but this was small consolation. Their Battery Commander tried to console them with the promise that this would not happen again. The new munitions factory at home was now in production and would ensure adequate supplies for future campaigns.

Chapter 50

Mrs Connor sat and gazed at the envelope in a state of shock as the awful significance of the telegram struck her. She was the only one in the post office when it came in and there was nobody to turn to for help. Her husband, the postmaster, was out and would not be back for some time. It was early closing day and not many customers were expected so he had happily left her in charge. She knew that she should call the telegraph boy and get him to deliver the wire immediately, but could not bring herself to touch it. As the horrible truth dawned on her she realised that this was not idle gossip to be indulged in and enjoyed after Mass on Sunday mornings. This was the horrible truth and she sat and burst into tears. She was still there several hours later when her husband returned, and the telegram remained undelivered.

· · ·

The artillery was now temporarily silent in Mesopotamia, but field guns were coming into action in Dublin. Sited in Phibsborough and at Trinity College the 18 pounders began to smash the rebel positions with high explosive shells. Bombardier Jack Quinlan and the artillerymen of the Tigris Corps would have been envious of the seemingly unlimited supply of ammunition available to the gunners in Dublin.

· · ·

Michael's funeral was held on Wednesday. James had managed to get a priest from Carlisle to conduct the committal. There was no time to take the body to the church on the evening before the funeral and left there overnight as would have happened at home but the priest, who had often officiated at funerals arranged by the local authority, assured James that his father would be buried in accordance with the requirements of the Catholic church.

Pete Casey had spent the morning with James but little was said. Sarah came with Commander Wilson and they brought flowers. They had managed to persuade the factory management to allow Kate a few hours off to attend. It was not usual for the Gretna Girls to be given time off to go to funerals other than for those of close personal relatives.

The service was conducted reverently and with dignity and Michael Quinlan was laid to rest at 2.30pm.

James had a single regret: His father's body had been brought to the cemetery in a motor hearse. The old coachman would have preferred horses.

. . .

"It's not Jack at all Ma, its Da. He died over in England of a heart attack, it was James who sent this." William was the first one to actually open and read the telegram since it had been delivered, with apologies for the delay, by the postmaster in person.

Annie was sitting in her chair crying and wondering why God had taken her son. William gently shook her out of her state of shock and showed her the telegram. She stared at it in disbelief. She had in some ways been prepared for news that Jack had been killed or wounded – he was after all a soldier at war. But Michael! Nothing could have prepared her for that.

William went out and called the children, and as gently as he could, told them that their father had died. It would be better for them to hear it from him now, rather than have them find their mother in tears and having to tell them why. He told young Michael to go as quickly as he could to the church and ask Father Murphy to come as quickly as he could. Then he went inside to try and console his mother.

A few days later, Annie received two letters in the same post: One from her son in Mesopotamia to let her know that he was fit and well and not to worry, the other from her son in Gretna to let her know the details of her husband's death and funeral.

Chapter 51

James stood and looked at the devastation that was the centre of Dublin. The Easter Rising was over. It had ended on Saturday April 29th 1916 when, with James Connolly badly wounded, the GPO on fire from the shelling and most of Sackville Street reduced to rubble, Padraig Pearse issued the order for all the rebel units to surrender. The insurrection had lasted a mere six days but the consequences would be felt for years, if not for ever. A member of *Cumann na mBann*, Elizabeth O'Farrell, acted as liaison and, under British supervision, carried the surrender order to the rebels still fighting.

As he stood amongst the rubble on that bright May morning James had difficulty in accepting that it was just four months since he had stood on the same spot with his father. Then, even in the rain, Dublin had seemed a happy vibrant city. Today as soon as he left the train at Westland Row Station he could not help but notice the difference. Then in the words of the song, Irish eyes had been smiling, but now those same eyes were filled with resentment, and he would notice this again and again as he travelled southward home to County Kerry. Anti-British feeling had replaced apathy and was growing daily. It had even been evident among the generally happy-go-lucky navvies at Gretna as news of the aftermath to the rebellion filtered through.

In Dublin the reasons for the change in Irish attitudes were obvious: firstly the destruction of their city by the British artillery, and secondly the casualty lists. The British authorities had lost 157 dead and 318 wounded – most of them soldiers but with a few policemen. The best estimate of Irish casualties put them at 302 dead and 1,617 wounded and of these 220 of the dead and 600 of the injured had been ordinary citizens. As in all such conflicts it was the civilians who had suffered most and rumours circulated, some of them substantiated, that not all civilian casualties had been accidental. James would have recognised one of the bodies pulled from the rubble of the GPO – 'Mick' had achieved his objective and died for The Cause.

Across the country, however, there was an even bigger cause for bitterness. The British reaction to the uprising: 3,430 men and 79 women, most of them members of *Cumman na mBann*, were arrested, and although most were eventually released, there was little evidence that all were rebels or even rebel sympathisers. 12 of the women, including Countess Contance Markievitz, were among those who remained in custody and sent to trial. Rather than be treated as prisoners of war, they were after all soldiers in uniform, the rebel leaders faced courts martial and were found guilty of treason. 90 were sentenced to death. Between May 3rd and May 12th, 15 of the leaders were shot. The seriously wounded James Connolly faced the firing squad tied to a chair. Nothing could have enraged the population more. Padraig Pearse had achieved his ultimate aim of uniting the Irish people.

James was reminded of Pete Casey's remark about the British creating a new crop of Irish martyrs.

But as James gazed at the piles of rubble he could not help but reflect on what had caused such devastation, and it gave him an uncomfortable feeling to realise that munitions manufactured at HM Factory Gretna could easily have been involved. Until now cordite to him had merely been the end product of the factory he worked in and had helped to build. When he thought any further about the purpose of the explosive cord it was in the context of helping his brother in the war against the Turks.

He had been touched when Kate said that while the other Gretna Girls were 'doing it for Tommy' she was doing it for Jack. The ruins of Dublin presented him with a very different viewpoint. If cordite could help to do this to solid masonry it was not difficult to imagine what it could do to human flesh. It confirmed what he already suspected; in spite of what he had said to Kate when he left, he would never go back to Gretna.

It had not been a tearful or emotional parting. After Michael's funeral his thoughts had been totally focused on when he could see his mother and what he would say to her. Kate was rapidly losing her shyness and becoming more involved in the life of the Gretna Girls. They remained friends but the romance had gone.

In truth James had found it more difficult to say goodbye to Pete Casey. This was after all the man who had saved his life and, although it proved fruitless in the end, that of his father. Soon after Michael had been laid to rest, James and Pete made the trip to Edinburgh for another funeral. Alistair McGregor was buried with full military honours not far from his son. When news came through that the rising in Ireland was over, James desperately wanted to go home, but Pete persuaded him to wait until 'the smoke cleared'. The last thing his mother would want, Pete argued, was to lose another family member in the confusion that was Ireland at the moment. He was only hanging on in Gretna himself until the time was right.

While they waited a new priest arrived at Gretna. The navvies soon repaired the fire damage to his living quarters, but could do little about the dark stains in the floor where blood had seeped into the wood. Father Conlon recovered and left Gretna for a quiet life in a seminary in Ireland after words had passed between London and the Archdiocese of Armagh.

When they eventually thought that it was safe to go they had a last drink together in Carlisle. Then they waited in the station buffet for their separate trains: one for the boat train to take him on the first leg of his journey home; the other for the train to London where he would see his sister before braving the U-boats to cross the Atlantic and a new life. Pete left with a promise that Sarah would join him after the war.

"Sure it'll take more than a German submarine to sink you Pete Casey," were James' last words to his friend.

He travelled overnight and arrived in Killarney on Sunday morning in time for early Mass at the cathedral. After mass he lingered to pray for his father and added one for Alistair and one for Pete. As he reached the door there was a crowd gathered outside being addressed by a man he recognised. He caught a snatch of what was being said: 'the Germans are treated as prisoners of war while Irish patriots are being shot and hanged as traitors.' The Man from Dublin was carrying out the last instructions he had been given by Pearse and Connolly. He was conveying the news of their patriotic deeds and glorious martyrdom to the Irish people. And now he did not have to talk to a mainly disinterested few in a back kitchen, he could speak openly to a large and listening crowd.

The James of yesterday would have joined the crowd and listened as enthusiastically as any. The James of today slipped out of the cathedral by a side door and left them to it. He thought about finding some form of transport but instead decided to walk. It was five Irish miles. He looked at his father's watch. If he stepped it out he would be there by the time they got home from Mass.

Epilogue

As we stood and looked at the place where he lay my mind was drawn to four other graves scattered around the world.

The first is in Wales. Jack survived the First World War only to die during the Second. Of all days he died on March 17th St Patrick's Day. Like his father he died from a sudden heart attack while performing a task he knew well – manhandling a field gun. But this was on a Home Guard exercise on a lush Welsh hillside rather than in a barren Middle Eastern desert. I wondered how he would have reacted to the news that modern British troops in Iraq had discovered three 18 pounder field guns left behind when that country was known as Mesopotamia.

There is a grave in America where James lies. He stayed at home for the remainder of the war and then left for America. He lived a long and quiet life, but it is not difficult to imagine him keeping abreast of the 'troubles' afflicting his homeland. After the Easter Rising some of the survivors joined the new Irish Republican Army (IRA) while the more politically inclined joined Sinn Fein, some of course joined both. I wondered what James, who had seen and had experience of both sides of the argument, would have to say as the 'troubles' persisted throughout his lifetime.

The third grave is in England. As soon as Jack came home from the war, William considered that it was his turn to seek adventure and joined the army. Like his brother he served in a war in a far off land (but that is another story to be told at another time). When he returned he followed in his father's footsteps and served the owners of Beaufort House. But unlike his father he drove a horseless carriage, a Rolls Royce motor car, rather than a team of horses. He eventually moved with his family to England and was the last of the brothers to die at the ripe old age of 98.

Michael had set out from Beaufort to try to keep his family together. But eventually they were overtaken by the tragedy that seems to have afflicted the Irish people throughout the ages. In the end, Annie was the only one to have died and be buried in Ireland.

We thought about trying to visit all four graves, but decided not to. They had lived through wars and revolutions and it was time to leave them in peace.

Go ndeanfar Dia trocaire ar a anam (May the Lord have mercy on their souls).

The End

Author's Notes
And Acknowledgements

This book is a work of fiction, but I believe that much of it is firmly grounded in fact.

The character of Michael Quinlan is based on my grandfather, Michael Doyle. I changed the family name to avoid the problem of his descendants believing the entire story to be true. Quinlan was my grandmother's maiden name. The leaders of the Easter Rising in Ireland were of course real historical figures as were some of the German officers.

All other characters are fictitious and any resemblance to real persons, living or dead, is purely coincidental.

The great munitions factory at Gretna was very real and by the end of the First World War was producing more cordite than all the other British factories combined. I am extremely grateful to **Gordon L. Routledge** for allowing me to draw freely from his excellent book, **Gretna's Secret War**, which is the definitive work on the subject. I believe that for the most part I have adhered closely to Mr Routledge's narrative and have deliberately strayed from it in just a few areas. Firstly, all of the characters, with the exception of Michael and James Quinlan, are pure fiction. Secondly the factory did not go fully into production until August 1916, but I have brought this date forward by a few months to fit with my fictitious plot. Finally the act of sabotage at the factory included in the story is based on a real accidental incident which occurred over a year later than the one I have described.

In the context of the factory I must also express my gratitude to the staff of the **'Devils Porridge' Exhibition**. My wife and I visited the exhibition in 2005 when staff members were able to confirm much of what we had managed to uncover about my grandfather's time there. It was there too that the idea for this book first entered my mind. The exhibition has since moved to Eastriggs & Gretna Heritage centre and further information is available on their internet site: www.devilsporridge.co.uk

The lodging house 'Solway View' is fictitious and any resemblance to any modern day building in the area is purely coincidental.

Beaufort House today, while still a family home, is available for holiday rentals. My thanks to **Donald & Rachel Cameron** for allowing me set part of my story there. Details can be found at www.beaufortireland.com

My basic knowledge of the Easter Rising stems from boyhood history lessons at school in Ireland and from listening as a young man to people who actually lived through those momentous events. But special thanks must go to **Mary Hardy**, not only for her invaluable help with all things Irish, but also for her time and effort in reading and correcting my first draft. For a comprehensive account of events in Ireland at the time, **Tim Patrick Coogan's** *Ireland in the Twentieth Century* is recommended.

Researching the First World War in Mesopotamia (modern Iraq) proved to be more difficult as most sources on the conflict tend to concentrate on the Western Front. In the end I found an excellent source with all of basic historic information I needed on: www.1914-1918.net which includes material from *The Long, Long Trail, The British Army in the Great War 1914-1918.* Thanks to **Chris Baker** for allowing me to use the information.

Finally, I must mention the other 'real' character in the book: my wife **Shireen**. She has been with me all the way from helping to locate the original coachman's grave, encouraging me to write, making numerous valid suggestions and being totally supportive throughout.

Thanks Darling.

John Michael Doyle 2009.

Historical Notes:

Chapter 4 – The 18 pounder field gun was a standard artillery piece of the British Army from 1904 to 1945. It weighed 1.5 tons and fired an 18.5 lb high explosive shell over a maximum range of 5,900 yards.

Chapter 5 – Daniel O'Connell (1775-1847) was born in Cahirciveen Co. Kerry. He was known as 'The Liberator' because of his efforts in support of Catholic Emancipation in Ireland. Although a staunch Nationalist he was opposed to armed insurrection due mainly to having witnessed the excesses of the French Revolution.

Chapter 6 – The Cunard liner 'Lusitania' was torpedoed by the German U-boat U20 off Old Kinsale Head in May 1915. Among the 1,153 passengers and crew to drown were 128 Americans. There were unsubstantiated rumours that the ship had been carrying ammunition which would have made it a legitimate wartime target. It was suggested that the British had allowed the vessel to be sunk in order to get the Americans to enter the war against Germany.

Chapter 10 – The rail crash at Quintinshill near Gretna Green on 22nd January 1915 was the worst railway accident ever to occur in Britain when a troop train carrying officers and men of the 7th Battalion Royal Scots was in collision with a local train. In total 277 people were killed and 246 injured, the vast majority of them soldiers.

Chapter 34 – On a visit to the Gretna factory the author Sir Arthur Conan Doyle, then a war correspondent, christened the cordite paste mixture 'The Devil's Porridge'. As a result of witnessing the dangers faced by the Gretna Girls he became a strong supporter of votes for women.